ART IS EVERYTHING

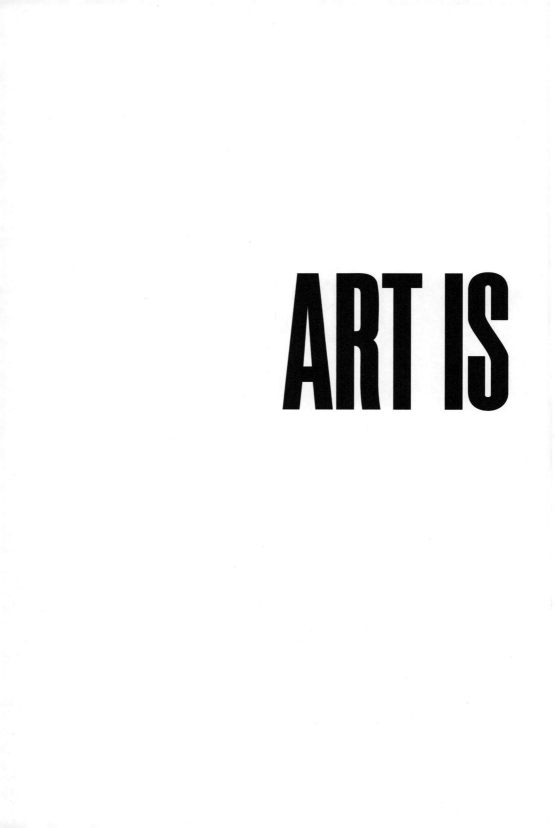

ART IS

YXTA MAYA MURRAY

EVERYTHING

A NOVEL

 TriQuarterly Books/Northwestern University Press
Evanston, Illinois

TriQuarterly Books
Northwestern University Press
www.nupress.northwestern.edu

Credits for images and text and acknowledgment of previously published
stories appear beginning on page 219, which should be considered a
continuation of this copyright page.

Printed in the United States of America

10   9   8   7   6   5   4   3   2   1

Library of Congress Cataloging-in-Publication Data

Names: Murray, Yxta Maya, author.
Title: Art is everything : a novel / Yxta Maya Murray.
Description: Evanston, Illinois : Curbstone Books/Northwestern University
    Press, 2021.
Identifiers: LCCN 2020021601 | ISBN 9780810142930 (paperback) | ISBN
    9780810142923 (ebook)
Subjects: LCSH: Art—Fiction. | Artists—Fiction. | Art criticism—Fiction.
Classification: LCC PS3563.U832 A89 2021 | DDC 813.54—dc23
LC record available at https://lccn.loc.gov/2020021601

To the memory of my father

Contents

CHAPTER ONE I DIDN'T EVEN KNOW THESE EXISTED

[This is a Wikipedia entry titled "Hey MOCA, why is Laura Aguilar's *Untitled Landscape* (1996) 'Unavailable' on Your Website?" that I posted on June 16, 2011, at 3:45 p.m. PST. On June 18, 2011, at 7:15 a.m. PST, Wikipedia administrators subjected the essay to "Speedy Deletion" for having (a) no context; (b) violating the policy against publishing Wiki biographies of living people; (c) being full of patent nonsense; (d) giving no indication of importance; and (e) violating MOCA's copyright of its own webpage. My entry came complete with a screenshot of MOCA's "Laura Aguilar" page, which looks something like this:
Collections>
Laura Aguilar
Clothed/Unclothed No. 19 (1992), No Image Available
Clothed/Unclothed No. 5 (1990), No Image Available
Untitled Landscape (1996), No Image Available.]

Xōchitl Hernández, I am in love with you. I am in fucking love with you. I love your eyes and your mouth. I love your teeth and your sweat. I love your hands and your knees. I love your sickness and your death. I love your hair and your dandruff. I love your dirt and your intelligence. I love your breasts and your cunt. I love your tendons. I love your tongue. I love your tongue inside of me. Xōchitl Hernández, I love your navel, with its fresh perfume. I love you Xōchitl. I love you I love it's you I love

*

Photographer Laura Aguilar was born in San Gabriel, California, in 1959, to the Mexican American Paul Aguilar and the half-Irish Juanita Grisham. Aguilar took some art classes at East LA College early in her career but remains largely self-taught. Her commitment to an autodidactic art practice has been hard-won, considering the personal forces that she grapples

1

with. Aguilar is dyslexic, large-bodied, queer, and of a complex racial background. She is also one of the best artists on the planet. Her talent impresses anyone who witnesses her celebratory late-1980s *Latina Lesbians* series, her agony-fueled early-1990s *Don't Tell Her Art Can't Hurt* images, or her incandescent mid-1990s *Nature Self-Portraits* suite.

However, very few people have seen these pictures.

As of this writing, only a scant number of museums and galleries own Laura Aguilars. Aguilar's work occupies space in the collections of the Los Angeles Museum of Art, UCLA's Chicano Studies Research Center, New York's New Museum of Contemporary Art, the Kinsey Institute for Research in Sex, Gender, and Reproduction, and the subject of this Wikipedia entry, MOCA. But, to the best of my knowledge, Aguilar's art does not appear in any of these museums' permanent gallery spaces. That's why most folks have not experienced the incredible joy of knowing what the *Latina Lesbians*, *Don't Tell Her Art Can't Hurt*, or *Nature Self-Portraits* series look like.

To come into contact with Aguilar's art, enthusiasts must time-travel to specific shows, like the Venice Biennale's 1993 *Aperto 93* exhibition, which displayed pieces whose names have been lost to history: except for a Wikipedia entry about the Biennale that cites Aguilar's name, the only archival news coverage of the exhibition that I can find mentions merely Damien Hirst, Maurizio Cattelan, Matthew Barney, Rudolf Stingel, Gabriel Orozco, Rirkrit Tiravanija, Pipilotti Rist, and John Currin, people like that.

Or, the motivated art lover could get into a space-time pod, zip off to San Antonio's Museo Alameda, and land there around the same time that the financial crisis hit. According to the web, a little newspaper called *My San Antonio* reported that the Museo Alameda, the foremost US museum dedicated to Latinx art, displayed Aguilar's *Clothed/Unclothed* series in 2008. However, the links that permitted aficionadas to see the pieces featured in that show are now all broken.

Not even obsessive Google research will offer connoisseurs sufficient exposure to Aguilar's work. The Los Angeles County Museum of Art *has* published twelve images on its web page, including the beautiful *Stillness #41* (1999). Yet, every other museum that I've looked up declines to reveal their Aguilar holdings on their websites.

The New Museum, for example, allows art detectives to type Aguilar's name in their magnifying glass function, but then it just says "Sorry, there are no results that match your search." When said gumshoes feed "Laura Aguilar" into the Kinsey Institute website, they are rewarded with "Unauthorized access to internal API. Please refer to https://support.google .com/customsearch/answer/4542055." And when they venture onto the

MOCA site, they discover that MOCA's listing for its three Aguilar holdings—*Clothed/Unclothed No. 19* (1992), *Clothed/Unclothed No. 5* (1990), and *Untitled Landscape* (1996)—only contains a thrice-repeated sign that says "No Image Available."

Why? Laura Aguilar is a great poet of queer Latina identity, passion, pain, and love.

But the museums either do not collect her, or they conceal her as if they are ashamed.

*

you it's you I love I love you Xōchitl. I love your eyes your laugh your sweat your hair your glands your big ass your feet your hate your rage your hands the way you look at me when you drink red wine the way you shop for vegetables the way you lick

*

In 1987–88, Aguilar produced her *Latina Lesbians* suite. Aguilar's self-portrait in this series (*Laura*) reveals her smiling in her bedroom, wearing shorts and a cowboy hat. Beneath the picture, she's written: "Im not comfortable with the word Lesbian but as each day go's by I'm more and more comfortable with the word LAURA." In *Yolanda*, we see an unsmiling, square-jawed heartbreaker wearing jeans and a navy Izod polo. Under her image, Yolanda has written, in cursive, "My latina side infuses my lesbian side with chispa & pasión." In *Lydia*, we meet a young woman holding a guitar and looking tenderly at the camera. In the white border of the photograph, the subject has printed neatly, "I have a long way to go to be who I would like to be."

*

In 1993, I was thirteen years old. I lived with my dad, Eddie Ruiz, in LA's Koreatown. I couldn't fly to Venice to see Laura Aguilar's *Aperto 93* pictures, which may have included the *Latina Lesbian* images. For one thing, I didn't know who Laura Aguilar was. I also didn't know what "Venice" was. And, even though I'd already fingered a seventh-grade Lego Leaguer named Marisela Valdez behind the CVS on Wilshire and Western, I didn't know what "Latina lesbian" actually meant.

What I did know: That if my dad saw me squeezing the little breasts of Marisela Valdez, his face would puff up and turn weirdly shiny like the foil top of a Jiffy Pop popcorn when you put it in the microwave. Then he'd start screaming.

What I also knew: That my mother, Flor Pérez, didn't care about my romance with Marisela Valdez because Mom's morphine, cocaine, marijuana, and Kirkland Signature cabernet addictions kept her too swamped to schedule giving a damn about crises involving non-drugs.

I knew two other things, too: Like Laura Aguilar, I already realized that if I didn't make art all the time, I would probably die from loneliness and insanity. But I grokked, too, that my family had no money. So, even if I had understood who Laura Aguilar was, what Venice was, and what being a Latina lesbian really entailed, I wouldn't have been able get a ticket to go see the inspirational Aguilars in *Aperto 93*, anyway.

In 1993, I would meet Marisela Valdez behind the CVS and kiss her until we both almost fainted. Marisela had long stringy brown hair and bowed legs. She wore boxy homemade dresses and Kivas. She liked chocolate, dogs, and *Family Matters*. She hugged me around the neck and bit me on the cheek.

Afterward, I would go home to my father and look into his beautiful pockmarked face. Dad has gold-brown eyes and a classically peaked Mayan nose. He would stare at me with his X-ray glare and my stomach would begin to flap and squeak.

"How's your friend, that girl Marisela?" he'd ask me sometimes, tense and not blinking.

I'd shrug. "She's all right." "She's cool." "I don't know."

But then, when he once didn't speak to me for three days, I clung onto him like a frightened kitten and cried, "I don't think I'm going to hang out with her anymore."

"I'm glad to hear that," Dad replied in a hot burst.

I broke up with Marisela the next day. She sat down on the concrete back steps of the CVS and wailed.

What would I have said to my father if I had seen those pictures of Laura, Yolanda, and Lydia?

Im not comfortable with the word Lesbian but as each day go's by I'm more and more comfortable with the word AMANDA?

*

me the way you scratch me the way you move. I waited for you for so long. I love your earlobes your snoring your disobedience your clothes your old socks how you grind your teeth your intransigence your myopia

*

Laura Aguilar is poor. Around the same time that she showed her undocumented photographs at the Venice Biennale, she made a suite titled *Will Work for AXCESS*. One of the black-and-white gelatin silver prints in this series shows her standing in front of a Santa Monica Bergamot Station art gallery while gripping a handwritten cardboard sign that contains the same words as the photograph's title. From her pose, Aguilar looks like she should be standing off the 101 Freeway holding out a baseball cap for coins. But she's just trying to be a working artist. In another photograph, she extends a cupped hand, so you can put quarters or folded dollars in it.

That same year, Aguilar also made her *Don't Tell Her Art Can't Hurt Her* tour de force. These gelatin silver prints include a traditional, bright-lit, head-and-shoulders portrait of Aguilar naked and putting the muzzle of a revolver in her mouth.

Beneath the image, she hand-wrote:

"If you're a person of color and take pride in yourself and your culture, and you use your art to give a voice, to show the positive, how do the bridges get built if the doors are closed to your voice and your vision?"

*

I learned about the existence of Venice, Italy, in 1996, when I was sixteen years old. I know that's an incredibly late age to get to grips with European geography, but Principal Hayden had slotted me into remedial because I was always drawing vaginas in class. I finally got to La Serenissima in 2003, on an $1,800 grant that I won from the California Arts Council for a critical race burlesque show I put on in Van Nuys. But I didn't see any Laura Aguilars that might have been left over from the *Aperto 93* exhibition. I just wound up running out of money after two weeks and shacking up with an intense blond Bulgarian curator named Gergana. I made all of these bad paintings of Gergana using my own blood and an Arteza Acrylics set that I commandeered from a store off the Riva Longa, and then fled Italy when she put me into a sleeperhold because of my commitment issues.

In 2008, I was twenty-eight years old, but I didn't hear about the Aguilar show at the Museo Alameda in San Antonio. Even if I had known about it, though, I was too busy to go. I got involved in this heavy polyamorous FUBAR involving a Maine-based choreographer named Vanessa Sutton and a Viennese otolaryngologist named Hoàng Truong. I was also super-overcommitted from staging a Happening in Tokyo that involved me running naked through the Nihonbashi District screaming a call-and-response shape-note song I'd written, which is titled *NED McCLINTOCK SHOULD*

BE IN JAIL. That intervention earned me a $10,000 Franklin Furnace award that I had to stretch out over two years, until I met Xōchitl.

I became so panic-attackingly poor that when I wasn't bunking with various females with vulnerability problems and a couple of man-dep male creatives, I homesteaded at the Saratoga Springs art colony Yaddo until I got almost arrested.

It's hard to make art when you have no money. At Yaddo, I hung out with a white female confessional harpist named Alicia who made $65,000 a year teaching in a tenured gig at Oberlin, a white male neo-abstractionist named Steven whose latest series of paintings had been sold at White Cube for $200K–$500K a pop, and a Black womxn composer named Treasure whose atonal protest chants had, within the last two years, earned her a $120 honorarium when she'd given a one-night concert at Yale.

Treasure had transformed her residency at the colony into a squat just like me. We both hated Alicia and Steven. Treasure and I spent so much time having sex and hysterically unpacking the texts of our unpayable credit card statements that Treasure only composed a quarter of a dirge titled "I Don't Have a 401K" during her year's stay. For my part, I just managed to write a handful of lines of *Texit*, a play about a neurotic anti-Mexican racist that I'd been drafting at that point for the past four years. I also indulged in my art hobby of writing institutional critique/pirate didactics like this one and hacking them into various museum websites: I posted Valerie Solanas's *SCUM MANIFESTO* (1967) on the Musée d'Orsay's webpage for Manet's *Olympia* (1863) and substituted a video of myself binge eating/Heimliching Cracker Barrel's Double Chocolate Fudge Coca-Cola® Cake for Paul Gauguin's *Two Tahitian Women* (1899) on the Metropolitan Museum of Art's website.

After I got kicked out of Yaddo, I had $572.88 left in my Wells Fargo account. I drove to Vail, Colorado, and stayed alive by making Arte Povera out of bits of string and dead leaves. I showed these sculptures in a pop-up on East Meadow Drive, and they sold out, which earned me $210.16 that I didn't get to bank because I got picked up on a vagrancy charge and escorted out of town before I could pick up the check.

I drove back to Los Angeles, where I tried to make art by sobbing into the dust on my Prius's windows and taking photographs of these action drawings with my iPhone. I sold the suite for $50 to an online feminist art magazine called *Kun(s)t*, but the PayPal got screwed up and I never received my money. Sometimes, after that, I'd create readymades out of my stained and bitten Styrofoam coffee cups I got from McDonald's. I couldn't sell those, though, so I took pictures of them and punked them onto the

Gagosian webpage because I'd just read in the *New York Times* that Larry G. had sold a limited-edition Jeff Koons BMW for eight figures. I also continued writing *Texit*, tweeting out the lines, and engaging in the typical compulsive validation-surveillance behavior one indulges in electronically when at a psychological low point.

What is it they say about being an artist? "The artist's vocation is to send light into the human heart"? Is that it?

Or, is it "The job of the artist is always to deepen the mystery"?

Oh, no, it's "The highest calling of the artist is to figure out sooner rather than later that being an artist is no bueno because $$$ is ❤❤❤ and so then go to dental school or at least get a teaching credential."

All I know is, at that point in my life, it would have really helped me to see Aguilar's *Will Work for AXCESS* and *Don't Tell Her Art Can't Hurt Her*. But I still didn't even know that they existed.

*

I first encountered Xōchitl Hernández at the Hammer Museum's absolutely unsurvivable 2011 "Gala in the Garden." It's a celebrity boozefest where donors eat nonfarmed salmon in the museum's heatlamped courtyard while sitting in white plastic chairs under glowy fairy lights and competitively understating their accomplishments. Hammer director Ann Philbin feted honorees Lari Pittman and Matt Groening with an adjectival speech that made me giggle helplessly. Neil Patrick Harris ran around in Tom Ford and Ed Ruscha wore a blue T-shirt. The Rodarte sisters slumped quietly. Art collector and Gala co-chair Rosette Delug stomped about in a bright-pink Vera Wang. Fashion designer Jenni Kayne fuckety blah blahed with that *Bound* actress Gina Gershon, who wore something black and hairy.

I stalked around the crudités (radical vegan). My couture for the evening was a slashed Reagan/Bush '84 T-shirt that I'd stolen from a WeHo gallerina named Bonita, whom I'd just dumped, and black Nike Zoom Hyperdunks that I jacked from a dude dancer named Tre, whom I was currently ghosting. I wore my laminated name tag aggressively over the nipple of my left boob. I had shaved half of my head and the other half was loose and curly. I got into the Gala because of my lingering Franklin Furnace "glow" and attended because it promised free and plentiful nutrition. As I hunched around the catering, my teeth bristled with hairy green shreds of broccoli and I felt increasingly hostile.

Xōchitl was talking to Jenni Kayne along with Gina Gershon by the shrimp. Xōchitl knew Kayne well enough from a 2010 Emily's List retreat in Taos that Kayne was one of Xōchitl's few Emergency Bypassers when her phone idled in DND mode. Xōchitl, like me, is a Mexican American. Unlike me, she's also a honcho actuary who had just made VP at Munger & Hanley's LA office, and had helped organize Kamala Harris's 2010 California AG nomination fund-raiser in Pacific Palisades.

I saw her before she saw me. Xōchitl's hair is hugely frizzy and a kind of stripy black-brown. She has the round, shining face of a Diego Rivera Madonna. She wore a navy-blue Land's End business suit and pink-and-white Sauconys with white socks.

Xōchitl chatted with Gina Gershon with her chin up and her mouth sort of softly hooting toward the sky, which I now know is how she gets when she's had a couple of drinks and is feeling "hawt n sexy." All of a sudden, she seemed to sense an unseen observer. She looked over her shoulder and saw me watching her. She fixed my gaze with her large, soft, golden eyes. I stood by the broccoli staring back at her. She smiled and said goodbye to Gina Gershon and Jenni Kayne. She walked straight over to the crudités table.

Xōchitl Hernández stood in front of me, a slow, slightly furry smile spreading over her dark strong features.

"Hi," she said. Her eyes darted to my name tag. "A-man-*da*."

She radiated light. She was as beautiful as Cassiopeia in the northern sky.

"Oh my God," I breathed.

*

your calluses your cough your insouciance the way you look in that white blouse with the tear in it the rough patch of skin on your right anklebone your fingerprints your moan your curses your teeth your

*

From the mid-1990s to the early 2000s, Laura Aguilar shot several series of herself nude in western landscapes. She traveled to the deserts and forests of New Mexico, Texas, and the California Mojave. She positioned her camera on a tripod, took off her clothes, and draped herself over huge stones while the remote shutter released. Her breasts hung down to her stomach, large and shining. She resembled the megaliths that she posed among: her chest and thighs are thick, dense, and powerfully built. Or she would curl up in a fetal position in the sand, her haunches exposed to the sun. Her flesh folded like the rocks' crags and whorls. Her dark hair fell over her face, obscuring her expression. Aguilar created three suites from these experiments. She titled them *Nature Self-Portraits* (1996), *Stillness* (1999), and *Grounded* (2006–2007).

Aguilar took the photographs in order to purge herself of self-loathing caused in part by difficulties she had with her father. In an unpublished artist's statement made circa 2003, she reflected: "*Stillness* drew from the experiences I had caring for my father and his dying process . . . As his caretaker, I was glad for the experience of caring for him, witnessing peace come over him as he surrendered to his illness and finding peace for the relationship between us."

Aguilar did not intend to circulate the pictures to the public. When she finally allowed her friends to see them, however, they convinced her to show and publish. So emboldened, Aguilar submitted the work for exhibitions, gave lectures about them, and sold them, until the images began to create expanding circles of influence among an elite tribe of alert artists and curators. *Stillness, Grounded,* and *Nature Self-Portraits* now stand as classics of Latinx and queer art. While the pictures remain imperceptible on most blue-chip museum websites, images from *Stillness* appeared eventually in the book *Women Artists of the American West,* which social documentary photographer Susan Ressler edited in 2003. UCLA gave a home to all three opuses in its archives. Scholar Rudi Bleys highlighted selections from *Nature Self-Portraits* in his 2000 survey *Homotextuality and Latin American Art.*

But I didn't see any of these masterpieces until about ten weeks ago, in April of 2011.

*

voice your words your breasts your intransigence your fragrance your lip prints on your wineglass your breath your teeth your memories your illness your poison your other lovers your nightmares your eyelashes your laughter your future your fingerprints your mutations your nipples your toes your cough your whole life your everything

*

Xōchitl and I attended an afterparty in Chelsea for the inaugural NYC Feminist Zinefest in spring '11. We had been together officially for three weeks. The first week and a half of our legit coupledom had been spent nearly killing each other in a huge bed/hot tub in the "Cliff House" at Big Sur's Post Ranch Inn, which indulges its inhabitants with an IMAX view of wind-tousled sequoias, custom-made burl wood furniture, and very hard, radiantly heated floors.

After we were asked to leave, Xōchitl and I returned to LA for six days. During that idyll we took my father to dinner at Dragon Chinese

Restaurant, his favorite, in Koreatown. The main course was sweet-and-sour ribs. Dessert was a dumpling-gagging debate that Dad and I engaged over the delicate question of whether queerphobia is a sign of mental illness or a respectable worldview based on Christian teachings. "I think he's cute," Xōchitl said after, kissing me in her pimento Volvo. The evening ended with a marathon Frenching/cunnilingus death match that cracked the rear window of her car and imbued me with an ice-cold fucking terror that somehow I would screw up this relationship, as I had kamikaze'd my romances with Marisela, Vanessa, Hoàng, Treasure, Bonita, and Tre.

I spent the rest of that week running up and down the streets of Burbank (where I lived) obsessively mentally composing Xōchitl passionate emails and cleaning up my squat so she wouldn't think I was a dealbreakingly "bad" homeless. Then a Nickelodeon producer/Emily's Lister scarily named Paula Verhoeven DM'd Xōchitl about the Feminist Zinefest. We got excited and used Xōchitl's miles to red-eye it to NY.

Now we were at the afterparty, in Paula's nineteenth-century Neo-Grec two-story brownstone on West 22nd Street. Rich boho feminists jammed the solarium while wearing Ann Demeulemeester and vaping. Xōchitl cackled over by the cassoulet kiosk as Paula, a seventy-year-old grand dame with silver dreads and dripping with turquoise, joked about how Tesla was already getting attacked by shorts. Every third wymyn there was a poet with a Guggenheim, sleeve tats, and a Seven Sisters chair. A tanned David Zwirner rainmaker called Bliss, who sat next to me on the bisectional Hans Wegner, whisper-talked to an unnamed skinny-sunglass-wearing art monograph buyer for the Strand about how Zinefest was her chance to "unwind." Glossy lesbian-feminist magazines lay scattered *Real Simply* style on the minimalist teak coffee table, which also boasted red radishes, white jicama, pot brownies, half-drunk glasses of pinot, and real cigarettes.

I wore the Reagan/Bush '84 and Superdunks again and chewed silently on the last of the jicama. I am not socially good. I stared at Paula making Xōchitl laugh. I side-eyed Bliss stretching out her pedicured toes while the Strand buyer talked about *Game of Thrones*. My love for Xōchitl was metastasizing into a combo of earthquakish chest-thumps and spiraled logic. I thought back to the torn cotton-poly bedsheet that marked off my "room" in my Burbank group crash and the twenty of my last dollars that I had used to buy a Whitman's chocolate sampler from CVS for Xōchitl as a special present. These thoughts boomeranged into doomful memories of my father yelling over the ribs at Dragon Chinese, my as yet undisclosed police record for shoplifting, and the time when Treasure had said I didn't have the "horsepower" for a real relationship.

Then I looked down. Among the feminist zines glowed a yellow fascicle titled *Latinx Babes from Outer Space*, which had a drawing of a USS *Enterprise*-ish *mons pubis* on its cover. I opened it up and paged through. On page seventeen I saw a reproduction of Laura Aguilar's *Nature Self-Portrait #14* (1996). A caption said *Laura Aguilar is a queer Latinx photog from San Gabriel, CA.*

The photocopied black-and-white gelatin silver print showed Aguilar in the Mojave. Aguilar poses at a small pond of water pooling up from a rocky outcropping. Tufts of acacia, brown grass, and wizened mesquite surround the little lagoon. The stones circling the water glow in tones of oyster and pure white. The sky stretches overhead in a thin marbled band. The water appears richly textured, glossy and rippled.

Aguilar is naked. She's taken off her clothes and crawled over the stones so that she rests on the rock's ridge, her head toward the pond. Her luminous left cheek and dark eyes glint like mica. The soft ends of her black hair fall into the water. Her hand grips the stone. The water reflects back Aguilar's face, shoulder, and round hip. The sun beats down.

I sat back on the sofa and breathed. The zine's page seemed to grow brighter the longer I looked at it. Aguilar's image entered and opened me. The room's chatter curled back like fog. I saw her. She made sense to me.

"Amanda?" Xōchitl walked over and stood in front of me. She looked down at me with her wide brown brow. She smiled her starlight at me.

"She's like you," I said. Tears started pouring down my face.

Xōchitl reached out her hands. "Honey, honey."

"You're so beautiful," I said, or tried to.

*

After I saw *Nature Self-Portrait #14* in *Latinx Babes from Outer Space*, I searched for Aguilars everywhere. I found her work on the LACMA site, and input her name into the Kinsey and New Museum search engines. I tracked her down to the UCLA archives. There, I learned about *Latina Lesbians, Don't Tell Her, Will Work for AXCESS, Stillness,* and *Grounded,* and saw almost all of the *Nature Self-Portraits.* After that, I found the reports about *Aperto 93* and the Museo Alameda show with the now-broken links. And then I learned that MOCA had purchased a small selection of her work.

On the MOCA website, it says that the museum possesses three of Aguilar's photographs. As I've mentioned, these photographs are *Clothed/*

Unclothed No. 19 (1992), *Clothed/Unclothed No. 5* (1990), and *Untitled Landscape* (1996). Instead of showing these pictures on their site, MOCA replaces the images with those little signs that say "No Image Available."

*

Available commonly means "accessible." But it bears a deeper etymology. The word hails from the fourteenth-century term *availen*, which means "to help" someone or "to assist" them. It also comes from the ancient Latin *valere*, which means "to be strong" and to be "of worth." *Valere* is the root of "valor."

I don't know what MOCA means by the title *Untitled Landscape* (1996). I'm not familiar with an *Untitled Landscape* series taken at the same time as *Nature Self-Portraits*. I wonder if the museum means that it possesses one of the nudes that Aguilar took in the Mojave. The picture it owns may indeed be the same one that I saw in Chelsea in April 2011.

If "available" means to help or assist, as well as to be strong, worthwhile, and valorous, then MOCA is incapable of making Laura Aguilar's work "unavailable."

But MOCA does cut us off from our history when it hides her away.

*

I love you, Xōchitl.

History

Saturday, May 7, 2016
3:17 AM artists who have children women failures?
Tuesday, July 19, 2016
12:58 PM 66 year old man prolonged cold normal?
Friday, October 28, 2016
11:04 AM Joint bank accounts how to get money when girlfriend mad
Wednesday, December 28 2016
9:15 AM marisa merz's dad died how why
1:56 PM Why

CHAPTER TWO A STRUGGLE THAT WILL NEVER, EVER PAY OFF IN THE END

[This is an experimental "didactic," which is otherwise known as an explanatory text accompanying an item in a museum collection. I posted it without authorization onto the Guggenheim Museum website page for Glenn Ligon's *Prisoner of Love #1* (1992) while doing a residency at the Guggenheim upon the invitation of director Richard Armstrong. I posted it on July 2, 2016; it was removed by a PR person or one of Richard's invisible interns on July 3, 2016. I was asked to leave on July 8, 2016: "It's not because of the sexual politics of it, Amanda, obviously not. It's the narcissism, the solipsism, the obstreperousness, your failure to recognize any kind of institutional culture or hierarchy or even understand this work of art outside of your own experience." *Prisoner of Love #1* is an 80" × 30" black-and-white oil and gesso on linen consisting of the repeatedly stenciled words "We Are the Ink That Gives the White Page a Meaning."]

Glenn Ligon, Prisoner of Love #1

Xōchitl's cheeks shone with an opal glow. She leaned across the table and touched my arm. "What do you think about us starting a family soon?" She flashed me a shining smile. "And by soon I mean now."

I didn't answer. I was thumb-typing stage directions into the Notes app on my phone, *ICE AGENTS, wearing bikinis made out of the American flag, enter stage right.*

"Amanda," Xōchitl said, still using her gentle voice. This was six weeks ago, before we came to New York for my residency. We sat in our regular corner table at Gjelina, in Venice. I had ordered the crispy purple potato with vegan lemon aioli, and Xōchitl had ordered the grilled Aspen "bistro" steak. Xōchitl began to pick at her dinner with her serrated knife, so a little blood sprayed. "Wouldn't that be nice?"

"Honey Bunny, it would be great—but I don't know if it's the exact right time," I answered, typing my notes under the table like a bastard. Looking up from my phone, I grabbed hold of my fresh glass of pinot grigio with my right hand. "I still have to do the Guggenheim rez, and then see if I get that NEA for the Mexico video, and then go to MacDowell, and then get *Texit* produced. And then we'll—"

"Yeah, except that we talked about me getting pregnant." Xōchitl is 5'3" and possesses an abundance of black-brown frizzly hair that puffs out from her temples like a beautiful Pomeranian's. Her eyes resemble gorgeous brown planets that now began to spin agitatedly on their axes.

I shrugged. "But how can you be pregnant when I'm dematerializing in the desert?"

Xōchitl tapped her left middle finger on the table, as if she were deleting a frivolous theorem. "Well, that's what I'm trying to talk to you about. Because, I've decided that you and I are gonna have a beautiful little baby together, not after the Guggenheim thing, or the desert thing, but as soon as my basal body temperature next hits between 97 and 99 degrees."

"But if I get the NEA, I have to commit," I said. "I can't do all of those things that people do when they have a kid."

Xōchitl cut up a piece of steak into tiny bites and didn't eat it. "You mean, be a parent?"

"It's just that, when I do my fast in Cabos Corrientes, I'm going to be high on ketones," I went on. "It'll be a Joseph Beuys level of nuts."

"I don't remember what that is," Xōchitl said.

"I told you," I said. "The guy with the felt."

"Anyway, I thought you said the NEA is fascist," Xōchitl said.

"Yeah, it is," I muttered. I stared down at my plate, suddenly catching a brainwave. With my phone on my knees, I surreptitiously thumb-typed, ICE AGENTS, *wearing flag bikinis and carrying babies in Babybjörns, enter stage right.*

Xōchitl tilted her head at me omnisciently. "No."

I stopped typing. "I'm not."

"Amanda, I love you. I want to start a family with you." Xōchitl pivoted her head back and forth, as if shaking water out of both ears. "We can have a baby together and be happy."

"I love you, too." I reached out and stroked her cheek. "And if we could just wait, say, six or seven years—"

"Six or seven *what?*"

"Five or six years," I said.

Xōchitl squinched up her eyes. "Is this about your dad?"

"Four and a half years."

Xōchitl put down her knife and fork and touched her fingertips to her temples. "You're not listening to me. I'm an old bag. I'll be thirty-eight in seven months. I gotta jack these eggs up now."

I stared down at my purple potato and blinked rapidly. "I promise that someday we will have a baby. A big, huge, perfect baby. A baby who gets multiple degrees but isn't a professional student. A baby who has a relatable emotional style and also fights crime."

Xōchitl nodded. "A girl."

I waved my hands in the air. "But the only thing is, after New York and Mexico and MacDowell, I thought that maybe I'd do a really massive project. I either want to skywrite an anti-rape-culture mural titled *NED McCLINTOCK SHOULD BE IN JAIL* above the US Capitol, or masturbate all over the White House in tribute to Sanja Iveković's 1970s anti-fascist interventions. How am I going to do that if we start a family now?"

Xōchitl speared a piece of her steak. She shrugged as she ate it. "You're not."

*

In 1986, Gallimard published *Prisoner of Love*, Jean Genet's memoir of living with the Palestinian fedayeen in northern Jordan in 1971–72 and his late '60s association with the Californian Black Panthers. Genet, a queer, white, French, child-free male novelist famous for *The Thief's Journal* and *Our Lady of the Flowers*, described the fedayeen as a transcendent but endangered language: "In 1970 an old word that had disappeared from political vocabularies was heard again: the word Palestinian," he wrote.

In *Prisoner of Love*, Genet also used this "endangered language" trope to describe Black people in the US. He put the metaphor to use when recounting his 1970 tour of American college campuses in support of Black Panther Bobby Seale, who was on trial for murder. Genet admired the Panthers' "rejection of the white world" and offered this poetic account of their trauma: "In white America the Blacks are . . . the ink that gives the white page a meaning . . . The abundance of whites is what the writing is set down on . . . But the poem is written by the absent Blacks."

Genet wrote *Prisoner of Love* more than ten years after his travels in Jordan and the United States. He composed this strange, vigorous work of nonfiction from 1983 to 1986, while he waged a final struggle with throat cancer. As he composed *Prisoner of Love* and fought to survive, Genet also maintained a personal life: In 1964, he'd abandoned his former boyfriend, Abdallah Bentaga, for the dashing race-car driver Jacky Maglia. Maglia remained Genet's companion, nurse, chatelaine, and inamorato to the end of Genet's days. But even though Genet lived with Maglia for a brief time, and bought him an expensive Lotus racing car, he apparently couldn't be happy/undepressed/sane if he wasn't constantly working at the level of maximum prejudice. So he moved out of the house he shared with Maglia and wrote his last book all alone in a Parisian garret.

Genet had long prized art over romance or family. When submitting to an interview with the journalist Madeleine Gobeil in the mid-'60s, he confessed that he regarded homosexuality as a "blessing" mostly because it had put him on "the path of writing." And when he mentioned his relationship with Maglia, he insinuated that their attachment served the greater god of literature. Maglia and his other lovers, Genet said, helped him engage with his "writing, that is, [to] return to society by other means."

Some people might think that Genet was a jerk, but most artists are jealous of Genet because he managed to make his obsessions pay off: Despite the demands of boyfriends and cancer, Genet finished *Prisoner of Love* in the summer of 1985. Then he collapsed in his apartment, hitting his head upon a hard surface. He died from his wounds. When Maglia found Genet the morning after his death, a clean manuscript of *Prisoner of Love* stood in a neat stack on Genet's night table. Soon thereafter, Gallimard issued the book, and it garnered rapturous reviews comparing the author to Proust and Céline.

Maglia continued to clamor for Genet's attention even after his lover was dead. As the self-appointed custodian of Genet's reputation, Maglia began to make belligerent appearances in books, films, and interviews about the author. Maglia fulminated at Genet's biographers that they did not understand how Genet's literary experiments changed the ways that we use language to describe the lives of despised people.

"He is very jealous of Genet's legacy and always fears that the events dedicated to the writer will betray the spirit of his works," curator Marie Redonnet told *Aujourd'hui le Maroc* magazine in 2002.

*

If I died, I would not have to worry about my girlfriend Xōchitl hysterically berating curators who sought to stage large exhibitions dedicated to the spirit of my work.

Xōchitl's full name is Xōchitl Juana Hernández. She's half Zacatecan and half Chihuahuan. At Munger & Hanley, where she works as an actuary, she earns almost $400,000 literal dollars a year. Xōchitl knows how best to predict when someone is going to get defenestrated in a car collision or outlive their reverse mortgage. She is also an excellent cook, bartender, carpenter, car mechanic, vacation itinerary organizer, hospital-corner bedmaker, checkbook balancer, nurse, therapist, and lover.

Xōchitl hasn't rejected the white world like the Black Panthers and maybe Jean Genet did. She reads books like *Backward Stochastic Differential Equations with Jumps and Their Actuarial and Financial Applications*. Xōchitl knows how to do complicated things like patch toilet flange leaks and arrange legal representation for girlfriends who receive threatening letters from MOCA lawyers and Wikipedia administrators, but she doesn't really get concepts like "the fedayeen are a transcendent but endangered language" or "Black people are the ink that gives the white page a meaning."

"Yeah, that doesn't make any sense," she'll say, looking up at me from her computer with her bangs in her eyes.

I, on the other hand, have rejected the white world. My parents are/were from Jalisco. For the past twelve years, I've been writing a mobile opera called *Texit*, which features a neurasthenically racist superhero named Texit. Texit wants Texas to secede because she doesn't like Mexicans, but she's also fallen into inconvenient love with an undocumented orthodontic hygienist named Josefina.

I'm a performance artist who fights the Anglo capitalist hegemony, unless my acceptance of fellowships and curation jobs with increasingly prestigious arts institutions means that I am a hypocrite with false consciousness. Even though I am a truculent institutional critic, I'm going to co-direct a show at the Whitney next year and right now I'm doing this residency at the Guggenheim! Also, last week Cornell emailed me about teaching a workshop on futurist body improvisation. None of it pays that great. Like other artists, I *could* do ad copy for capitalist art institutions to supplement my income, but Xōchitl is an active supporter of my vision. Also, I would never sink that low.

Sometimes, when I am in an "elevated mood," I do gratis Situationist interventions, like this Ligon text. Right now I'm most famous for my Laura Aguilar trespass, which got speedily deleted for violating one federal and seven Wikipedia statutes, and then triggered an internecine and viral web war between #lesbiantwitter and #ricksantorumrocks. Future projects include a residency at MacDowell and my maybe staging *Texit* next year at the Geffen. And in a month Xōchitl and I are going to Cabo Corrientes to film a still untitled autocritical documentary that I will hopefully get an NEA for.

I'm going to starve myself nearly to death and film it. It'll be very anti-white supremacy and Vito Acconci. The logistics are complicated, though, which Xōchitl doesn't completely understand. I hope she soon figures out that baby manufacturing is inconsistent with fasting so hard that you hallucinate like the hate child of Cesar Chavez and Emmeline Pankhurst.

"You're fucking crazy," Xōchitl often says. Sometimes, she smiles and adds: "Take off your clothes."

I love Xōchitl so much. She is inside of my marrow and my vagina and my pores and my dreams and all of my thoughts.

But this baby thing is a blocker. How do you make a person like Xōchitl stall their bio clock for, say, four years or so? Anybody out there got any tips? I'm busy enough as it is taking care of my father. I used to cook for my dad just once a week, but lately he's had a cold or something. Before we came to New York, I was there almost every day to help him out, and he made me watch the entirety of some eternally long PBS miniseries called *A Man for All Seasons*, which definitely cut into my dedicated *Texit* time.

I really have to get some work done.

*

From 1991 to 1992, the Black American, queer, and child-free artist Glenn Ligon began to work on his *Door Paintings* series, where he used black oil stick to write quotes from Zora Neale Hurston, John Howard Griffin, and Jesse Jackson onto white wooden doors that he'd covered with primer. In late '92, Ligon added to this body of work by appropriating Jean Genet's *Prisoner of Love*. He converted Genet's line "They are the ink that gives the white page a meaning" to "We are the ink that gives the white page a meaning," and stenciled it in an increasingly messy manner all over a door.

Ligon once participated in an interview with a MoMA curator where he described his practice of rendering endangered language in his painting:

"I use a plastic letter stencil that has every letter of the alphabet on it and the painting is made by doing each letter one at a time, from the top of the painting to the bottom of the painting, and then when I reach the bottom I start over again. The more I go over those letters with this oil stick the blacker and denser the surface of the painting becomes to the point where it is entirely blacked out, so the text is visible and not visible, legible and not legible. [Reading it is] . . . a struggle that will never, ever pay off in the end."

*

Xōchitl and I are delicately negotiating our family dynamic. The more we debate having a baby the messier and denser the problem becomes. I think she may be a *little* pissed at me.

But she can't stay mad at me for very long.

Our bedroom is white and minimal. I decorated it, as opposed to the rest of the house, which she stocked with bourgeois wicker and gallery-purchased paintings. I threw out everything from the boudoir except for one chair from Ikea and a massive Goodwill bed that we put to very good use.

When Xōchitl fucks me, she grips my jaw gently with her left hand and stares me in the eyes.

"Hey, there you are," she says.

I am slow and ferocious. I touch her until she bucks.

I do each of her letters, one at a time. When I reach her bottom I start over again. I keep going until Xōchitl is visible and not visible, legible and not legible.

"Aman—" she gasps, which would be funny except that she's so full of passion and emotion.

I love Xōchitl more than art.

*

In 1955, at the age of forty-five, Jean Genet met the eighteen-year-old juggler and tightrope walker Abdallah Bentaga. Genet quickly formed a passion for this young and beautiful man, who was born of a German mother and Algerian father. Genet paid for Bentaga's circus arts training and found himself so inspired that he wrote an essay titled "The Tightrope Walker" in 1958. He even rented an apartment in Paris, instead of living in the hotels he favored, because it made Bentaga feel more secure. Genet and Bentaga remained partners for over a decade.

But in 1959, Bentaga fell from a tightrope and injured his knee permanently. Genet, watching Bentaga struggle with his disability, lost interest. He eventually formed an attachment to the race-car driver and future biographer-heckler Jacky Maglia. Though Genet continued to finance Bentaga, the castaway could not withstand his losses and committed suicide in 1964. Genet reeled from this death. He tore up his manuscripts and swore that he would never write again.

Genet's biographies understandably grow a little thin at this stage. There aren't a lot of forensic evaluations of how he spent the next several artless years, except that we do know that, at one point in 1967, he drank a lot of alcohol that was packed with tranquilizers. After this failed attempt on his own life, Genet realized that, if he was to survive, he had to break his promise about the not-writing. He found himself re-inspired after visiting with the Black Panthers in '70 and then traveling to Palestine to work with the fedayeen in Jordan in '71–'72. These experiences led to his composing magazine articles about global racial activism and feeling like a real human being again. Eventually, his efforts grew into his solitary work in his Parisian garret and his successful completion of *Prisoner of Love.*

Despite his book's title, Genet was not a prisoner of love. He proved unable to make either Bentaga or Maglia the annihilating center of his life. In "The Tightrope Walker," written in that fiery period when Genet was in the first thrall to Bentaga, he explains the insuperable distance between himself and his lovers by observing that human beings can never escape their damage: "I wonder where it resides, where the secret wound is hidden . . . It is into this wound . . . that [the artist] must throw himself, it is there he will be able to discover the strength, the audacity and the skill necessary to his art."

For Genet, the only answer to life's suffering existed in his work.

*

The childless artist Glenn Ligon may well be a prisoner to love, but if he is, he conducts that drama in secret. Despite repeated web searches, I can find no information on a boyfriend, husband, paramour, daughter, or son.

The only available data about Glenn Ligon's love life exists in the web documents that report on Ligon's relationship with Thelma Golden, who is the child-free director and chief curator of the Studio Museum in Harlem, which exhibits art made by artists of African descent.

Glenn Ligon was born in 1960 in the Bronx. He is deservedly one of the most revered artists in the whole world, and his résumé boasts shows at the Hammer, the Guggenheim, MoMA, and the Whitney. Thelma Golden was born in Queens in 1965. She is one of the most celebrated curators on the earth. Art world insiders mention her regularly as a possible future leader of the Metropolitan Museum of Art and the Brooklyn Museum. She is a genius and spends a lot of her time creating a staggering number of curatorial products and/or championing Ligon's art.

One of the reasons why Thelma Golden promotes Glenn Ligon so energetically is that she appears to love him very much.

As just one illustration, consider a spring 2016 video showing Golden and Ligon speaking together at Chelsea's Luhring Augustine Gallery. Their discussion promoted Ligon's film exhibit *We Need to Wake Up Cause That's What Time It Is*, which sampled footage from comedian Richard Pryor's early 1980s show *Live on the Sunset Strip.*

The video opens with Golden and Ligon seated close together in a book-filled salon. They face a glass coffee table. Papers fan out on the table in front of Golden and a champagne glass stands in easy reach of Ligon. Both Golden and Ligon wear chic black outfits with silver accents.

Golden perches on the very edge of a large oatmeal-colored wing chair. She fixes her huge radiant eyes on Ligon and holds her hands between her knees. Ligon leans back into his chair and tries unsuccessfully to seem relaxed.

Ligon is an artist and so he doesn't remember a lot of details about his art. At around minute four of the video, while describing Richard Pryor's comedy, Ligon forgets the year that Pryor filmed *Live on the Sunset Strip*. "Eighty-two," Golden says, quickly. "My film runs the length of the original film," Ligon goes on, hesitating. "Which goes on for . . ."

"Eighty minutes," Golden interjects, smiling and laughing.

Soon after, Golden begins to read a rapturous *New York Times* review of the show, authored by the eminent critic Holland Carter (" 'It was a tribute, but also a statement about the punishing work that's required to add new kinds of motion to the world' "). Ligon deflects, confessing that he "thinks that is incredibly generous," and then arguing that "Pryor has done much of the work." But Golden leaps to Ligon's defense: "That's not true!"

The video closes with an invisible audience member asking Ligon, "Why did [your] paintings take so long to find their legs?" This question could be read as containing an assessment of Ligon's work as having gone through a period of depressing unrecognition before it achieved its current Luhring Augustine magnificence. "I don't know," Ligon replies in a muffled voice. He pauses for several seconds, at the end of which Golden leans forward and says, "I—I." During this brief interlude, Ligon stares out into the middle distance, but you can practically see the invisible love-tendrils that shoot out between him and Golden. The tendrils touch. Then Ligon recovers: "I don't know if I always believe in a linear progress," he murmurs. All the while, Golden sits upright, her wrists nestled between her knees, as she blinks supportively at Ligon.

"Thank you, Glenn," she says softly, at the end.

*

"Babe, I don't think I really understand what you're trying to do here," Xōchitl said to me two years ago, as she looked at my eleventh draft of *Texit*. We lounged on our bed, Xōchitl sitting back on the large white pillows I'd bought at Target. I perched at the very edge of the mattress, clenching my hands together. "I can tell it's really good, you know," she went on. "But I don't know why everything has to be so dark and horrible."

"It's all right," I'd said, tears running down my face. "All I care about is that you're here, in my life."

"It's just that, we're so happy. Why's your writing so sad?"

I looked down at my bare feet. Xōchitl loved their arches, their thick athletic callouses. That morning, when I'd stuck my foot up in the air and started shaming it, she'd said I was an artist and that meant I didn't need to do dumb things like get professional pedicures.

I now blinked mutely at my multicolored toenails. I didn't say, *Why's my writing SAD? Have you read the news lately?*

I didn't say, *I'm a fucking performance artist, not a comic.*

I didn't say, *If you have to ask me that question then you have no idea who I am.*

Instead, I lay back on the bed. I felt the danger in the moment. But I didn't give in. I began to softly stroke Xōchitl's short, muscular legs. I pressed my cheek to her warm thigh.

"We are happy," I said.

*

For many of the world's great artists, all of life goes into the work. Not even love escapes this utilitarianism.

Abdallah Bentaga loved Jean Genet so much he killed himself when Genet left him. And Jacky Maglia loved Genet so much that he became the nervous, mouthy guardian of Genet's writings and reputation.

Jean Genet loved Abdallah Bentaga and Jacky Maglia, too, but not as much as they loved him. Maybe this isn't fair to say, but Genet did return to writing even though he promised to give up his career after Bentaga committed suicide. And he spent his last years dedicating himself to *Prisoner of Love* instead of Maglia. Also, Genet did not consider his homosexuality a blessing because it gave him the gift of the two men's company, but rather because it put him on the path of writing, as he told journalist Madeleine Gobeil in 1964, the same year that Bentaga killed himself.

Thelma Golden loves Glenn Ligon so much that when she sits down with him in a gallery to talk about art her eyes glimmer like full moons and she seems ready to launch herself into the air.

I must believe that Glenn Ligon loves Thelma Golden back because no artist or human being who had a soul like Thelma Golden in their life would not love her. Of course, maybe I'm projecting or romanticizing. Probably. Yet, you can't fake love, and love is what I see passing between them in that spring 2016 video.

Thelma Golden and Glenn Ligon together have achieved something so important that it exceeds the boundaries of a love story. Their friendship, genius, and work ethics created not only the ink but also the phrases and the paper upon which the story of Black and American history appears.

But their platonic romance deserves a special mention in their CVs, too.

I could be wrong, but Thelma Golden and Glenn Ligon do not seem to be prisoners of love, though for reasons altogether different from Jean Genet. They may have discovered a way to share an affection that does not suck the energy out of the insane will-to-power that most creatives need to do their work.

In fact, their love may even make art possible.

*

Part of me wishes that, if I died, Xōchitl would Magliaishly berate biographers, curators, critics, and art institutions for recognizing inadequately the supreme importance of my work and explain to them in ranting monologues that my performances altered the ways human beings use language to describe despised people.

All of me wishes that I had a Thelma Golden in my life. I don't know if an artist can achieve escape velocity without that kind of help.

But what I want most of all is to be with Xōchitl. Xōchitl does not put me on the path to art and she does not understand *Texit*. She also does not comprehend that crap in my life "secretly wounded" me so that I am crazy like Jean Genet.

That doesn't matter to me. I am the real prisoner of love, you see.

Still, readers of this unauthorized didactic may have noticed that neither the amazingly productive Jean Genet, Glenn Ligon, or Thelma Golden ever had children. I can't help but do the math. If Xōchitl could just give me three years before we have a baby—or *two* years, then maybe I can strategize a way to both be an art sociopath and also selflessly do what is necessary to keep micro-humans alive.

I'd even take just one year, so that I can finish this residency, make my movie, and either skywrite the Ned McClintock anti-rape thing in the prohibited airspace above the Capitol or execute a heritage self-pleasuring protocol in the White House's foyer in honor of the body-positive Croatian dissident artist Sanja Iveković.

It's not that I'm afraid of having a child. I'm just seriously scared that if I stop making art I will disappear.

CHAPTER THREE MAYBE I SHOULDN'T HAVE INSISTED ON TAKING THIS TRIP

[These are lines from my mobile opera, titled *Texit*, which I tweeted on the flight to Cabo Corrientes. That is where I would film my untitled autocritical documentary upon having received the NEA grant. N.B., you can italicize on Twitter using a Unicode converter.]

ICE AGENTS, wearing flag bikinis and carrying babies in Babybjörns, enter stage right #texit
3:30 PM—August 10, 2016

ICE AGENTS: Don't you understand / We will clear the fatherland! / Those Mexicans don't stand a chance! / But we still need our work-life balance!
3:32 PM—August 10, 2016

[These are lines from *Texit* that I tweeted on my way back from Cabo Corrientes, three months later.]

Josefina: Ur an enemy of the state / we can no longer date #texit
7:44 AM—Oct 3 2016

Texit: but I thought u said opposites attract / babe you know you'll come back #texit
7:45 AM—Oct 3 2016

Josefina: I told u I wanted u to listen and not just hear when I explained / that ur anti-family values are super lame #texit
7:46 AM—Oct 3 2016

Texit: PLEASE DON'T LEAVE ME #texit

CHAPTER FOUR HEY CAN I COME BACK HOME NOW

[I posted a photo of Thomas "Painter of Light" Kinkade's *A Peaceful Retreat* (2002) onto SmugMug with the accompanying comment on November 5, 2016. Kinkade's monstrosity hung in the living room of my father's apartment in Koreatown, which is where I took up residence temporarily when Xōchitl made me move out of her house.

Thomas Kinkade is a flabbergastingly popular artist and probable billionaire who has made his fortune by painting placidly bad William Turner rip-offs, using a heavily pastel palette. *A Peaceful Retreat* shows a rustically quaint yet expensively huge cabin in some place like Wyoming. Pine trees and pink clouds and frosted mountains surround the cabin/mansion. The house also fronts a sloping verdant lawn, which is empty but for a meaningfully empty Adirondack chair. A babbling brook cuts through the grass and hosts a little wooden rowboat floating in the water so that fed-up actuaries could make a river escape from their clingy megalomaniac artist girlfriends if they really, really decided that this was not just a "break." A limited edition of the painting may be purchased for $280-$5,350 from Thomas Kinkade's website, though my father bought it from a garage sale in 2008 for $55.]

Xōchitl yes I screwed up I made a mistake we can have a baby you can impregnate me ASAP I'M SORRY look at what I'm reduced to without you here in my dad's house which is where im living while you work through your thing of not wanting to talk to or see me right now dad has this really bad art in his house and I have to look at it every morning when I wake up WITHOUT YOU and feel dead inside also my dad in case you want to know is actually not doing that great he's got this extremely bad flu I think the doctor wants to do some more tests anyway so that's why I haven't taken this painting out to the trash or burned it in a cleansing flame b/c hes just not doing that well anyway I miss you so much xochitl so much

CHAPTER FIVE I DIDN'T SEE THAT ONE COMING

[This was a now-vanished Snapchat of a red, white, and blue
Hillary for President poster depicting a failed female
presidential candidate standing by a US flag and smiling
widely into the camera while wearing red lipstick in an
unsuccessful effort to soothe patriarchal terrors over
her supposedly inescapably impending penisless rule. Over
the image, I scrawled the words *What Just Fucking Happened*
using Snapchat's drawing tool. I composed the Snapchat in
order to send it to Xōchitl Hernández on November 9, 2016,
at 1:16 a.m., but then I couldn't find her in my contacts
list and so I knew that I'd been blocked.]

CHAPTER SIX WEIRD SOCIAL MEDIA STUFF YOU DO WHEN YOUR DAD DIES

[This is an Instagram of three of Marisa Merz's circa 1980s zoomorphic figurines, with a circle drawn around the sculpture *Untitled, Undated, 8*. I posted this with the comment below on December 28, 2016, at 3:13 a.m. and deleted it at 3:15 a.m. *Untitled, Undated, 8* is a small, unfired clay bust of a zoomorphic creature, which might be a cat. The cat looks unhappy. Its little lips are tinted pink and its forehead looks glazed with silver dust.]

Marisa Merz's sculpture *Untitled, Undated, 8*, made of unfired kaolinite and pigment, stands apart in Merz's circa 1980s series of clay zoomorphic figurines, otherwise known as *"Testine"* (heads). While some of these statuettes look like creepy Georgia O'Keeffe skulls or hooded victims of wartime rendition, *Untitled, Undated, 8* resembles a grief-stricken cat-head. The cat-head opens its mouth and squeezes shut its eyes, as if it has just found itself utterly alone in a hospital room noisy with life-support equipment. Its forehead shines with silver dust and its lips and nose glow with pink paint, so that it resembles a human face that has grown mottled from too much sobbing.

While the cat-head expresses limitless heartbreak, its creator, Marisa Merz, seems well adjusted and happy. Marisa Merz, a small, brown-haired, bespectacled librarian-type born in 1926, is a Turinese superstar of the Italian Arte Povera school of art. Arte Povera emerged in the 1960s as a mostly macho and male aesthetic movement. The Arte Povera school included a lot of dudes like Michelangelo Pistoletto, who stuck photographs on mirrors, and Mario Merz—Marisa's own husband—who made igloos out of glass and wire. Marisa Merz feels happy because she harnessed her genius and enormous will-to-power to successfully distinguish herself in this phallo collective: she crafted eye-dazzling art like the clay heads and also made aluminum squid monsters and weird drawings of birds and angels. Gallerists and fancy exhibitors soon came calling. In 2001, she won the Special Jury Prize awarded at the Venice Biennale, and then, three years ago, she won the Golden Lion for Lifetime Achievement, also at the Venice Biennale.

Marisa Merz must also feel pretty good because she became a world-famous artist while getting married to igloo man Mario Merz and, at the same time, was smart enough not to say, "I don't think the timing is great for having a family right now, because, you know, my career." IOW, Marisa Merz made award-winning art at the same time that she had a baby with her husband, Mario Merz. The baby was born in 1960 and is now a full-grown person named Beatrice.

Marisa Merz is a wizard not just because of the aluminum squid monsters and the Venice Biennale but also because she had that baby. She apparently knew what I did not, which is that you should spawn despite the hassle so that Xōchitl doesn't leave you and also so when your father dies you have somebody brand-new and happy around the house. This brand-new human could give you something to live for, instead of the nothing that you now have to live for as you sit on your futon not giving a solitary damn about art, prizes, career, or anything. Marisa Merz's own father, by the way, was a mechanic who worked at the Fiat plant for Mario Merz's padre, who was an upper-middle-class car engineer. The art histories only give this one detail about Marisa Merz's pop, and I can't find any book or article that gives his name or the exact date of his death, but her dad must have had a name and then died at some point because we all do. As proof, I offer the example of my own personal father, Eddie Ruiz. Like Marisa Merz's father, Eddie Ruiz was a mechanic who worked on cars. My dad is now also similarly dead. He died ninety-eight hours ago.

But maybe Marisa Merz is not completely and everlastingly always cheerful on account of the protective force field created by the spectacular art career and the baby/husband. Maybe the great and lucky Marisa Merz did not find herself immune from mother and father death and its accompanying desolation, and so she wanted to leave a subtle little sign as a consolation for the helplessly bereaved. Because, if she was so implacably happy, why else would she make *Untitled, Undated, 8*? As I have mentioned, *it is* a melancholy and dented figurine made of unfired clay. Artists typically put their clay works in a kiln because otherwise the clay slowly flakes off until the object disappears, like life and love and parents. Unfired clay also finds itself deeply vulnerable to moisture; if a glass of water were poured upon *Untitled, Undated, 8*, say, it would melt back in into the earth. Unlike Marisa Merz, most artists are monomaniacs who want to make sure that their art will remain in museums for millions of years or at least until the replicants and cyborgs colonize the earth and make human beings and their cultural products redundant. Her humble gesture makes her work, paradoxically, deathless.

Marisa Merz's cat is crying and disappearing at the same time, which is terrible, but if you think about it, it's also a mercy. The self-exterminating feature of *Untitled, Undated, 8* makes me love the little cat-head a whole bunch, or it would make me love it if I could feel anything. Or maybe I am feeling so much that my circuits are blowing and it just feels like I can't feel anything? My thesis for this Instagram post keeps getting muddled in the midst of my evidently unstoppable compulsion to write art criticism even in the face of unfucking believable dad mortality, but it essentially boils down to the fact that I, too, keep squeezing my eyes shut tight in shock, and my haggard face looks as if it were streaked with pink and silver paint. I wish I could just pour a glass of water over my head and vanish like *Untitled, Undated, 8*. Because then I could forget my father's face in the ICU, his blind eye, the sweat on his forehead, the nurses coming in, the syringe, the last rise of his chest, and then the moments after—when there was no ghost, no small still voice, nothing but the machines whirring and the sound of my own gasping breath.

History

Wednesday, December 29, 2016
6:56 PM Heartbreak why physiologically danger of dying tips
Monday, July 31, 2017
10:28 AM Object petit a Lacan
Friday, August 18, 2017
2:15 PM that time that Sonia ivekovich masturbated and almost got arrested in croatia
Monday, August 28, 2017
12:14 agnes martin schizophrenic went sort of crazy
Sunday, January 28, 2018
11:11 PM Xōchitl Hernández girlfriend wife married?
11:46 PM Xōchitl Hernández baby shower
11: 52 PM Effects of cortisol and adrenaline too much
Sunday, March 4, 2018
10: 59 PM Brandon Chu lawyer wife girlfriend married?
12: 38 PM Crystallization love Stendhal

CHAPTER SEVEN THIS NEW JOB ISN'T THAT GREAT

[This is ad copy that I wrote for the Whitney Museum's new "collab," being the 2017 Max Mara Whitney Anniversary Bag Designed by Renzo Piano's Building Workshop. I posted it on the Max Mara website on July 31, 2017, at 7:46 p.m. EST, after being pulled off a co-curation gig for the Whitney's upcoming *Jimmie Durham: At the Center of the World* show and then involuntarily subcontracted out to Whitney affiliate Max Mara's marketing department because of my "disruptive, incessant crying." Removed at 8:04 p.m. EST.]

Making a cultural impact, having a unique look, and representing a way of life—these three factors can turn a fashion accessory from an item into an icon. One bag that checks all three boxes? Step forward Max Mara's Whitney Bag. We're all. over. it.

Ever since its launch in 2015, the bag has been seen on the arms of former *Elle* cover stars Karlie Kloss and Amy Adams as well as *Scandal*'s Bellamy Young. So how did one bag become so much more than a fashion accessory? Let's break it down . . .
—Isabella Silvers, "The Stars Can't Get Enough of This Must-Have Bag, and Here's Why (The Hadid Sisters Fully Approve)," Elle, July 27, 2017

Max Mara Whitney Bag
Designed by Renzo Piano Building Workshop
Colors: Tobacco, Dark Gray, and Bordeaux
Sizes: Medium, Small, Mini
Limited edition
Details:

The Whitney Anniversary Bag is made of soft leather and comes in three arbitrary sizes. It is decorated with slashy vertical stripes on each side, which resemble the scratch marks that our girlfriend used to leave on our back, and when it is unfilled it looks like an empty mind. The Bag is designed by an anonymous artisan who works for Renzo Piano, an architect who makes money from the sale of the bags, along with the Whitney Museum and the fashion retailer Max Mara. The Bag is a metaphor that sits at the highest reaches of luxury and longing, and its only function is to make its owner look wealthy and to feel temporarily free from grief and pain.

The objective of art is to make us *look* and also feel something disturbingly authentic, but these utilities are unlikely to be discovered in the Whitney Anniversary Bag. The Whitney Anniversary Bag costs between $948 and $1,560, though not all of these Bags manufactured by the anonymous wretch toiling in Renzo Piano's bag factory have been sold for actual money. While some of the bags have been sold to susceptible women in the brick-and-mortar Max Mara stores, others remain what the philosopher Jacques Lacan called the *objet petit a*, which Lacan never wanted translated except by an algebraic sign that means an "unattainable object of desire."

In other words, a large fraction of the Whitney Anniversary Bags remains unavailable to regular humans, since they are reserved as free-with-strings gifts for Karlie Kloss, Max Mara ambassador Amy Adams, *Scandal*'s Bellamy Young, and the Hadid sisters. The bags are also set aside for generous museum donors, such as our desired yet unattainable ex-girlfriend Xōchitl. The Whitney Anniversary Bag's artificial scarcity, actually, also resembles Xōchitl's, since Xōchitl could see us at any time she likes but won't. All in all, the Whitney Anniversary Bag's "it's not me, it's you" quality makes it perfect to put on one's Wish List, because it represents Lacan's ungrabbable Other, in this case the paparazzi-trailing Hadid sister whose unexplainably vast surplusages of human capital entitle her to a free bag that signifies, as Sigmund Freud teaches us, an unoccupied vagina.

There was once a point at which our vagina was occupied and we occupied the vagina of Xōchitl, but after our father died she moved permanently to New York and blocked us on media. Thus, the only way to send her a love letter is to write it here, on the Max Mara/Whitney website, and post it before our boss rips it down. Though Xōchitl just wears Land's End suits to work, and vegan clothes on the weekends, we know that her actuarial firm partners are the type of ghouls who would wear Max Mara. We pray that they will see this valentine, snap a screenshot of it, and forward it to her via email or text.

We hope that when Xōchitl reads this ad she remembers how much we still love her. Yes, for five years we loved Xōchitl so terribly that we became deluded and cherished expectations that in our dotage we would be old and shrunken and yet still murmuring sweet nothings to her until we gacked. But now all we possess is the memory of her dark mouth and her naughty mounds, along with the devastated hollow dead-eyed self-destructive longing of a woman in the grip of the *objet petit a.*

Similarly, the Whitney Anniversary Bag is an *object petit a* for the bonehead who wants to purchase purses instead of love or sex, but can't get her hands on it or pay between $948 and $1,560 before tax. It is not clear whether this shopper is Team Gigi or Team Bella, but regardless, she would love to fondle a Mini, Small, or Medium purse made by a dogsbody of Renzo Piano's instead of feeling genuine emotions. "Genuine emotions," actually, sound better than they are. Maybe love is a deadly illusion in the same way that consumerist celebrity worship is a fatal waste of time because in the end you are left with no money, no girlfriend, no father, and no reason to live.

We have hinted that the Whitney Anniversary Bag is sold empty, but that is not quite correct. It holds something invisible, but very precious. A long, long time ago we believed that museums, such as the bag-flogging Whitney, were churches uncontaminated by the soul-numbing problems of money. Back in our ignorant youth, we would bring Xōchitl to this paradise and worship beauty, though pointing out to her that MOCA's web curation qualified as cybercolonialism or that the omniscient third-person narrative style of the Guggenheim's object labels trafficked in a false form of point-of-viewlessness.

Yes, within each sold or gifted Whitney Anniversary Bag hides a small cinder of that dream of what art means and what it should be, which turns out to constitute the real *objet petit a* for not only Max Mara customers, Karlie Kloss, Amy Adams, Bellamy Young, and Gigi and Bella Hadid, but also for anyone who has ever felt passion. Hearing the cinder rattle around your new Bag is sure to add a *frisson* to any occasion that requires the carrying of status objects crafted out of skin and American exceptionalism, though whether that excitement triggers manic epiphanies or tingly self-satisfaction is up to you.

Add to Shopping Bag
Add to Wish List

CHAPTER EIGHT I'M NOT SURE IF I SHOULD HAVE PRESSED SEND

[This is an email that I sent to Xōchitl and a bunch of her cronies. One of her Munger & Hanley partners sent me fifty dollars.]

To: Xōchitl Hernández, undisclosed recipients
From: Amanda Ruiz
Re: Triangle
Date: August 18, 2017

One day, the artist Sanja Iveković performed a radical act of love. That is, she pretended to masturbate as the Yugoslav strongman Josip Broz Tito drove by her apartment in a cavalcade. This was Zagreb, May 1979. My ex-girlfriend Xōchitl will remember me talking about this. On the day that Josip Broz Tito paraded past Sanja Iveković's apartment in his huge black car surrounded by his armed entourage, Iveković sat on her sixth-story balcony overlooking her street and performed erotic sign language between her legs. The erotic sign language said, *Fuck you and your tyranny, sir.* It also said, *I am dematerializing the art object.* Then it said, *My symbolic queefing is an action in the tradition of Joseph Beuys and Martin Luther King Jr.* Sanja Iveković fluttered her fingers above her pudendum until it began to sing protest songs. The protest songs were in Croatian.

One plainclothes police officer assigned to the presidential security detail stood on the roof of the apartment opposite Sanja Iveković's. This plainclothesman carried a walkie-talkie on his belt. A uniformed police officer stood watch on the street below. Both men observed the huge mandatory crowd that awaited the greatness of Josip Broz Tito. The uniformed police officer also had a walkie-talkie, in order to ensure open communication, but not the kind of "open lines of communication" that I told Xōchitl that I wanted her and I to have after I read she was living on the Upper West Side with Greta Weber, M.D., and having her baby, but another kind, a worse kind: surveillance.

41

The uniformed police officer on the street and the plainclothed roof-stander believed themselves to be autonomous agents in the wide web that is the patriarchy's panopticon. What they did *not* realize is that, together with Iveković, they also formed a feminine sign, being a triangle. You have to visualize it—draw an imaginary line connecting the roof-stander, Iveković on the sixth floor of her apartment across the street, and the street-level officer, and you'll see.

That's what Sanja Iveković called her performance: *Triangle*.

Sanja Iveković loved her country, and women, and art so much that she risked her freedom and her reputation for them. She expressed this love during the amazing Croatian Spring. As Xōchitl will recall hearing about during our previous disagreements about whether having a baby would destroy *our* freedom, the Croatian Spring was a free expression movement that artists and intellectuals initiated in the 1970s in response to Tito's repression. Sanja Iveković was a child-free video artist within that uprising, and she did unconventional things like artistically give herself a couple of sweet little honks while Josip Broz Tito motored by.

So President Josip Broz Tito drove past Sanja Iveković's apartment, in his big black Mercedes that flamed with flags. He had jailed the rebel poet Vlado Gotovac in the dungeon known as the Stara Gradiska, and he popped free elections into his mouth like fun-sized Butterfingers. He thought gender critique was a capitalist plot to destroy the world's supply of extrajudicial manspreading.

Up on her balcony, overlooking Tito's cavalcade, Sanja Iveković leaned back in her chair and began to simulate the act of self-love with her fingers. Xōchitl, I know this is difficult for you on account that I am cc'ing your colleagues at Munger & Hanley but please keep reading. The roof-stander eventually looked over and saw a woman jizzing herself in the presence of the president. Both walkie-talkies began twinkling. The roof-standing officer used his walkie-talkie to express his patriotic suspicion of dissident female taco touching to the police officer on the street. The police officer ran valiantly to Sanja Iveković's apartment and told her that if she didn't stop stroking her lotus of bliss that he would throw her into the Stara Gradiska, which was full of hairy screaming dissidents in chains and personality testing.

Then the artist Sanja Iveković took pictures of everything and wrote up a little report wherein she documented the violent absurdities of the overreaching state. This report can today be found in art books and so we can worship Sanja Iveković, artist-guerrilla of the Croatian Spring, by looking her up at the library.

Now it is 2017. I think it would be a good idea to do an *homage*. We have lived through interesting times, as the Chinese are falsely reputed to say, but now the times seem to be getting ever so more fascinating since our new US president has said that white supremacists are "fine people" and also triggered mass fear at airports with the Muslim ban. As such, I believe our era has ripened into the perfect political climate for a resistant performance of heritage wymynist onanism. I have been practicing and submitted my *précis* to both the Rockefeller and Ford Foundations. I haven't heard back yet from them, though, and my Kickstarter pitch was misinterpreted and so I had to give back the money.

That's why I am now emailing you, you who are the wealthy and reputedly left-leaning colleagues of Xōchitl Hernández, the love of my life. I am hoping that you will help me with the funding I need to do my performance. Maybe I should have said that at the start. I am Fund-raising for Art. There is a PayPal button that you can press at the end of this email, which is kind of semiotic and Gertrude Stein if you think about it.

I need $13,000 for transportation and food, gas, film, rent, bribes, and batteries. I plan on re-creating *Triangle* at the many sites of American tyranny. My first performance will be at the Guantanamo Bay Naval Base. After I land in Havana and climb up the Peninsula using crampons and hired guides, I will stage an action in the detention camp. I will dematerialize the art object with a peaceable gesture of woe and dissent that will hopefully be witnessed by the detainees, who numbered forty at the last available count. If I have an orgasm, I will still be faking like Sanja Iveković. I am joking on that last point, just in case you don't know me that well and don't understand my sense of humor. To wit, my queefery will all be safely pantomimed and Beuysian, as it was in Zagreb in 1979.

After that, I will masturbate at Mar-a-Lago in Palm Beach, Florida. I will ask Carol Ann Duffy to stand on a podium next to me and give a speech on late capitalism's responsibility for the US's 14.5 percent poverty rate and for the lead-water disaster in Flint, Michigan, among other crimes. After that I am hoping that I will be indicted for trespass, public indecency, or treason and be convicted in a highly publicized show trial. I know that my inevitable criminal conviction will not increase my market potential in the standard economy, though N.B. that Chris Burden was arrested for making a sculpture out of a dead person once and that didn't hurt his career.

When I masturbate at one of Supreme Court Chief Justice John Roberts's two summer homes in Saint George, Maine, I anticipate that a SWAT team will use enhanced interrogation on me until I confess that

I hate Roberts's destruction of the Voting Rights Act and his *Obergefell* dissent, and that's why I masturbated extra-long, not because he's attractive.

When I masturbate like a champion at the White House, the Secret Service will chase me around the Mall with their tasers and guns. I am pretty confident that Melania Trump will save me, though, because I'm starting to get the idea that she hates Donald's guts and is one of the secret leaders of the Resistance. The way I imagine it in my head is that Melania will wade out into the vast disbelieving crowd and say, "Wait, don't shoot her, she's a queer Latin@ performance artist speaking truth to power. Her message is one of love and nonviolence. Yours are the kinds of misreadings that happen when you cut the humanities," she'll yell out. "She's making a sly allusion to the work of my sister Yugoslav, the Croatian performance artist Sanja Iveković. This lady is being *épater le bourgeoisie*." I will have written my intentions up in a memo and distributed it beforehand, and so I hope that my expectations are not too unrealistic. At the very least, some people will get it.

I will then stop masturbating and take a bow. At first I will not say anything to the assembled masses. I will let the power of the feminine principle speak for itself. I will hope that I have helped people understand via my metaphor of liberatory pearl polishing that in this world of hate and war and fear there is nothing left to do but love any old way you can. You can love yourself, *ipso facto*. You can also love detainees and poor people and voters and your dead dad and even the president, whom I actually hate. You can love the work of Sanja Iveković so much that you will repeat her art in front of anyone who will watch. You can risk being taken for a lunatic by the beloved community and that is better than being alone. You can express your love for your ex-girlfriend Xōchitl and the unborn baby you were maybe going to have with her, if Xōchitl had been even minimally patient and didn't instead get pregnant with Greta Weber, M.D. You can also embrace your love for everybody you know, including the entirety of this cracked and bananas country.

You can also recognize that the ideas that seemed so good in your bedroom look crazy out in society, and that maybe you are really not going to do this at all but just write about it, and that the art is in this writing and the response that you get to your writing. Except, you should actually do it, shouldn't you? Because the job of the artist is to challenge herself and trust her voice. Imagine if Sanja Iveković had not fake-masturbated at all but just wrote down the idea, it would be nothing. Think about the courage she had to muster to actually do her work.

Anyway, the Secret Service will have arrested me by this time. This is when I will sing my own protest song. I will stand up to my full height and to the mob of police officers and furious tourists I will say, *My piece is called Triangle. "Triangle" refers not only to my vagina. And it doesn't just signify my ex-girlfriend Xōchitl, our unborn baby, and me. It also refers to a cosmic configuration: You, me, and the United States. You, me, and the world! Together we make a beautiful design. Because we are all connected, we are all a family. If you draw invisible lines between us, you'll see.*

Thanks for considering this request for artistic financing. I also take checks.

Love, Amanda

CHAPTER NINE IS THIS HEALING ME OR IS IT PROPAGANDA

[This is my overlong and thus unsuccessfully submitted Yelp review of the *Agnes Martin* show at the Los Angeles County Museum of Art (April 24–September 11, 2017).]

In 1967, just as her art was gaining acclaim, Martin abandoned New York City and her practice in pursuit of silence and solitude, traversing the United States and Canada. Settling on a remote mesa outside of Cuba, New Mexico, Martin returned to art-making in 1973.
—https://www.lacma.org/art/exhibition
/agnes-martin

The work of minimalist painter Agnes Martin is difficult to understand under the best of circumstances, and the best of circumstances are not to be discovered at LACMA's April–September 2017 retrospective of her work, *Agnes Martin*. If you love Agnes Martin with the same bone-deep cultism that you reserve for your ex-girlfriend who dumped you in Cabo Corrientes while you were making a logistically challenging and NEA-funded autocritical documentary, then I recommend you go view *Agnes Martin*. However, before you do, you should read a good Martin biography, such as Nancy Princenthal's Google Books–accessible *Agnes Martin: Her Life and Art* (2015), so that you do not become confused. You should make sure also that you have taken all of your medications in anticipation of your visit.

When you first look at the work of Agnes Martin, all you see are blank, dumb graphs. That's what she's known for, graph paintings. Martin began to invent these baffling schematics in the late 1950s, when she lived in New York's Coenties Slip neighborhood alongside artists like Ellsworth Kelly and Lenore Tawney. Unlike most women, Martin became as famous as Kelly, but at first you can't tell why.

What is so special about monotonous canvases painted blue-gray and plaster-white and light yellow and hatched all over with pencil lines? The question pops up at the LACMA retrospective as you stand before, say, *Falling Blue* (1963). *Falling Blue* is a large brown canvas threaded with thin indigo lines of oil paint. It is just a bunch of lines, you mumble silently. This would not be very hard to do. Then you look at something like *White Stone* (1964), which was painted a year later than *Falling Blue*, and looks about as challenging. *White Stone* is just a huge canvas painted white and marked all over with little penciled squares. You might be inclined to walk out of the retrospective as you stare at *White Stone*. The work probably strikes you as pretty, yet boring and meaningless. Then you see 1967's *Grass*, where the boxes are even tinier and the canvas is painted intricately with two different shades of light green. You turn away. You think about going home and doing the work that you have somehow scratched together in the gig economy, which is barely allowing you to remain afloat. You think that maybe you have wasted your time and your limited money by buying a ticket to *Agnes Martin*.

But then, if you have just a bit of patience, you might get lucky. It is possible that at this moment a little shaft of light will begin to illuminate the dark cavern of your mind like an actual angel. That angel is the revelation that possessed Agnes Martin when she painted these seemingly monotonous works of muted colors and pencil lead. You might be in dire need of this angel because you have been struggling as an artist and a woman of color in Los Angeles for over fifteen years, and now your crisis has reached full flower: Your dad is dead of something called multiple myeloma, and your beloved Xóchitl—that goddess of the Chicklet teeth, strong rough hands, and $400K/yr. job in an actuarial firm—took a long hard look at your badly aging bohemianism and vanished like a leprechaun.

What is this message of hope, precisely? Turn to the paintings again. What do you see? You detect that *Falling Blue, White Stone*, and *Grass* are stunningly repetitive. You observe that Martin treated these three themes almost without distinguishing between them, which, as it turns out, has the interesting effect of imparting to the sky, the stone, and the grass a marvelous hedonic equality. *Equality*, you think suddenly. The word has the force of epiphany. It shimmers through you. Your brain-angel flaps its wings. And this is when, if you're, maybe, in Libra rising or your Moon is in Cancer, you'll have the very good fortune to realize:

Agnes Martin thinks they're all the same.

It is at this point that Agnes Martin's work stops looking to you like so many shabby chic painting swatches and more like an idea or a philosophy.

And it is. And if you have been witness to the nuclear destruction of your own personal dreams of love and professional fulfillment, then you will want to know if this philosophy contains any helpful advice. They're all the same . . . what? At LACMA, you get very few hints. *Agnes Martin was familiar with Taoist, Zen, and Buddhist thought,* says a didactic text block lettered on the wall, like an informational pamphlet or a curator's talk. *Agnes Martin was meditative,* it goes on.

Well, you know something about this because *you* have studied the Tao, Zen, and Buddhism, at least a little. *You* have meditated, sometimes. And so you are well familiar with the koans of radical equality that purport "everything is one" and "happiness is the path" and "what you think, you will be." However, it bears noting that, though these bumper stickers dazzled you when you were a freshman at RISD and drunk on the honeyed mead of life, today these clichés strike you as dangerous placebos. Just around the same time that Xōchitl left you, you realized that they had sabotaged the mercenarily critical thinking that you should have practiced when filling out your college applications, because it would have led you to medical school and a mortgage and a family.

Still, this isn't the time for nihilism. You are now breathlessly leaning way past the gray "do not cross" line marked on the floor, which creates a fascist capitalist barrier between you and the canvases. As you verge perilously close to Agnes Martin's paintings, you see that *Falling Blue, White Stone,* and *Grass* are made with compulsive attention to detail. They must have taken a terrifically long time for Martin to execute. The pencil markings are nearly perfect yet handmade. The brushwork is as precise as mathematics but also loose and free. You start to feel a rumbling in your bowels, which is gastritis occasioned by your reawakening suspicion that Art is not the dark force that has hijacked your life, but rather the only human invention that can afford spiritual rescue. You feel the rumblings syncopate with your swiftly beating heart, and then your combined nervous system and soul effervesce into joy that sparkles lightly through your body.

You look at yet more signs that have been applied helpfully onto the walls by LACMA factotums, who have been directed to do so by the museum's Yale-trained curators. *In 1967, having achieved considerable acclaim, Martin jettisoned most of her possessions and left New York forever. She moved to a remote mesa in New Mexico and had an artistic hiatus that lasted until 1972.*

An artistic hiatus that lasted five years sounds like a lot. What happened after that? LACMA does not tell you, at least not in this room. It makes you depart from *Falling Blue, White Stone,* and *Grass,* and move through a little hallway. You pass through this intestinal passage and go to another series of galleries. And once you have scurried through the rat-run, and come out into the museum's massive, naturally lit cathedrals that host Martin's 1973 paintings, you are at first astonished.

Instead of the pre-1973 work's limitations to a white and cream palette, these huge canvases are all beautifully colored. They are layered with faint, gauzy tones of blue and pink. These illuminations recall the first delirious moments of waking, when the sun drifts onto your forehead like a holy benediction, and you have not yet remembered that Xōchitl has fled you, your relationship, and the entire state of California.

It's overwhelming. These pastel paintings recall the southwestern sky, but when you read their titles you do not see *Wind*, *Clouds*, or some such, but instead that they have all been titled *Untitled*. Such is the case, for example, of 1974's *Untitled #3*, which assembles deep blush and blue hues in an exhilarating astronomy made of six rectangles. Another wondrous work is the quartz-pink *Untitled IX* (1982), which envelops the viewer in glowing rose pleasure. Why has Martin not named these radiant paintings after specific nouns? Because, instead of limiting herself to marveling at the syntheses of air, water, sky, and stone, in the 1970s she embraced the ecstatic marriage of *all* existence, even that which cannot be described in language. It seems that after that curious unexplained lacuna between 1967 and 1972, she had her breakthrough, you think. She found the Source.

You move from wall to wall, noting that Martin's documentation of supernal communion lasted for decades and is to be found in works such as 2000's *Blessings*, which is a series of blue and white stripes—sky, spirit, air, soul—stitched together with a *taijitu* line of pink and blue. Also recognizing eternal harmonies is *Untitled* (2004), a series of pearl-white and dove-gray bands rendered in delicate, feathered strokes. Deeper into the retrospective, your shoulders begin to hunch and your eyes overflow as you see that Martin shifted her colors to darker, more mournful grays in the 1990s, which LACMA deigns to assess in its didactics as Martin's acknowledgment of "the impending end."

You go back to the pink and blue ones, and feel jubilation. If you are like me, you think about your annihilated love life, your cluttered shared sublease, and your horrible job writing gig copy for underpaying art world behemoths like Max Mara/The Whitney, and realize that all of these pains are necessary parts of life's transcendent paradox. Without sadness there can be no bliss, you exult. Without suffering there cannot be enlightenment. Without dad death and girlfriend loss there cannot be the epiphany that the entire world is your community, and that you have enough love to share with this whole exhausted planet. Everyone, everyone you know and have never met is your lover and your family.

Yes, if you are like me you stand in this cathedral of Martinalia, wearing your father's huge yellow Nordstrom sweater and your at-home haircut, and you weave your own difficult life story into this illumination. You think of the moment that Xōchitl left you, after a fight on a beautiful if drought-ridden Mexican beach. *I told you I wanted a baby, and that I need you to be an equal partner*, Xōchitl had said. *Don't overreact*, yours truly had replied. *Everything happens when it's supposed to happen, and what's supposed to happen now is that I'm supposed to finish this autocritical documentary and then go to MacDowell for that residency and then we can have a baby in maybe like one to five years.*

I'm leaving you, Amanda, Xōchitl had replied, before running off to New York and setting up impenetrable shields on social media.

But everything is fine now. As you shiver in front of Agnes Martin's *Untitled* paintings, you smile at your overwhelming store of horrible memories, because Martin's pinks and blues are healing your many wounds. You reconsider the dark and terrible moments of your life, and see them brightened by a universal tenderness that forgives us everything.

Though, it is at this moment, when you hear yourself thinking that there is "a universal tenderness that forgives us everything," you realize there might be a problem. Recall that you prefer critical thinking to the kinds of yogic bumper stickers sold at Whole Foods. Indeed, you have dedicated the entirety of your life and often shocking performance art practice to rejecting propaganda and embracing the suck. After all, you are an artist, which means that you must live within truth. Is this truth? you start to worry, squinting at the pink and blue canvases that shine on the walls. Isn't this all a little . . . *baby shower????* And now maybe the beautiful canvases start to look to you like soothing misinformation campaigns broadcast by the government to keep down unrest despite war and unemployment. You stare at the *Untitled*s aghast as you discern their resemblance to "artworks" that J. Crew and Soft Surroundings deploy in their advertisements as Heideggerean concealments of your cheerful participation in a neoliberal world order that destroys minorities and the Global South. It is distinctly possible, you fret, that you are not actually achieving a spiritual eureka in the church of LACMA, but rather are being lulled into obedience by LACMA, corporate overlord. That is, you are buying into the free market's hallucination that pinky-blue fake-Taoist happiness is a good substitute for resisting the hard political realities that artists like Otto Dix and Nancy Spero and Romaine Brooks painted.

This is why I said that Agnes Martin is difficult to understand under the best of circumstances, and the best of circumstances are not to be discovered at LACMA. Look again at the text on the walls, the didactics. They tell you about Martin living in New York and New Mexico and being meditative and taking a five-year break. Like most other mainstream arts institutions that omit from their exhibitions' PR such unnerving details as Alice Neel's suicide attempt or Hannah Gluckenstein's annihilating WWII–era depression, LACMA's didactics fail to tell you about the difficult parts of Martin's life. Why? Toxic heteronormativity? Certainly "sanism."

For (as you discover by Googling Princenthal's book as you wander awkwardly around LACMA's galleries) Agnes Martin was schizophrenic. The reason Martin had an "artistic hiatus" between 1967 and 1972 was because in 1967 she was found wandering New York's Park Avenue in a psychotic state. The authorities dumped her into Bellevue, which at the time was the proverbial python pit. Martin endured one hundred electroshock therapy treatments there and in other institutions. *That's* when she ran away to New Mexico. One other factoid about Agnes Martin that will not be found written on LACMA's tall white walls: she was a lesbian. She had a relationship with her Coenties roommate Lenore Tawney and also with the Greek sculptor Chryssa. And she had these love affairs while the American Psychiatric Association still classified homosexuality as a mental illness, and while anti-sodomy statutes were still being upheld under the US Constitution. Agnes Martin, in other words, was not living in a pretty pinky world of totally easy universal sameness. She couldn't have sold you J. Crew hegemony or Soft Surroundings mind control because her straitjacket was too tight and her pussy too mutinous.

It's only when you know this information that Agnes Martin's galactic importance reveals itself to you, as you stand there weeping and nodding your head *yes*. Martin painted the union of all life, the beauty and perfection of all beings, even though she was labeled a monster and electrified like Frankenstein. Realizing this, you no longer worry about Agnes Martin J. Crewishly brainwashing you, because when she made paintings that say "everything is one" and "happiness is the path" and "what you think, you will be," it really means something. Agnes Martin paid the hard price of alienation and terror to access these authentic, loving truths.

Maybe at this point you're digging into your vegan purse for your Paxil or Remeron. The thing about realizing that your suffering is one of a zillion colored strands in the universe's radiant cat's cradle is that this enlightenment can feel like a kissy Ayahuasca trip but still trigger your generalized anxiety disorder. Knowing that you have been seen and named by these paintings does not relieve you of your poverty or loneliness, it just clarifies those sorrows, like *ujjayi* breathing or getting fired does. This clarification is making you cry too hard for a public place like a museum, and by now people are staring. Actually, LACMA should be zoned for participatory convulsive wailing and not just for selling Klimt posters. Museum docents should smile with empathy at sobbing patrons and explain Stendhal Syndrome to the tourist groups taking pictures on their phones. Because art can strengthen the cortisol-flooded heart but also crack it wide open. Art can make you fizz up with religious awe, but it can also thrust a poison-tipped spear deep into your chest. Art performs a difficult consolation that's part group hug and part curb stomp. Museums like the Los Angeles County Museum of Art that are lucky enough to host the sacerdotal paintings of Agnes Martin are not just sites of commerce and pedantry, of luxury and status. They are altars of love and suffering. They are locations of grandeur. They are a place for the world's broken and beaten to call home.

CHAPTER TEN I AM TRYING TO CARE ABOUT THIS BUT IT'S NOT REALLY WORKING

[This is the acceptance speech that I gave at the Slamdance Film Festival on January 25, 2018, upon winning a 2018 Sparky Award for *Ain't Nobody Leaving*, an autocritical documentary that Xōchitl and I filmed at Cabo Corrientes.]

"Um, I don't know, that's uh . . . that's . . . yeah, that's OK."

CHAPTER ELEVEN **UNLOBSTERING**

[This is a Wikipedia entry for Mickalene Thomas's *Le Déjeuner sur l'herbe: Les Trois Femmes Noires* (2010), which I posted to Wikipedia on March 4, 2018. Anonymous Wikipedians nominated the essay for deletion on March 4, 2018, and unreachable authoritarians deleted it on March 11, 2018, for "not containing reliable sources" and "violating the policy against novel theories." *Le Dejeuner sur l'herbe: Les Trois Femmes Noires* is a collaged and rhinestone-bedecked photograph depicting three Black women gazing directly at the viewer while enjoying a picnic.]

Mickalene Thomas's *Le Déjeuner sur l'herbe: Les Trois Femmes Noires* (2010) is a 10' × 24' photo-work of three Black women foregrounded against a multicolored forest. Some academics who have written scholarly articles about the collage argue that one of the models was born a man. That claim, however, is most certainly an error, as people aren't "born" anything but instead create themselves through extraordinary efforts of will made possible by hope and stubbornness and love.

Le Déjeuner sur l'herbe: Les Trois Femmes Noires refers to the famous 1863 painting *Le Déjeuner sur l'herbe* by the white French artist Édouard Manet. *Le Déjeuner sur l'herbe* features two white men dressed in suits having an alfresco meal with a naked white woman. As Wikipedia readers can probably tell from this description, Mickalene Thomas's version is better than Édouard Manet's male-gazy pornography.

The subjects of *Le Déjeuner sur l'herbe: Les Trois Femmes Noires* sit on bright quilts in their golden forest while eating lunch. They wear glamorous dresses, and their Afros and curls sparkle. They wear full makeup and hoop earrings. Each of the women stares at the viewer with a serene, fierce expression. They all appear to be barefoot. They do not smile. If you look at them with any attention, you will see that they shimmer and glow. They do not twinkle only because of their inherent radiance. The women refract light because Mickalene Thomas famously uses Swarovski crystals in her artworks. The crystals glitter on the women's lips and eyelids, like small stars. The rhinestones give viewers the sensation that they witness a special occasion, and lend the art a dress-up party feeling.

Thomas celebrates these women with the shine and fire of crystals because she loves them, and they help her survive. When once talking about other subjects she's featured in her art, like Eartha Kitt and Betty Davis, Thomas said:

> I like women who have a sense of grit and a sort of hard edge while remaining incredibly sexy. These are the women I look to as mentors, because I want to remember that whatever I'm going through, as long as I have my own faith and do what I know is right, I'm going to come out okay.

In the early 2000s, Mickalene Thomas hit on the idea of expressing this wymynist reverence with the rhinestones, which anoint her subjects like halos. Thomas is getting sick of the Swarovskis now, though. She's said as much in interviews, because that's all anyone can talk about, the rhinestones. She would like to be known as more than the "rhinestone lady." She's begun making films and taking photographs of built environments. She's trying to change as an artist.

Thomas was born in 1971, lives in Brooklyn, and graduated from Yale. She is Black and a lesbian, and a mother to a daughter. Her own mother died a couple of years ago; she did not react to that loss by leaning super hard into a nervous breakdown but instead amped up her production of yet greater quantities of even more spectacular art.

Thomas's life strategy has paid off handsomely. *Vogue* magazine reported in January 2016 that Thomas has a partner named Racquel, and "splits her time" between her studio, Racquel's Chelsea apartment, their country house in Connecticut, and her own Brooklyn brownstone, which Thomas described to a *Vogue* interviewer as a "sanctuary." Artists with less emotional discipline than Mickalene Thomas can only gaze upon her career and personal life with awe verging onto catatonic depression. However, Thomas's life is not perfect. Beyond the aforementioned parental loss that Thomas suffered, and the seemingly inevitable societal oppression that women of color experience in this unspeakable society, sometimes also Thomas finds herself boxed in as an artist because of a kind of aesthetic typecasting.

That is, Mickalene Thomas has a problem with art critics' intentional fallacies. In other interviews, she's said that people misinterpret her work as a mindless celebration of beauty. It's unclear why onlookers fall prey to this hermeneutic temptation. For, Thomas says, she does not ignore beauty's huge predicament:

> Beauty . . . comes from an ugly place, [I mean, consider the] corset . . . and the painful sort of beautiful notions that women put themselves through . . . When I think of beauty . . . it's not because I think life is all, sort of, you know, "oh well you're beautiful and seductive and have this allure and so it's all good." Because it's not.

Instead of people focusing so much on the beauty and the rhinestones, Thomas would like us to respect her art more because of its message of female resilience. She'd also like some credit for her work's formal qualities, such as her use of constructed spaces and her allusions to Romare Bearden and Henri Matisse.

It's hard to do that, though.

The rhinestones make us feel cheerful, which is no small thing. Thomas has used them in a lot of her paintings and photo works, particularly the early ones. The rhinestones, actually, might be "deeper" than Thomas gives them credit for. Those shiny bits make us wonder how we should live, and how we should view our lives. Mickalene Thomas takes a racist and sexist legacy (Manet, exploitation) and metamorphoses it into something glimmeringly personal and beautiful, a beauty that is unsmilingly painful but joyous nevertheless.

I thought about this a lot last week when I went shopping at Ralphs. I was very sad, in part because I had been researching the amazing art of Mickalene Thomas and stumbled across that *Vogue* article. *Vogue*, I had thought, was just some massive advertorial filled with pictures of white people wearing obscene status symbols. But apparently its editors have also gotten into the business of publishing real estate hagiographies of successful artists so that artists who are finding themselves skidding on the big banana peel of life can use their iPad *Vogue*s as sleeping masks when they collapse onto their futon after reading its essays.

Anyway, last Wednesday I felt old and withered and covered with a hard carapace. I was like a lobster. I crawled around the Ralphs wearing my dad's old yellow Nordstrom sweater as a dress, and chucked bread and broccoli into my cart with my big clacky claws. It has been a hard year. My dad died of a blood thing, and I don't want to talk about my ex-girlfriend anymore. I had been fired from my gig curating/propaganda jobs at the Guggenheim and The Whitney/Max Mara. And, though I am an award-winning performance artist, I am currently broke and am having trouble producing my mobile all-wymyn opera, *Texit*.

So there I was, clattering around the supermarket with my little beady lobster eyes and my gnarled yellow shell, while mournfully purchasing vegan carbs.

But then, there was this guy in check-out. The guy stood next to an older woman, his mother. The man's mother was Latin American, and her body had a soft luscious bean-shape that reminded me of my dad before the doctors diagnosed him.

"I like your sweater," the man said, and smiled.

"Thank you," I answered.

"Pretty girl," the man's mother said, so that he laughed and gave her a squeeze on her shoulder.

The man stood about 5'10" and looked like he had a mix of Latinx and Asian ancestry. He had muscled forearms, glowing brown eyes, and wore khaki cargo shorts. We stood in line side by side, quietly. He met my gaze twice and smiled again, revealing very white, very square teeth. The mother smiled, too. She had the same clean bright grin.

"My name is Brandon," he said, after he'd paid up and was about to leave.

"Mine's Amanda," I replied.

"He's a lawyer at Paul, Weiss," said his mother.

Then they left Ralphs and I haven't seen them again.

Now, I do realize that art criticism and Wikipedia pages do not usually traffic in confessional journaling. Also, I understand that this supermarket exchange doesn't have anything to do directly with *Le Déjeuner sur l'herbe: Les Trois Femmes Noires*, or with the genius of Mickalene Thomas.

My conversation with Brandon and his mom bears a remote synchronicity to Thomas's photograph, however. The link exists in her use of rhinestones.

While I crawled around Ralphs like a lobster, I wondered about the work of the nineteenth-century French philosopher Gabriel Marcel. Marcel was an existentialist, though he didn't like being called that. He gained fame for his concept of *crispation*, which occurs when we form a brittle, hard shell over our authentic selves. When we "crispify," we shrink and withdraw into our carapaces, like crustaceans. Marcel tried to figure out ways to free people from these jail-like egocentric shells, but he didn't. He remains in the philosophy books only because of his articulation of this particular human problem.

How *do* you stop being a miserable shellfish? It's a good question.

A first step might be in reading Stendhal.

Stendhal was another nineteenth-century Frenchman, though he worked as a novelist. Among other things, he authored *The Red and the Black*. Unlike Gabriel Marcel, he *wanted* to be covered with hard, shiny things. He associated such an armature with falling in love.

One summer, Stendhal went for vacation to a Salzburg salt mine, and took with him as a companion a lady named Madame Gherardi. Madame Gherardi did not suffer from the burden of flawless beauty, as she had contracted smallpox in her earlier youth. It left her with some light scarring. When Stendhal looked at Madame Gherardi, that's what he saw—scars, imperfections. Stendhal's lack of romantic interest in Madame Gherardi freed him to notice the world around him. He looked down and observed a smattering of crystallized tree branches that decorated the floor of the mine. Stendhal learned that in the winter, right before they took a three-month break, the Salzburg miners threw the branches onto the mine's wet floor. In the ensuing months, the branches accumulated a crisp covering of delicate crystals from soaking in the salted water. While the effect lasted, the branches emitted beautiful shafts of refracting light.

Along the way, Stendhal and Madame Gherardi had gained a fellow traveler in the form of a Bavarian officer. The officer looked at Madame Gherardi and at first saw just what Stendhal did—a disfigured woman, nothing special. But then he began to fall in love with her. Stendhal watched the Bavarian officer go through the process of love-falling, and it took the form of a wonderful madness: the officer soon became blind to the flaws of Madame Gherardi and he could only perceive her virtues. In lieu of a pocked hand, he saw a soft and pretty hand. The officer looked down and spied a twig covered with the crystals, and in his lunacy mistook them for diamonds. He tried to give the diamond-stick to Madame Gherardi while she patiently explained its worthlessness. And all the while the officer stared at pockmarked Madame Gherardi, who had been transfigured into a gorgeous goddess.

Stendhal later called the process of falling in love *crystallization*. "What I call *crystallization* is the operation of the mind that draws from everything around it the discovery that the beloved object has new perfection," he wrote.

Sometimes, then, a person will find themselves covered by a horrible lobster's crispy shell, as Gabriel Marcel teaches us. Other times, though, they might find themselves enrobed with beautiful Stendhalian love crystals. What most people want to know is how to become unlobstered and yet crystallized.

Mickalene Thomas resolves this uncertainty. Her work says: you are covered with crystals rather than in Western Civilization's crap when you go to

61

the store, buy a bunch of rhinestones, and with great tenacity and patience glue them on until you are a shimmering beauty. Still, the process is not easy: gluing rhinestones won't make everything *all good*, and you can't just run away from the *ugly place*—that is, your history. You're just going to have to wear your rhinestones *and* your history, Thomas says. It's complicated, like a woman whom heteronormatives say was born a man, or Eartha Kitt's hard-edged sexiness, or Madame Gherardi's pocked hand, which becomes prettily soft and ready to be kissed when looked at in the right way.

In other words, Mickalene Thomas resolves to cover herself and those she adores in Stendhal's crystallization rather than Marcel's crispation by dint of hard work and trust in the promise of a better day.

I am not in love with a man and his mother whom I met for two minutes in a Ralphs. I know the three of us will not turn into a splendid family picnicking in the golden forest. I have been in love before, the real thing, and I know what it feels like.

But I also know that a person cannot travel from crispation to crystallization all by herself. You must at least glimpse love first in order to transcend your history. Mickalene Thomas said as much when she talked about Betty Davis and Eartha Kitt, and how they help her know she's going to be OK.

Glimpsing love is like dipping your lobster claw into the dark water pooling at the bottom of the Salzburg mine. When you lift your claw back up, you see it is a human hand, your hand. Yet it defies your expectations, because it has a new perfection. It shines just perceptibly with a beautiful, salty, rhinestone brightness. Your life will remain unmanageably difficult, but you can look down at your fingers and see that inspiring crystalline gleam.

That's what happened to me that day. I drove away from Ralphs and came home to my sub-sublet in Palms. I put away my broccoli and bread in my small brown-and-orange kitchen. I put on a vinyl of Diamanda Galás's *You Must Be Certain of the Devil* ("Break out the great teeth of the young lions, O Lord"), a song that I like to blast out of my southwest window because my neighbor is a red-capped superfan of the current administration. I went into my bedroom, which is also my studio. The room was fluffy with mailed notices of overdue tuition debt payments and dust. Also, I had been doing a little bit of clay sculpting to open up my creative kundalini, and a small dented bust of a sad cat stared at me from its perch on the worktable I'd propped up in the room's east corner.

I didn't work on the cat-head, though. I sat on my bed, next to my laptop. I briefly looked at my email—I had just received an offer from a web company (Snapchat, Inc.) to be a temp replacement in marketing, and the prospect made me face-plant into my quilt. I *was* moping; *definitely* crispifying.

But then I thought about Brandon and his mom, and how they'd liked my dad's sweater, which I still wore. I rubbed the sweater's yellow cotton weave with my fingers and thought about the way that Brandon had smiled at me. I felt that little flush of happiness come back, that glimpse of love. I thought about his nice mother.

Then I thought about Mickalene Thomas and her *Le Déjeuner sur l'herbe: Les Trois Femmes Noires*. I imagined all the hurdles she'd had to get through to make such an incredible photo collage. I thought about the Stendhalian rhinestones on the women's eyes and lips. I thought about their beautiful Afros and curls. I thought about how one of them had made herself into a woman, and how she'd rhinestoned *herself*. I thought about their picnic in the gold forest, and my fantasy of Brandon and his mom and me having a picnic, too.

I opened up a new screen and began typing this Wikipedia page.

Even though I felt depressed and like a lobster, and even though I had Diamanda screaming through the house like that torture music military interrogators play for suspected terrorists, I started to feel good, for the first time in over a year. I mean, even though I do not have a Brooklyn brownstone or a Connecticut farmhouse, and will never be with Xōchitl again—I actually started to feel happy. Happy, even though I was sad at the same time. I was a crustacean, but as I typed and remembered the transformations of the forest-lounging women, the Bavarian officer, Mickalene Thomas, and suddenly-smiling Brandon, I felt myself getting covered in luminous crystals. I had this sense of being renewed by lovely fragments of light, a delicately radiant feeling that filled me with hope. This sensation gave me the strength to maybe try to remake my life, and it lasted for almost the rest of the day.

History

Monday, March 6, 2018
12:57 PM Brandon Chu Los Angeles lawyer Paul Weiss wife
girlfriend boyfriend husband
Friday, April 13, 2018
1:12 AM Chris Burden lamps LACMA crappy art but people
like it why
1:42 AM street lamps invented why racism
Saturday, June 2, 2018
11:01 PM Robert Barry Untitled (1968)
12:51 PM Invisibility the science of

CHAPTER TWELVE IT'S NOT STALKING, IT'S JUST FINDING SOMEBODY'S NUMBER AND CALLING THEM ON THE PHONE

[This is yet another *Texit* tweet.]

Texit (*glissando*): Why do my bowels tremble? Could it be the rapture of white supremacy or is it my passion for Josefina? #texit
7:06 AM—12 March 2018
0 Retweet 1 Like

CHAPTER THIRTEEN CRUCIFIXION AND HAPPINESS

[I posted this essay and photo of Chris Burden's *Urban Light* (2008) on Instagram on April 5, 2018.]

amandapanda
Amanda Ruiz
Los Angeles County Museum of Art >
16 likes

Urban Light (2008) consists of 202 vintage cast-iron lamps collected and painted pale gray by the American artist Chris Burden (1946–2015). The lamps create an illuminated forest bordering the Los Angeles County Museum of Art at its Wilshire Boulevard entrance. They hail from the 1920s and 1930s. Between-the-wars cast-iron lamps are rarities that collectors pursue with tenacity, and Burden assembled his vast inventory during heroic flea market carousals. Burden began collecting the lamps in 2001, during the last, sociable stage of his career.

At dusk, *Urban Light* envelops the LACMA entry pavilion with a soft silver nimbus. With their curving basal motifs, the lamps recall an old Hollywood glamour; they might be the complexion-flattering incandescents under which Fred Astaire and Cyd Charisse danced in the 1950s.

The prettiness of *Urban Light* can make us worry that it's not very good.

Urban Light was at first laughed at as simple and insipid. Architecture critic Christopher Hawthorne called it "sizable" and "insistent." But today it provides a popular meeting place where likably gender-conforming Angelenos make iPhone spectacles of themselves before perusing the galleries. *Urban Light* also offers a good spot for smoking before a date at one of Wilshire's nearby clubby bars. The smoker can lean on a lamp and light his cigarette while an atypically fetching native wearing a huge yellow sweater and baggy cargo pants—a local female artist, say—chatters to him about aesthetic integrity. The smoker will appear pensively amused to have such a beautiful space within which to glamorously exhale black smoke like a dragon. The female artist will take a snapshot of him doing this, and then feel embarrassed.

Chris Burden made *Urban Light* into a symbol of seemingly untroubled metropolism, but his work used to be far less picturesque. He began as a horrifying performance artist in Irvine, California. In 1971, he ordered an assistant to fire at his left arm with a .22 rifle while filming his alarming *Shoot* on Super 8. Three years later, in Venice, he presented *Trans-Fixed*. In this action, he drove a Volkswagen Beetle into a garage. He lay down on the hood of the car and an assistant crucified him to the metal: the assistant actually hammered Burden's hands into the Beetle's steel carapace. After Burden had bled all over the car for a while, the nails were extruded from his extremities and saved as precious relics.

Critics remain confounded by *Shoot* and *Trans-Fixed*, but the works prove almost too easy to read. The Vietnam War was not "over there"; it was at home. Also, we can try to transform the savagery of history and technology into a cute VW Bug, but we cannot escape from it. We are nailed to history and technology like Christ was nailed to the cross.

A week after Burden had himself impaled to a car, he flew to New York. There he performed *White Light/White Heat* at the Ronald Feldman Gallery. For *White Light/White Heat*, Burden's assistants built a triangular platform in a corner of the gallery. The platform rose ten feet off the floor and hung two feet below the ceiling. Burden climbed up to the platform and crawled back into its recesses and lay down. He brought with him no food or water. No one standing on the floor of the gallery could see him and he could not see anyone. We do not know what Burden did with his bodily waste. He stayed up there for twenty-two days.

It is also not hard to read *White Light/White Heat*. Chris Burden wanted to die.

How does a man go from risking his own extinction by shooting, self-crucifying, starving, and hiding, to then building a garden of light for the people? Have we misinterpreted Burden's motivations for *Urban Light*, which may be more hostile than we admit? It's worth noting that Burden's other light-focused work, *Fist of Light* (1992), consisted of a metal box jammed with hundreds of metal halide light bulbs and required a mechanism for cooling its display space at the Whitney Biennial. In other words, *Fist of Light* was a kind of bomb.

But beauty did creep into Burden's later projects. In 2005, Burden made a crewless, computer-navigated sea vessel called *Ghost Ship*, which sailed dreamily around Scotland. And in the months before he succumbed to melanoma in 2015, he made a fabulous flying dirigible titled *Ode to Santos Dumont*. The installation referred to the idealistic yet suicidally doomed inventor of the hot air balloon and the airplane. Burden denied that he expressed new positivity in his work, though. "I don't think art has a moral imperative," he cautioned an *LA Times* reporter at the start of the millennium. Yet since Chris Burden passed away, the evaluations of his oeuvre have grown ever more friendly. Critics now see his late-stage fabrications as a congenial about-face from his previous self-harming compulsions. In the end, this art appears to say, he just wanted to make people happy.

Does that make *Urban Light* excruciatingly bad? Is Christopher Hawthorne right?

I wondered about this yesterday evening while out on my eighth date with Brandon Chu. Brandon is a lawyer at Paul, Weiss, Rifkind, Wharton & Garrison LLP. I met him at a Ralphs supermarket about six weeks ago and then fished him out of the deep waters of the interweb after some heavyish IG creeping. He is thirty-four years old and enjoys Italian food, progressive bluegrass, and slow, deep kissing. He has large intense dark eyes like a matador. He has a very nice mother who unfortunately does not live in California but rather in New Jersey. Other than that, there is nothing really wrong with him, except perhaps for the way his focus grows prismatic when extracurricular cisgender cleavage wafts into his frame. Maybe smoking is also a wrong thing but I am in that phase of a relationship where it seems charming.

My Stage 4 limerence explains my agreement to meet Brandon after 9 p.m., which is the earliest I could get free from my brand-new but already exhausting temp job at the social media juggernaut Snapchat. Brandon wanted to start the evening with a burger because he felt "zombied" from his commute. I managed to drag him first to *Urban Light*, Burden's installation that I have always had questions about but also tried to enjoy in that dumb easy way that other people do.

"We could go for a long weekend to New York," Brandon said, as we swung around the lamps and he took periodic glances at his phone. "I have credit at the Waldorf."

"I don't know." Since I had split from my ex, l had lost some of my gastric panache. There had been a time when I could straddle an unspeakable hole in front of a mosh-pit at the Ohio Lesbian Festival. Now, I secretly worried about the bathroom situation, the intimacy.

Brandon's Adam's apple jerked sideways in the elevator of his throat. He slowly widened his eyes. "Okayyyyyyyy . . ."

I squinted up at *Urban Light* again. I blinked at the fizzy halogens and pretended not to notice as Brandon sneaked a look at a woman who had just manifested among the lamps. The woman wore a pink dress and bounced up and down unrestrainedly as she greeted two male friends. Her neckline revealed significant bosoms that soon lost their equipoise when her pals initiated a self-portraiture ritual.

I scowled at the vanishing point between Brandon's eyeballs and the woman's breasts. I inwardly supported in sisterly solidarity the pink-dressed woman's use of technology to subvert the male gaze with her expensively purchased body confidence—but actually I didn't. While Brandon remained utterly verbally silent and yet audibly breathing, I struggled to affirm my own commitment to polymorphous perversity and not cathect onto one particular person. Sexual possessiveness is a symptom of patriarchal capitalism's cult of private property. Also I am bisexual, so I could exploit the woman with my own predatory scopophilia if I wished. Also what does it matter who looks at whom because as the early work of Chris Burden teaches us we're all going to die anyway and fuckety fuck fuck fuck.

"Ha ha ha!" the girl said, as she and her pals shimmied away.

"You're not even performing right now," Brandon finally said. He took a deep, Freudian drag on his cigarette. "You just got this great job, and they give you weekends off. You should take advantage of it."

"I'm still working on *Texit* when I'm not at Snapchat." I watched his sexy lips curve as he dragon-smoked.

"Yesterday you said you were 'subverting social media with authentic intelligence.'" He frowned. "What does that mean again? You're posting stuff and making comments on Reddit?"

"It's all art," I said, making sure the woman in pink was really gone.

"Is this why you and Xōchitl broke up?" he asked. "Because your work makes you crazy?"

"Sort of." I blinked in surprise at his question. I felt briefly like crying, but didn't. "She just somehow got away."

Brandon dropped his red-glinting butt to the ground. He gave me a kiss and raised his face to the lamplight. He closed his eyes. A few seconds passed. "I could just fall asleep right now, standing right here," he murmured.

The question is how to live, I thought, watching Brandon take a nap. It's a universal quandary, as Chris Burden himself well knew. After all, Chris Burden was disfigured in a motorcycle accident at the age of twelve, had to have surgery without anesthesia, and afterwards became obsessed with technology and alienation. The ordeal led eventually to Burden's suffering from drug addiction, which blossomed into a quarter-life crisis that he expressed by literally tucking an Uzi between his butt-cheeks and running around like a long-armed kangaroo. But at the end of his life, Burden resided in Topanga with his second wife, Nancy Rubins, and reputedly felt so happy that he believed humans could love even in the mechanical age. He made an adorable miniature race track called *Metropolis II* (2011), which is also installed at LACMA. People crowd around and giggle affectionately at the cars whizzing by in eternal circles. And then Burden built the whimsical dirigible in empathetic honor of the ill-fated airplane inventor Santos Dumont, who hung himself in Brazil in 1932 because he felt awful about enabling deadly aerial warfare during WWI.

Maybe it is more important to be happy than to do great work, I wondered, weakening slightly as I watched Brandon wake up and handsomely light another cigarette. I could age out of anger, too, couldn't I? Like I aged out of success and self-confidence. I don't have to write a scathing autopsy of this evening on Instagram. Instead, I could move to Topanga and be poignantly frivolous like old man Chris Burden.

"This is the worst art installation in the entire world," I blurted suddenly, waving my hands at *Urban Light*.

Brandon brooded at me. "I'll try to get up the energy to hate it more."

"We should crash your car into it."

"That would do the trick."

"Did he give up?" I asked. "It just makes me insane to think he changed his mind and decided to sell people an idiotic Hollywood fantasy."

"Now I don't know what you're talking about again," Brandon said.

"Chris Burden," I said. "The guy who put all these lamps together."

Brandon looked up. "OK."

I said, "Chris Burden started his career as this amazing, miserable, scary person. But then he made this feel-good stupid lamp thing that everybody loves. But they shouldn't. No real artist in the whole world ever has said, 'My style break is now going to take the form of offering up unequivocally happy endings.' Take Kafka as an example. Kafka started out *The Metamorphosis* with, 'When Gregor Samsa woke up one morning from unsettling dreams, he found himself changed in his bed into a monstrous vermin.' And at the end of his life, his last gesture was to tell Max Brod to burn everything. *That's* a career arc." I rested against one of the lamps and tilted my chin up to glare at the installation's starlike canopy. "Right?"

"Huh," Brandon said, smoking some more.

"An artist can only transform in some super happy way when they're like Agnes Martin, and they are actually suffering from schizophrenia," I went on. "Otherwise, the artist isn't really making art. She's just doing yoga."

"At least the street's lit up now, it makes it safer around here." Brandon yawned. "I was once mugged two blocks up by a guy who'd made a Glock out of electric tape."

I was still staring up at the lamps.

"Yup," I said.

"I gave the robber my wallet and my car keys, which I later realized was a mistake. But he had this scarily deep voice that made me believe everything he said. Also I was on two tabs of Klonopin."

I stepped back from the pillar I had been leaning on, nodding as if I was actively listening. But, as I studied the way the lamps' luminosity altered the landscape, I started to realize something. "Wait. You're right."

Brandon blinked rapidly. "I don't even remember what I just said."

"You were just saying that you're scared of the dark," I murmured.

"I did?" Brandon peered hard at his cigarette, which was just a menthol.

I gripped onto one of the pale and slippery lampstands. I glared at the foliate designs at the lamps' tops and bases. I continued to inspect the swath of visibility that the lights shone onto Wilshire Boulevard. There was a noise somewhere, which was Brandon, who had started talking again, about subjects that I was going to, in just one second, respond to with lots of specific questions, even if said subjects were not nearly as interesting as what he had just unintentionally suggested.

Had Brandon this very moment accidentally explained the deeper meanings of *Urban Light*?

"Don't you just think it was easier to date when you were younger? I mean, it's always hard to get to know a new person, but it just seems lately that . . . ," Brandon said.

I thought back to Chris Burden's early terrifying works, *Shoot* and *Trans-Fixed* and *White Light/White Heat*. I thought about *Fist of Light*'s aggression. Then I considered the seemingly beautiful or harmonious works, like *Ghost Ship* and *Metropolis II*. For all of my creative life, I had regarded these installations as symptoms of a genius-sacrificing genre shift, like how formerly screamy Edvard Munch began painting flirty pastel nudes after his 1908 nervous breakdown, or how, after William Wordsworth grew rich and famous in his forties, he stopped writing odes to lonely clouds and commenced scribbling NIMBY song cycles about how flowerbeds shouldn't be bulldozed to make way for affordable housing.

But now I began to grok that Chris Burden had stayed frosty in his dotage. Brandon's throw-away aside about his Klonopin mugging revealed that the artist's conceptualism does not divide into scary/dumbly sweet messaging. Instead, Chris Burden's projects engage a persistent, though increasingly complicated conversation about how civilization's advancements not only enable joy, but also kill you and turn you into an idiot ghost with a Sisyphean commute.

Really *think* about it! You, the Instagram viewer, are looking at a picture of a sparkling constellation emanating from vintage lamps Chris Burden collected post-2001. This photogenic atmosphere may delight you, particularly if you seek to showcase your secondary sex characteristics on a post-Hollywood panopticon and hashtag them #nofilter.

Yet recall why the lights were designed. From their earliest incarnations, streetlights had two morbid purposes: they repelled "tramps" and "hobos" from gathering on public byways and also increased worker productivity. So, today, you can stand beneath the lamps, but beyond their silvery perimeter lurks . . . what? Robbers with electric-tape Glocks? Scared homeless people? Trump? You dither beneath *Urban Light* because you have worked past 8:30 and arrived at your destination in the post–Charlie Hebdo afterhours. Note that no malevolent alien force has nailed you to technology, making you tardy and endangered by the dark. You have nailed *yourself* to technology, and consensually work late at a law firm or at Snapchat because you are a fungible agent of "war capitalism." But, then again, all the pretty lamps are nice, too. Because of this collection of outdated fixtures, you can stand in front of LACMA after 9 p.m. and talk to a real live person. Indeed, if you are me, you can harness Los Angeles's oil-dependent infrastructure as you attempt to attract the attentions of a fellow bourgeois by participating in the city's cutthroat sexual market.

What this means is, maybe Chris Burden did not betray his art with his Topanga bliss. *Urban Light* is anodyne, but if read in a certain way, we can see it is also just as ghastly as *Trans-Fixed*. This teaches us something great: maybe not all positive artistic transformation is moronic yoga. You can have both—crucifixion *and* happiness. Technology *and* analogue love. Antennae-waving Gregor Samsa can get crushed to death by society's big boot but also get to a place in his life where he's ordering up a chicken cobb at the Waldorf after a night of amazing sex.

Brandon chomped down on his cigarette and looked at me sideways. I wriggled around the lamps. My new reading of the installation combined with the lunacy of freshly baked infatuation made me ecstatic. And about the bathroom situation if Brandon and I went away together on vacation—I resolved suddenly that I could just hide all evidence of my waste like Chris Burden did in *White Light/White Heat*.

Brandon squashed out his cigarette with the heel of his shoe and frowned at his feet. "Are we having fun right now?"

"Let's go to New York," I said.

1 minute ago

CHAPTER FOURTEEN AUTHENTICITY
CULTURE IS DUMB

[This is an email that I sent to my boss during my second week working at Snapchat.]

To: Francesca Maroni, head of Snapchat Marketing Dept
From: Amanda Ruiz, Temporary Program Development Associate
    While Haidar is on Parental Leave
Subject: Memo on Snapchat's Capacity to Kill Instagram While
    Staying Authentic
Date: April 16, 2018
Dear Francesca,

Please find here the requested recommendation report on how to remain competitive with our main rival Instagram while not (as you put it) "sacrificing our culture of authenticity." As I understand it, Snapchat's famous "authenticity culture" requires that Snapchat desperately try to make money while simultaneously saying that it is really *not* interested in making money but just in creating world-improving networks for IRL friends. In this way, Snapchat distinguishes itself from Instagram, which stomps gleefully over supposedly noncommodifiable values like love and community in its fast march to convert all humans into visual products that may be monetized via delivery systems such as social confessionals and mass hypnosis.

How to Beat Instagram While Remaining "Authentic"

∞ That sounds impossible

∞ Sabotage?

∞ Assassination

∞ Anna Wintour

∞ Install prostitution and drug distribution circuits via a PayPal option on Snapchat stories

∞ Support the Russian annexation of Ukraine

CHAPTER FIFTEEN THE SCIENCE OF INVISIBILITY

[I posted a picture of an exhausted guard standing watch over Robert Barry's *Untitled* (1968) and this accompanying essay on Instagram on June 4, 2018. I can't reproduce the picture here, however, as an official has explained to me that the Museum of Modern Art does not permit publication of photographs taken inside of its buildings. *Untitled* (1968) is a metal weight affixed to a translucent string.]

On the fourth story of the Museum of Modern Art in New York City, my boyfriend Brandon and I encountered a man attending to a nearly invisible piece of string. Like many of MoMA's guards, the man was Black, and had donned a neat sharp black suit with a white shirt. He also wore black-rimmed spectacles. He stood before the string, which I soon discovered was a length of translucent nylon filament. A heavy stainless steel weight anchored the tendril to the ground, and the string extended to the ceiling, to which it was attached. The fibril proved so difficult to detect visually that, at first, I thought the man only guarded the steel weight. I took Brandon's arm and tugged him across the floor as I approached the guard.

"Is this an installation?" I asked, looking down at the piece of metal while Brandon thrust his hands into the pockets of his navy blazer and made a soft *put put putting* sound with his lips.

The man had seconds before worn a blank and exhausted expression, but now smiled at us. He thrust his head forward from his shoulders to indicate the diaphanous art product. "I'm here to make sure that no one runs into it."

Now I saw the plastic string. "What is this?"

"A ha ha," he said. "I don't know. Art."

"How long do you stand here?" I asked.

"All day," he said. "My whole shift. Then I go home and soak my feet."

"Amanda," Brandon said.

"That sounds hard," I said, to the man.

"I soak my feet at the end of the day," he said again.

"I would too," I said.

"I'm sure this nice guard would rather just do his job without being both—ugh, OK," Brandon said, as I grabbed his hand and dragged him to the little wall sign supposedly explaining the artwork, in order to see who had made it and why.

As I later found out by doing my own research, the conceptual artist Robert Barry built *Untitled* in 1968, during a period from the mid-1960s to the 1970s when string works dominated minimalism. For example, the sculptor Fred Sandback made large installations out of black acrylic yarn. Similarly, Eva Hesse crafted squiggly clouds out of string, rope, wire, and latex.

But Barry, an Anglo man born in the Bronx in 1936, was different. While Sandback made outlines, and Hesse created levitating graffiti that quoted the body, Barry wanted to represent nothing at all. In a 1968 interview with the critic Lucy Lippard, he explained: "Nothing seems to me the most potent thing in the world." He pursued this obsession by playing with transparency and undetectability, which found expression in this work guarded, in the manner of Sisyphus, by the sore-footed man in the black suit and black spectacles.

After Brandon and I read the uninformative wall didactic for *Untitled* (1968), we walked back to the string-protecting man, who continued staring out at the room with expressionless eyes as visitors swirled around him.

"May I take your photograph?" I asked.

"Sure," he said, looking at me shyly.

While Brandon made a distressed coughing sound, I took out my iPhone. The guard's face grew somber again as I snapped him. I wanted to ask his name, but did not. He seemed too exhausted to talk, and I did not want to treat him as a specimen in the diorama that is MoMA. Or maybe I ceased conversing with him because I didn't want to depart from protocol, which in this space demanded that art patrons look at the art and not really see the guards. Or, I stopped asking him questions because I was awkward and stupid.

Brandon and I left.

*

"That was upsetting," I told Brandon, when we walked out of the museum a few minutes later and onto West 54th Street.

Brandon stood tall above me and nodded. His white shirt opened at the throat, revealing the slim shelf of his clavicle. "Because you made him uncomfortable?"

"If you weren't here, I'd protest MoMA's labor practices by hyperventilating until I passed out." I stared at the press of humans rushing back and forth on the sidewalk and the slow crush of cars trundling on the street. I wore Brandon's green-and-black plaid shirt, a white tank top, and skinny jeans that revealed the contours of my buttocks in a cheerful salute to the male gaze.

"Like Marina Abramović in *Rhythm 4*," Brandon said.

I looked up, into his face. His dark irises locked gently onto mine.

Brandon and I sometimes have difficulties communicating. A month and a half ago, while frolicking in front of Chris Burden's *Urban Light* installation, we had a fight about whether we would go on this very trip. And then, just now, I had worried that Brandon had been stifling my efforts to engage in a human way with the museum guard, because he thought I was being weird and inappropriate.

During moments like those, my feelings about Brandon grew so imperceptible that I worried they were no longer there.

But now they came back. I felt something like actual love irradiate my whole body with golden light. Brandon and I were bonding over the famous tale of how, in 1974, the performance artist Marina Abramović protested fascism by traveling to Milan and then nakedly crouched in front of a huge fan and inhaled so fast and hard that she collapsed, unconscious. It occurred to me briefly that the mere fact that Brandon had remembered an Abramović story that I'd once told him constituted a slender ledge upon which to hang my intense emotions.

That was OK with me, though. I reached up and placed my fingers on Brandon's gorgeous clavicle.

"I'm wild about you," I said.

*

Robert Barry became interested in Nothing in the mid-1960s, and made art that resembled the absence of something in its invisibility.

However, as many racial minorities and older white women well know, being invisible is not the same thing as being nothing.

One way of thinking about the relationship between imperceptibility and existence is to investigate the science of invisibility.

In the seventeenth century, Pierre de Fermat discovered that light will always travel on the shortest possible path between points. This is the principle of *least time* or *least action*. We see the principle of least time or action at work when we look at objects half-submerged in water and they appear to us in a position other than where they rest: when light travels from the air to the water, it bends so that the path it takes from one point to another requires the minimal possible action, which causes the immersed portion of the object to look distorted.

The science of invisibility exploits Fermat's breakthrough: if space curves wholly around an entity, then this swell determines the shortest distance for light to travel. If space can somehow be pushed out around the thing—a string, a weight, a person—then light will also journey around it, rendering it undetectable.

*

On June 2, 2018, the Museum of Modern Art was a place full of invisibility.

On its fourth floor, I felt depressed because the security guard has an unendurable job and I may have exacerbated his suffering by asking him questions about it.

At the next moment, after having escaped from Robert Barry's *Untitled* (1968) to West 54th Street, I looked up at Brandon and felt love illuminate my soul with golden light.

This golden halo pushed space out around the museum guard, *Untitled* (1968), West 54th Street, and my troubling memories of an actuary ex-girlfriend whom I am no longer going to write, think, or talk about. All I could fathom were Brandon's beautiful matador eyes and the seeming perfection of my own happiness.

Everything else disappeared.

*

"We could have a baby," Brandon said, later that night in our hotel.

The Waldorf has outrageously nice rooms. Our huge bed had clean, bright linens that swaddled both of us like togas. The walls shimmered with tones of cream and beige. Wing chairs upholstered with striped fabrics had been arranged thoughtfully next to cut-glass coffee tables, where room service people could rest silver trays laden with champagne and strawberries.

"I never imagined myself as a mother," I said, touching the tender mohair on Brandon's sternum and batting away annoying recollections about how this very issue of interrupted child-freedom had nuked a previous thing that is really nothing now, a true nothing like Robert Barry wanted to make art about.

"That's not saying no," Brandon said.

"I love you." I started crying messily, like Marina Abramović had after waking up from her hyperventilation-induced pass out.

"Yes, yes, yes," he crooned. He tucked me into his armpit and kissed my ear. "Yes, yes."

I had completely forgotten that the museum guard had ever existed at all.

*

Now that I am not completely fixated by oxytocin, empathy allows me to deduce that a person who stares at the space around a translucent string all day gets an education on the real meaning of Nothing—the most potent thing in the world.

A person who becomes an expert in Nothing, I think, would learn that its related concept, *least action*, is a misleading phrase. In physics, Fermat's *least action* indicates that universal powers conspire to conserve energy by executing the fastest, most efficient space-time processes. This resourcefulness is accepted as a piece of cosmic cleverness. It explains, as mentioned above, why light always seeks to travel the shortest distance.

In security guarding, however, the guard acquires the job of least action because he or she cannot do anything but stand watch, unless something bad transpires. *Least action* is not as great when practiced by human beings in this way.

In 2012, a scientific paper published in the *International Journal of Psychology and Behavioral Sciences* described a study of Malay security guards who worked in a bank. Its authors reported that "a considerable number of participants were screened positive for depression (25.4 percent) and 14.8 percent were positively screened with psychosis . . . Overall, there is significant presence of mental health problems among the participants."

The authors did not suggest that metastasizing boredom or feelings of invisibility or perpetually hurting feet contributed to these mental ills. Instead, they looked to childhood traumas and the stress that comes with monitoring other human beings and conceivably being called upon to repel a violent affront to an employer's safety or possessions.

Still, I think that if I had to look at a transparent string all day to make rent I would go completely crazy.

*

Robert Barry's art teaches us that the stuff of life—the elements, thoughts, emotions, the mysterious vitalities that keep us alive—remains as ephemeral as a nylon fiber. It will vanish before your eyes.

That's really interesting. But we still all want to live for something, even if we're scared that it will yet again fade or disappear.

Everybody deserves a lot of something. It's a human right.

*

If Nothing is the most potent force in the world, then no one should have it thrust upon them as a condition of work. Invisibility is the scientific product of mind-bending racism and social inattention to sore feet and weathered peace of mind.

Art is supposed to be the visible energy that impels us to look with passion at reality. But what happens when art is held in an environment that trains your gaze away from inequality and suffering? And what occurs when your passions cause you to grow blind to what's in front of you?

Something, rather than nothing, does take place—and it's awful.

So why am I still so happy?

1 minute ago

History

Friday, June 22, 2018
6:19 PM wtf rogue one
Monday, June 25, 2018
9:45 AM How not to sabotage your healthy relationship
10:45 Xōchitl Hernández Munger & Hanley wife baby address images
Saturday, June 30, 2018
1:32 AM Radical feminist performance art videos crazier the better
3:02 AM Did Wittgenstein kill a kid
Monday, July 2, 2018
4:02 PM Craig Wallace schmoozer or real thing
Thursday, August 9, 2018
9:57 PM when do you know that you're becoming a hack warning signs
11:13 PM pretty woman

CHAPTER SIXTEEN PRIVATE LANGUAGE

[Vimeo Comment #1 that I posted to Lindsay Tunkl's *Is This What Feeling Feels Like? -First Attempt* on June 30, 2018. This video features the performance artist Lindsay Tunkl singing "I Will Always Love You" while drowning herself in a bowl filled with water.]

Amanda 1 hour ago

A person who wants to be destroyed by love is normal. The human wish to be ravished, despite its bearer's avowed feminist principles and self-possessed public persona, does not present an anomaly. At rare yet foreseeable intervals, erotic desire will offer most mortals an expensive, all-inclusive trip to a magical land where they will engage in mutually confusing flagellations with other reasonable people who are similarly, if temporarily, afflicted.

So, no, it is not strange to want to be bent painfully over a headboard while wailing with happiness. Even famous people like Herman Melville aspired to be slayed like a babbling lamb. Indeed, this ambition proves so common that it often crawls to the depths of banality. Maybe Melville wrote the great *Moby-Dick* about Nathaniel Hawthorne, but think about the thousands of cliché-flamed films that have been made in passion's name. Desiring another person to drink from your flagon of life is a well-worn theme in the history of love.

What *is* strange is articulating this longing in language.

"Grab my ass! Pull my hair! Harder!" goes the mantra.

"Spank me! Say my name!" goes another.

*

Brandon is a thirty-four-year-old corporate lawyer I met in a Ralphs. He is imposingly tall and possesses buoyant pectoral muscles. I am a thirty-eight-year-old former performance artist, an aspiring writer, and now a platform strategist for Snapchat (that is, until Haidar comes back from baby leave). Brandon is half Chinese and half Peruvian, and likes *Star Wars* prequels. I am a bisexual Chicana with large eyes and sturdy legs. We have been dating for four months.

When I visited Brandon's two-bedroom condominium in Culver City tonight, I arrived at its walnut parquet foyer ready to talk. I had been reading Wittgenstein's late philosophy on the Metro and wanted to ask Brandon about his thoughts on indeterminacy. But then I saw his blue-veined biceps and bloodshot aura of overwork, and became incredibly excited.

"Hi, you look really pretty," he said, backing into the living room as I threw my recycled canvas Snapchat work bag to the ground and tore at his shirt buttons. "Babe. Baaaaabe. Whoa, this is so exciting. But. Hold on, wait—" *Plop* we fell on the sofa, which is covered in tweedy wool.

"I am holding on, I *am* waiting a minute," I gasped back, until I heard myself yelling, "TAKE ME NOW, YOU MONSTER! LOVE ME LIKE A STEVEDORE! MAKE ME BEG!"

"Oh my God," Brandon said. "OK, OK. OK."

I think that I love Brandon a lot.

"What's a stevedore again?" Brandon asked afterwards. We cuddled in his queen-sized bed, in his small blue-walled bedroom. "It sounds like something out of *Moby-Dick*."

"It's a figure of speech," I said, stroking his arm hairs.

"Not one I ever heard." Brandon pursed his lips to the far right side, as if his mouth were running away from something.

"It's a compliment." I laughed.

"Uhhhhhh . . ." Brandon lay on his back and looked at the ceiling with eyes that kept widening. "Do I have sex like a postal worker?"

"What do you mean, like, homicidal?" I asked.

"No, like boring," he said.

I stretched out my legs. "No, you have sex like a lawyer." Brandon *is* a lawyer, but I immediately understood my mistake. "A really amazing lawyer. An ACLU person who fights for justice and stuff like that."

"Oh, Jesus." Brandon rolled over and closed his eyes and stopped talking.

"Like Ruth Bader Ginsburg," I said. "That's good, right?"

"I do mergers, Amanda," Brandon said, his voice muffled under the blanket.

Now he is asleep.

*

I am awake, web surfing. When Brandon started snoring around midnight, I padded out to the living room and retrieved my bag, which contained my Wittgenstein and my laptop. I returned to bed and turned on the small white lamp on the stand next to me. I took out my paperback copy of *Philosophical Investigations* and read until I reached the last page.

After that, I leaned over and whispered into Brandon's ear: "You have sex like a superhero."

He remained unconscious.

"I am fanatically in love with you," I barely breathed.

Still no response.

"I want you to tie me up like I'm a Victorian femme fatale and you are an evil villain with a mustache and a top hat," I said.

"What?" he said.

"You're dreaming," I said.

Brandon fell back asleep.

I turned off the lamp. I tried to sleep, too. When that didn't work, I dug through my bag again and this time fished out my laptop. I opened my computer and balanced it on my knees. I started looking at feminist art videos on Vimeo, which is one of my favored distractions during uneasy times. After a while, I found the work of Lindsay Tunkl.

It is 3:01 in the morning.

*

You have likely never heard of Lindsay Tunkl. You have probably found this Vimeo page in the same way that I did, which is to say, on accident. According to her website's *CV/Bio* section, Lindsay Tunkl graduated from CalArts with a BFA in 2010 and, as of this writing, is attempting to complete an MFA in Studio Practice and an MA in Visual + Critical Studies at California College of the Arts in San Francisco. From her videos on Vimeo, and her still shots on her website, we can see that Lindsay Tunkl is a white woman in her twenties. She has long dark hair, with streaks of early gray in it. She also has a big silver lip piercing, and bears a metal stud below her left eye, which seems painful. Lindsay Tunkl is pretty and large-framed, with fleshy arms and formidable breasts and thighs.

Lindsay Tunkl has made a series of conceptual art perfumes based on the apocalypse. One of the perfumes is called "Tsunami," and another is called "Nuclear Blast." They do not appear to be available for purchase on her website and doubtlessly smell bad.

Lindsay Tunkl has the word "HOLOCENE" tattooed on the inside of her lower lip, as a memento mori. She is in mourning for the Holocene, which has been replaced by the apocalyptic era of the Anthropocene, the age of global warming and atomic annihilation. In 2010, Tunkl took a self-portrait. In this photograph, she sticks out her lower lip so that you can read *Holocene* on her mouth's shiny underside. She made this image into a 36" × 48" print, which also does not seem purchasable from her website.

The same year that she made *Holocene*, Lindsay Tunkl executed a performance called *This Is How the iPhone Didn't Save My Love Life*. *This is How the iPhone Didn't Save My Love Life* consisted of Tunkl sending plaintive text messages to a lover who never replied to her even once, despite the fact that she sent those text messages while driving across California to reach her, him, or them in the middle of the night.

I love you and I'm not ready for this to be over, she wrote.

I'm not leaving until you tell me that you're not coming.

This is all very good, but Lindsay Tunkl's best work product may be a short video that she posted on this Vimeo page in 2014. It is titled *Is This What Feeling Feels Like?—First Attempt*. In *Is This What Feeling Feels Like?*, Lindsay Tunkl wears a blue dress and her dark hair loose. In a wide shot, we see her walk into a white room that hosts a white table with a white enamel bowl on it. The bowl brims with water. Lindsay Tunkl stands before the table and the bowl and stretches out her arms. She begins to yell-sing the Dolly Parton/Whitney Houston hit, "I Will Always Love You," and periodically dunk her head into the enamel bowl, continuing to screamingly sing while her head remains underwater.

This video lasts for one minute and fifty-one seconds, and has been played sixteen times, mostly by me. Except for the comments that I am now writing, *Is This What Feeling Feels Like?—First Attempt* has elicited 0 comments. It has not been Shared with anyone. It has not been Liked by anyone, nor included in any collections.

Lindsay Tunkl's work is a study of human solitude. Tunkl craves a whole and healed earth, but sees only destruction and death. She loves, but remains apart. She adores, but is drowning. She cries out for union with her beloved, but feels like she is dying.

Lindsay Tunkl is alone. She is abandoned as a human on a dying planet, deserted as a woman in an affectionless world, and she is also forsaken as an unLiked and unCommented-on artist.

Lindsay Tunkl's loneliness dooms her to speak in what Ludwig Wittgenstein once referred to as a *private language*.

Ludwig Wittgenstein studied the problems of private language at the late stage of his career, in his vulnerable old age. Wittgenstein had conceived this idea after an early, more foolish, period: during the Great War, Wittgenstein believed that language mirrored the logic of reality (as he explained in his *Tractatus Logico-Philosophicus*, published in 1922), and thought that in so mapping existence and its reflectively lucid attendant discourse that he, Wittgenstein, had solved every single philosophical problem that ever existed. "Whereof one cannot speak, thereof one must be silent," he wrote.

Wittgenstein was gay, Jewish, and an intellectual during the rise of Hitler, but he would not be persuaded that reality was actually a confusing mess except after he began working as a grammar teacher in Lower Austria in 1922. Wittgenstein did not prove a natural educator. He reviled provincial life and called his pupils "worms." In 1926, in the municipality of Otterthal, Wittgenstein beat a hemophiliac eleven-year-old student named Josef Haidbauer, who died shortly thereafter, possibly because of his injuries. Wittgenstein's family was rich, and Wittgenstein did not suffer any consequences for killing this child.

But maybe Wittgenstein did suffer internally. Ten years later, he no longer believed that he had solved every philosophical problem that ever existed. He had moved away to Vienna but returned to Otterthal in 1936 to apologize for committing murder and other student abuses. The people of the region remained unreceptive. They did not look him in the eye, and just said *Ja, ja*.

After that, Wittgenstein went back to Vienna and repudiated all of his work. He spent the last years of his life trashing his earlier philosophy by writing *Philosophical Investigations*, which was published posthumously in 1953. In *Philosophical Investigations* Wittgenstein now said that words don't have any inherent logic, but only derive their coherence from their ordinary vernacular usages. People agree to use words for certain purposes, and in that way create their meaning. Perhaps Wittgenstein was thinking of the ambiguity of *Ja, ja* when he wrote this. No linguistic significance exists outside of these agreements, which are formed out of elongated human exchanges, Wittgenstein explained. These personal connections, however, are difficult to attain. They require more than refraining from homicide. Relationships also require a feat of the imagination.

"If one has to imagine someone else's pain on the model of one's own, this is none too easy a thing to do," Wittgenstein wrote. "I can only *believe* that someone else is in pain, but I know it if I am.—Yes: one can make the decision to say 'I believe he is in pain' instead of 'He is in pain.'"

But what if you have imperfect relationships and no one is trying to imagine your subjectivity? What if you are a loner who is obsessed with the apocalypse? What if, left to your own devices, you spend your afternoons singing "I Will Always Love You" while drowning and filming it? What if you only have sixteen downloads and no one Likes your videos? Does anyone believe that you are in pain? And is anyone hearing or understanding you? To this last question, Wittgenstein might say *Not really* or *Are you joking?* He might also say *Ja, ja.*

"Now, what about the dialect which describes my inner experiences and which only I myself can understand?" he asked in *Philosophical Investigations*, and in so doing defined his theory of private language. Wittgenstein did not answer this question outright, but he suggested that such a solitary vernacular does not bear a "criterion of correctness" and thus would "give no information." A brief review of his biography also makes us suspect that if we could conjure the spirit of Wittgenstein in a séance, he would additionally warn us that a person with a private language is crazy and likely to beat up a hemophiliac child when in a bad mood.

It is too bad that Wittgenstein did not live in the age of the Anthropocene so that he might watch Lindsay Tunkl videos. Lindsay Tunkl shows us that private languages persist as inescapable parts of life. Indeed, her work reveals that the most compelling of all grammars remains the private language that we are each condemned to speak. This private language does not necessarily evidence murderous craziness, even if we use it to talk about the apocalypse or to express "babbling lamb" desires for erotic possession. However, this language possesses no criterion of correctness except for its verification of our solitude.

Lindsay Tunkl teaches us that the community of empaths that Wittgenstein alludes to consists of people who speak their own grammars of solitude together. Every once in a while these individuals may understand each other. But a lot of the time, they don't. "Having a relationship" occurs when a person agrees to continue loving another person despite the fact that their reciprocal comprehension remains sporadic and without guarantee.

*

Art is like unrequited love.

As a maybe former performance artist, I can tell you that there exists a lot of art that very few people look at, even if that art was made by somebody who won a Franklin Furnace in 2009 and a Slamdance Sparky in 2018. A huge number of artists work without any support at all, and even those who have had the honor of being fired by the Guggenheim may find themselves making unheralded Vimeo comment art at four in the morning.

Artists post their art to the web and wait to see if anyone can hear their private language.

Commenting on and liking videos, paintings, stories, and also other comments now form new, often fruitless, practices of bridging this unbearable silence in the modern era.

*

For a short while, the nineteenth-century novelists Herman Melville and Nathaniel Hawthorne provided each other with a life-sustaining community that proved even more powerful than that found in web commentary: They both loved and occasionally even apprehended each other. However, though Wittgenstein observed that reciprocal recognition must be manifested by people helpfully imagining one another's suffering, Melville and Hawthorne's corporate sympathy did not protect them from pain.

Melville lived near Hawthorne in western Massachusetts in 1850 and 1851, the same years that he wrote *Moby-Dick*. Melville was thirty-one and unknown. Hawthorne was forty-six and had just published *The Scarlet Letter* to much acclaim. Both men were married, but this did not matter. They met often and walked in silence in the Berkshire woods, enjoying the sunbeams, the trees, and the sounds of the birds.

On November 17, 1851, Melville wrote Hawthorne: "Whence come you, Hawthorne? By what right do you drink from my flagon of life? And when I put it to my lips—lo, they are yours and not mine."

We cannot know the precise right that Hawthorne claimed when drinking from Melville's flagon of life. Though he wrote many letters to Melville, they do not survive, because Melville burned them. But by studying Hawthorne's actions and writings, we may discern that Hawthorne and Melville enjoyed some forms of agreement on this aspect of the human condition that Wittgenstein described as the *inner experience.*

We begin to suspect that the two men shared some sort of private revelation when we learn that Hawthorne ran away from Melville. In early 1852, he moved himself and his wife, the dark-eyed Sophia Peabody, to the stevedoreless safety of Concord, Massachusetts.

That same year, Hawthorne wrote *The Blithedale Romance.* The novel concerns the relationship between a young poet named Miles Coverdale and one Hollingsworth, an older fellow with a vocation for penal reform. The men form a passionate attachment in the utopian community of Blithedale but then have a savage falling-out over a disagreement about the socialist philosophies of Charles Fourier. Coverdale and Hollingsworth's spat, however, probably concerns their romantic frustrations more than their commitments to the universal laws of social progress. They break up, Hollingsworth taking up with a lady named Priscilla and Coverdale moving to the city, where he begins spying on strange married men.

Coverdale, the novel's narrator, admits that he cannot cope with his loss of Hollingsworth.

"The heart-pang was not merely figurative, but an absolute torture of the breast," he says.

*

Earlier this month, while standing with Brandon on West 54th Street in Manhattan, I felt bad about the working conditions suffered by a guard at the Museum of Modern Art. I thought that Brandon had not understood my response to this man and believed I was inappropriate and weird. But when I made a context-free reference to antifascism and hyperventilation, Brandon had understood that I attempted to defend my reaction by connecting it to the famous story of how, in 1974, a performance artist once resisted oppression by gulping down air so hard and fast that she collapsed to the ground.

"Like Marina Abramović in *Rhythm 4,*" Brandon had said, looking at me intently with his beautiful eyes.

For the past couple of years, I had felt dead inside because of the loss of my father et cetera. But at that moment, I felt suddenly the feathered wings of my spirit terrifyingly expand like the golden wings of those emotional angels described by Plato in the *Phaedrus.*

I looked back at him.

My heart beat and beat.

Eight days ago, though, Brandon and I "crossed wires." We sat in his living room, on the sofa covered with the fuzzy fabric. With the aid of his iPad, Brandon attempted to show me a scene of violent young people dueling with big glow sticks. He explained that he wished me to watch this bit of *cinéma improbabilité* because he felt very excited introducing me to his favorite installment in the current incarnation of the *Star Wars* franchise, which is a movie called *Rogue One*.

Rogue One, as I quickly learned in enormous detail, is a prequel to the Luke Skywalker, Princess Leia, and Han Solo tale. It tells the doomed love story of two binary interstellar Resistance Fighters who waste a lot of time misunderstanding each other's private languages via interminable debates over a primordial, tech-savvy version of Fourierism that requires the subservience of individualism to the greater good. The female eventually submits to the ideology of the male, which causes them to fall deeply and hysterically in love. The female and the male then perish demi-*in flagrante* while getting planet-bombed by the Empire.

"Here, look," Brandon said, pressing the iPad up to my face.

I have already mentioned Brandon's physical attractions, such as the chest muscles and the tallness. These gorgeous temptations prevented me from caring about *Rogue One*. All I wanted to do, as Brandon leaned close to pressure me to watch interstellar decapitations, was nuzzle my mouth into his warm, musky neck, and to bite him and maybe lick and also perhaps in my enthusiasm leave a hickey.

So, instead of admiring the iPad, I pressed my mouth directly under his jaw. I tried to kiss the tender flesh next to his thorax. This stimulus caused Brandon to swiftly jerk his shoulder up so that my face, briefly if brutally, smushed between his head and shoulder. Brandon then snapped his head away, leaving me squish-eyed and politely smiling as I sat stiffly next to him.

"No, come on, watch it," he said.

"OK," I said.

Nodding, I observed the space murder.

"See?" Brandon said, raising his eyebrows. "It's so good."

My eye hurt.

"That's really neat," I said.

*

I cannot say for certain what exactly Brandon had in mind when he said *See? It's so good*. I suspect that he attempted to communicate to me a hope that we shared similar cultural and aesthetic values that would bode well in our future together as deeply committed life partners. He also, of course, could have simply meant to convey a ludicrously positive assessment of the film's quality.

I can say for certain, however, what *I* meant when I said *That's really neat.* I did not mean *That's really neat* in the least. I actually meant *It is super important for me not to compare this relationship to my last relationship because in my last relationship I was constantly covered in hickeys and felt like I was a god.*

For a moment, I also meant *I sort of hate you right now, Brandon.*

What had passed between us to explain this deterioration? What sin had we committed to fall from our psychic declarations of love on West 54th Street to the depths of our mutual ignorance in Brandon's living room?

Earlier in our romance, when Brandon had understood my reference to Marina Abramović, our Plato-like passion to fuse into one person had impregnated every moment with agreed-upon meaning. But then, love appears to have cooled. And once this horizontality began to dissipate, a creeping hierarchy of affection started to reveal discrepancies, that is, the existence of our separate private languages.

While sitting on Brandon's sofa, we had a choice to endure the risks of empathetic imagination, as Wittgenstein teaches us. For example, I could have submitted my ideology to the male's, like in *Rogue One*. Or, Brandon could have seen a look of disappointment flash across my features and said, *This heart-pang is not merely figurative, but an absolute torture of the breast,* like Hawthorne wrote in semi-code about Melville. Or, we could have stared into each other's eyes and said *I will always love you*, like Lindsay Tunkl sang as she drowned in a bowl of water in *Is This What Feeling Feels Like?* and like Xōchitl told me every goddamned day of our life together until she decided to get pregnant with Greta Weber, M.D.

None of that happened, though.

*

ste·ve·dore / ˈstēvəˌdôr/ *noun*

1. a person who loves you by fucking you so blindingly hard and passionately that he, she, or they destroys the separateness between you.

*

There are three types of language. The first type of language voices a fellow-feeling. One need not say a word to pronounce this idiom. Wittgenstein says that this expression is *none too easy* to achieve, but Brandon and I spoke it effortlessly on West 54th Street when he said "Marina Abramović," and looked into my eyes. I know that the message that passed between us signaled *I love you*.

When Herman Melville and Nathaniel Hawthorne walked together in the Berkshires, they, too, co-wrote the story of their fatal love by marking their footprints into the leaf-mold of the Massachusetts forest. I cannot say if it was none too easy for them to do so, but the violent queerphobia plaguing the United States at the time (and, now) suggests that they had to fight to secure these precious moments of affective telepathy.

Lindsay Tunkl and her lover also spoke this language in *This Is How the iPhone Didn't Save My Love Live*, where she clamored at her, him, or them via text to return her devotion, but only silence followed. Like Brandon and me on West 54th Street, Melville and Hawthorne in the forest, and Xōchitl and me when Xōchitl blocked me even after my dad died, Lindsay Tunkl understood eventually the magnitude of her beloved's communiqué. It created an arduous yet necessary mutuality between them.

*

The second type of language bears words whose meanings arrive corroded and warped, but partially understood. This is the language of *Ja, ja*. Lovers live in terror of this vocabulary. It is the patois that leads to heartbreaking disagreements over Fourierism, singing "I Will Always Love You," and drowning. *Ja, ja* has double, triple meanings, untrue meanings, builds false hopes, and lays secret traps. A person may hear a phrase spoken in Language Number 2 and believe that they discern an existential *yes* within its syntax, but later realize the damnation of their dreams. A particularly exquisite suffering ensues.

When Melville asked Hawthorne *by what right* he *drank from the flagon* of his life, Hawthorne replied with a Yankee *Ja, ja* by fleeing the soft mossy forests of the Berkshires for the redoubts of Concord and then writing *The Blithedale Romance*. In so doing Hawthorne tried to convince Melville that he had no idea what in the hell Melville was talking about but simultaneously also explain that he would love Melville for the rest of his life.

In my case, I fear that when I said *That's neat* about the *Rogue One* prequel, and actually meant *I sort of hate you right now, Brandon*, I cracked the mechanism that translates Brandon's and my words when we speak to one another. I worry that the injury I inflicted on this love technology continued to lethally spread and widen in the week after our conversation about *Rogue One*, since I did not immediately superglue the damage with sex or authentic ideological submission. Thus, when I made erotic overtures to Brandon this evening, and he responded by saying *Wait* and *Hold on*, I am scared that what he actually tried to tell me was *Stop, I do not want you anymore*.

The third type of language cannot be understood, either as a single or double entendre. This private language is the shibboleth of a different type of wasteland. In this vernacular, the word "stevedore" may be written by an island castaway on a paper scrap that is then stuffed into a bottle and thrown into the ocean. When a beachcomber on the mainland sees the bottle bobbing in the water many months or years later, and opens it up, he reads the word and thinks that it refers to a character out of a novel by Herman Melville that treats the themes of masculine madness and whales. The castaway remains on her faraway sandbar, unable to translate her nouns and verbs into shapes that will attract a rescue party. She sits on the beach and contemplates tsunamis and nuclear blasts—the end of the world.

*

It is 4:45 in the morning. Brandon's breathing remains deep and steady. In Los Angeles's pre-dawn, sepia light, I can make out the hedgehog spikes of his hair. I smell his skin, the clove of him under his cologne. He moves lightly. The cotton sheets make crinkling noises.

I want you to love me like a tornado, like a plague, like a fire.

I want you to destroy me with your light saber.

I am over Xōchitl, for real this time.

I lean over to him again. "I love you," I say instead. I say it now so that he can hear it.

Brandon's rhythmic breathing stops. He shifts and turns toward me. He reaches out under the sheets and grasps my thigh.

"Yeah, I love you too," he says after several seconds. Then he falls silent again.

I look up, at the blue-opal sky captured in his window.

I don't really know what he means.

*

Lindsay Tunkl, keep working.

CHAPTER SEVENTEEN HOPE IN A PHONE

[Text sent from Craig Wallace to Amanda Ruiz, July 2, 2018, 3:41 PM.]

Hey Amanda it was great to
meet you at the Snap/Murakami
collab party last nite i was
wondering if you wanted to
send me your script it sounded
very NOW considering all the shit
that's going on politically and i
think we could do something with
it at the gallery if ur interested
cw

[More meaningfully subtextual lines that I tweeted from *Texit* throughout the amazing month of July 2018.]

Josefina: Texit, ur getting overexcited / Mexicans r not to blame #texit

Texit: Don't hate just cuz I'm starting to get some fame #texit

Josefina: Just because one guy emailed u doesn't mean u got game #texit

Texit: Don't harsh my buzz / In a mad world only the mad are sane #texit

Josefina: You're just quoting Kurosawa that's lame #texit

Texit: When u understand my references I feel totally seen #texit

Josefina: Baby the world's your burrito you're not a has-been. #texit

CHAPTER EIGHTEEN IT'S FINE TO BE EDITED BY YOUR GALLERIST

[These are new lines tweeted from a *Texit* rewrite that I composed after several extensive conversations with Craig Wallace. They are followed by replies tweeted by Xōchitl Hernández in the first week of August 2018.]

Texit (pointing Colt 9mm submachine gun at Josefina): We will deport you and make America Great Again #texit
Josefina: I am a Strong Brown Woman you can't talk to me like that bird-brain #texit
Texit: When I see you standing there so proud and tall I am ashamed of my racism and xenophobia #texit
Josefina (taking gun from Texit): Only my righteous anger can cure you of your myopia #texit
Texit: But if you are a person with equal dignity then I am confused #texit
Josefina: You are a poor white fentanyl addict caught in Donald Trump's ruse #texit
Texit: Perhaps then we shouldn't be building a wall #texit
Josefina: Yes we shouldn't be doing that at all #texit
Texit: I now see that you are a Strong Intersectional Female deserving of rights #texit
Josefina: Si se puede baby together we will win this fight #texit

Xōchitlhernández @xochhern   Aug 7
Replying to @amandapanda
but i thought texit was going to be evil throughout and she & josefina were going to have a complicated relationship

AmandaRuiz @amandapanda   Aug 7
Replying to @xochhern
so now ur talking to me again hows Greta

Xōchitlhernández @xochhern   Aug 7
Replying to @amandapanda
I unblocked u weeks ago why are u still yelling at me about that. gretas great
but what about this weird dialogue

AmandaRuiz @amandapanda   Aug 7
Replying to @xochhern
i got some notes from my gallerist

Xōchitlhernández @xochhern   Aug 7
Replying to @amandapanda
u said u didn't want to "conform to the noble savage stereotype" in your
work that u were going to write a "complex & disturbing piece about

Xōchitlhernández @xochhern   Aug 7
Replying to @amandapanda
racism and sexism's invasive pathology"

AmandaRuiz @amandapanda   Aug 7
Replying to @xochhern
my gallerist thought I should maybe make #texit more likable and not be
wholly dismissive of audience expectations and also

AmandaRuiz @amandapanda   Aug 7
Replying to @xochhern
tell a story of redemption

Xōchitlhernández @xochhern   Aug 7
Replying to @amandapanda
wtf that doesn't sound like you at all

AmandaRuiz @amandapanda   Aug 7
Replying to @xochhern
i thought you would have liked this you hated #texit when you read the 11th
ms u said it was depressing

Xōchitlhernández @xochhern   Aug 7
Replying to @amandapanda
I NEVER SAID THAT

CHAPTER NINETEEN MAYBE THIS WILL MAKE ME SOME MONEY

[Essay I wrote for Hatchfund Create a Project on August 10, 2018; Hatchfund is a fund-raising site for artists.]

Project Title

Texit: A Mobile Opera, Opening at the Craig Wallace Gallery Late Summer 2018

Project Description (max 6000 characters)

Here's a story about a sellout: J. F. Lawton. That's the guy who wrote the first draft of the screenplay that ultimately became the blockbuster movie *Pretty Woman*. However, you have probably never heard about J. F. Lawton. You have heard about *Pretty Woman*, though. When *Pretty Woman* opened in 1990, it earned $11,280,591 domestic in its first weekend and $12,471,670 on its second weekend, and then it was number one at the box office for four weeks and after that it was in the top 10 for sixteen weeks. *Pretty Woman* made ultimately $178,406,268 in the US and $285,000,000 everywhere else, leading to a worldwide victory of $463,406,268. *Pretty Woman* remains number four on the list of all-time highest-grossing films in the US and number three worldwide. It endures as Disney's biggest R-rated earner in history. It also earned millions more than the G-rated phenomenons *Bambi*, *Finding Nemo*, and *Lady and the Tramp*.

    Pretty Woman earned all that money because people like it. The movie as aired stars Julia Roberts and Richard Gere. It revolves around a gruesomely hackneyed plot about an attractive white female prostitute who has sex with an attractive white male businessman who then uses the female prostitute as a beard but then after she shops and he buys her a necklace and some roses and escargot they fall in true authentic love and she stops being a prostitute and everything is super good forevermore.

    This is not the story that J. F. Lawton first wrote way back in the 1980s, however. J. F. Lawton is a white man from Riverside, California, whose parents were both artists, a novelist and a pianist. J. F. Lawton wanted to be an artist, too, so he wrote a dark, sad, and gritty tale about Wall Street corruption during apex Reagan. J. F. Lawton titled his precious project *3,000* after the number of ducats exchanged between his script's sleazy Wall Street robber baron and broken-hearted female sex worker. In *3,000* the protags don't fall in love but have lots of bad mechanical sex, where the sex worker's main contribution is staring dead-faced at televised cartoons. In the second act, after proving her ability to give decent fellatio, the sex worker is then hired for the aforementioned sum to continue committing soul-destroying fornication with the Wall Streeter for an elongated period of time, but during this idyll she finds herself unable to withstand her exploitation and debasement. Her emotional turmoil culminates in a fourth act catharsis after the Wall Streeter leaves her in a gutter covered with dollars and she realizes that capitalism and patriarchy are toxins that have eroded her will to live. The End.

In the 1980s Disney Studios had a deal with Garry Marshall, a popular director of such hits as *The Odd Couple, Beaches, Happy Days, The Princess Diaries,* and *The Princess Diaries 2.* Garry Marshall made a lot of money in his contract with Disney, and based on this list of his films and TV series we might surmise that he might not have very high aesthetic standards. Nevertheless, Garry Marshall had reached that point in his life where he Spielbergishly wanted to prove himself as a serious artist. He told Disney execs that his next project had to be dark and edgy and gritty and meaningful and cool, instead of a tepid romantic vehicle for a fungible white star with an apex Q score that also contained copious opportunities for product tie-ins.

The cowed Disney subalterns duly scoured the earth for a script that would fit this description. They stumbled eventually into a Sundance Lab where the youngish J. F. Lawton had been admitted on the strength of *3,000*'s challenging and anticapitalist qualities. Disney bought the script and gave it to Garry Marshall, who loved it. But then Garry Marshall, aforementioned director of *The Princess Diaries 2* and *Beaches,* couldn't help himself. Garry Marshall unceremoniously threw J. F. Lawton off the project and had his script dogs rewrite *3,000* so that the prostitute loved her subordination and the Wall Streeter's sleaziness was magically hidden behind distractions like the escargot and shopping. Thus *3,000* turned into *Pretty Woman,* a piece of patriarchal propaganda that brainwashed millions of women with the fantasy that they could be a happy whore and bark "Big mistake, huge" triumphantly in the faces of only slightly less oppressed female retail workers.

After Garry Marshall called security to drag J. F. Lawton off the Disney lot, J. F. Lawton continue to ply his trade, but whatever muse of true creativity and risk-taking that had allowed him to write *3,000* got murdered on the day that the Disney suits darkened the Sundance Lab door. J. F. Lawton's muse was so dead she was now a zombie, who re-rose in such a gory form that he later wrote gems like the Steven Seagal vehicles *Under Siege* and *Under Siege 2*. Thereafter, when J. F. Lawton's career was almost completely defunct, he changed his name to J. D. Athens so that people wouldn't know that he was J. F. Lawton, the *Under Siege* guy, and under that subterfuge managed to get a few other movies made. The most notable of these are *Cannibal Women in the Avocado Jungle of Death* (1989) and *Pizza Man* (1991).

This essay is supposed to be a description about my Hatchfund venture, which is titled *Texit*. But, before I fully get into the details of *Texit*, which is a Brechtian mobile opera about a neurotically xenophobic anti-Mexican named Texit who falls in love with an undocumented orthodontic hygienist named Josefina, I need everybody interested in undertaking the frankly awesome responsibility of *financially* supporting this art performance to remember the cautionary tale of J. F. Lawton. Because I have been working on *Texit* for the past fourteen years, through father death and girlfriend abandonment and neoliberalist spirit murder, so all prospective patrons must understand that no matter how much money you decide to contribute to this project I AM AN ARTIST AND I WILL NEVER LET CAPITALISM, WHITE SUPREMACY, OR PATRIARCHY CORRUPT MY PROC

Shorter Version (140 characters)

Texit is a racial mobile opera w/ lots of sex, nudity, violence, karate, Marxism, babies, Mexicans, ICE agents in bikinis, and swordfights.

Keywords

Texit, Mexicans, Latinx liberatory performance art, #notmypresident, #nobannowall, #keepfamiliestogether, ICE abolition, wymyn-defined eroticism, nipple freedom, Bertolt Brecht, Craig Williams Gallery

CHAPTER TWENTY **CRUSHING IT**

[This was a mass-mailed Snapchat invitation. It featured
an embroidery of the single-starred, red, white, and
blue Texas flag, which I punctuated with a Word "exit"
icon and overlaid with the following text: "Texit table
reading at Craig Wallace next Tues. seating limited RSVP to
amandapanda@gmail.com." I have titled the embroidery *Texit*
(2018) (silk thread and ribbon on undyed linen).]

History

Tuesday, September 18, 2018
9:42 PM gun near me
9:43 PM where can I buy a gun near me
Saturday, November 17, 2018
10:16 PM California Penal Code 243.4(e)(1)
Saturday, November 18, 2018
4:55 AM Isaac Newton nervous breakdown why
Thursday, December 27, 2018
5:06 PM David Hume nervous breakdown why
Saturday, March 2, 2019
3:29 AM Rosa Rolanda why freaked out
6:16 AM why do women stop making art
Tuesday, April 23, 2019
6:51 PM Did Tracey Emin go crazy why
Monday, September 26, 2019
3:17 PM Hilma af Klint parsifal portraits

CHAPTER TWENTY-ONE I DON'T THINK I'M HANDLING THIS VERY WELL

[I posted this unauthorized essay on Rosa Rolanda on Metmuseum.org's "Online Features" page on March 2, 2019, at 4:11 p.m. PST, after securing a three-month contract to create web content for the Metropolitan Museum of Art. My boss removed it on March 3, 2019, at 10:31 a.m. PST. Rosa Rolanda's *Autorretrato (Self-Portrait*, 1952) depicts a beautiful, green-eyed Rolanda holding her head while skeletons and tiny stylized dancers swarm around her like wasps or nightmares. The painting also features an off-the-hook phone and a vibrant color scheme.]

Rosa could have been a great painter, but she lacked the drive.
              —Adriana Williams, *Covarrubias*

In 1970, the former artist Rosa Rolanda died of undetermined causes in Mexico City. Rolanda had an active art practice in her thirties, forties, and fifties. Then, it appears that she stopped making art altogether, a catastrophe that few people noticed. A perusal of Rolanda's scattered archives reveals that her output began to dwindle in the 1950s, before collapsing entirely sometime in the early 1960s. In 1960, Rolanda was just sixty-five years old. Sixty-five years old is still too early for an artist to retire, particularly if you think about the obscenely long career of Pablo Picasso, who ceased painting and sculpting just weeks before he died of congestive heart failure at the age of ninety-one. Rolanda's farewell to the art world also compares embarrassingly to the enduring triumphalism of the portraitist John Singer Sargent, who still made exquisite charcoal drawings in 1925, the same year that he died, at sixty-nine, also of heart disease. Actually, this Metmuseum .org essay could go on to list hundreds of celebrated artists who made copious amounts of work throughout their lives, most of these old masters being white, and typically male—Michelangelo, Leonardo da Vinci, Julian Schnabel, Francisco Goya, Claude Monet, Joseph Beuys, Jackson Pollock, Auguste Rodin, Alberto Giacometti, Phidias, Donatello, and Marcel Duchamp, as well as the exceptional Louise Bourgeois, Marisa Merz, Mary Cassatt, Artemisia Gentileschi, Lee Bontecou, Georgia O'Keeffe, Helen Frankenthaler . . . but, this essay is supposed to be about the Mexican American female artist Rosa Rolanda, so perhaps we should stop there.

Rosa Rolanda was a woman of color who stopped making art in her seventh decade, and we would like to know why. People who are ignorant might suggest that Rolanda quit the struggle because she had a nervous breakdown after her husband abandoned her for a teenaged ballerina around 1952. Rolanda's husband was the renowned polymath and world traveler Miguel Covarrubias, who never stopped painting epic murals of Pacific Islanders, sketching lively caricatures of the glitterati for *Vanity Fair*, and being famous. That is, he didn't stop until he had to: Miguel Covarrubias died in February 1957, at the age of fifty-three, of what the *New York Times* called "septicemia, a blood poisoning" in its dithyrambic obituary. Miguel Covarrubias enjoyed a tenacious art practice, like Picasso and Sargent and Beuys and Goya and Frankenthaler. Mere months before he contracted septicemia, he made a solemn black-and-white lithograph titled *Man and Woman*, which now hangs in the Art Institute of Chicago.

Though it is difficult to know the precise contours of Rosa Rolanda's career arc because so few scholars have paid attention to it, a tiny tribe of heroic art historians have tried to reconstruct her efforts. From their writings, we learn that Rolanda's work habits deliquesced from a rigorously maintained art regimen into a fugue of angsty dabbling, whose early onset arrived shortly after she painted her remarkable self-portrait, *Autorretrato* (1952), which I have posted above.

The lavish yet melancholy *Autorretrato* shows Rolanda holding her head and freaking out because she is surrounded by lithe dancers and skeletons, which are unsubtle references to her husband's baby-skinned ballerina girlfriend and the way that time destroys our dreams and our lives. Readers of this unsolicited and unsanctioned Metmuseum.org essay will see that Rolanda's attractive avatar appears in the center of the canvas, wearing a green dress and a fashionable red scarf. The figure possesses giant greenish alien-like eyes and an unsmiling mouth. Some of the dancers tangle in her dark hair, perhaps in a complicated reference to the Rogers and Hammerstein hit song "I'm Gonna Wash That Man Right Outa My Hair," from the musical *South Pacific*. Rolanda reaches up and paws at her head, attempting to "wash out" the dancer demons but failing to succeed, and so she just stares balefully out at the viewer. Other dancers spill out across the canvas, leaping and cavorting around a few other troubling symbols like an unringing telephone, wee skulls, and a ticking clock.

Autorretrato is a sad painting and a fine one too, and in hindsight we might read it as a harbinger of the letdowns to come. At the beginning of her art career, though, it seemed like Rolanda's future was full of promise and that everything would turn out really good and not in tears and failure. Rolanda began her professional life as a dancer, when she fled her boring hometown of Asuza, California, and began can-canning on Broadway at the age of sixteen. Her life as a visual artist flowered shortly after 1925, which is when she met Covarrubias, moved with him to Mexico, and began taking photographs under the tutelage of Edward Weston. During this period, she experimented with the rayograph technique invented by Man Ray, and her resulting still lifes of apples, lace, crystal, and skyscrapers radiate with intense inky blacks and starry whites, as well as displaying Rolanda's exquisite flair for composition. Few of these pictures sold, however. As the tenaciously feminist art critic Dawn Adès has noted in *In Wonderland: The Surrealist Adventures of Women Artists in Mexico and the United States* (2012), "Rolanda's experiments with photograms seem to have remained unknown during her lifetime. Perhaps they found no natural outlet because their experimental look did not fit with the dominantly realist styles of *mexicanidad*."

Rolanda dealt with this fiasco by moving onto gouache in 1926, commencing a career that would see her painting glamorous movie stars like Dolores del Río, an ever-more-interesting progression of self-portraits that would culminate in the fabulously disturbing *Autorretrato* (1952), and then diminishing into *meh* and OK paintings of orchids until she appears to have ceased making art entirely. After that, the glimpses of Rolanda that we can espy in Covarrubias and Weston biographies indicate that she directed her energies into hosting large, ambitiously catered parties for celebrity friends and staring forlornly at the wall.

What happened? A woman of color artist (WOCA) who has been hired to write anodyne copy about Richard Prince and Willem de Kooning by the Sackler-funded art aggregator Metmuseum.com, and who completely stopped making art herself after getting sexually assaulted by her quondam gallerist in a Lyft six months ago, will likely find herself worrying about the significance of Rosa Rolanda's vanishing from the art scene. This sensitive and disappointed WOCA will anxiously compare Rolanda's amputated career to that of sister historical WOCAs. She could, for example, be pathologically inclined to brood over the obstructed vocation of the

Black writer Zora Neale Hurston, who had enormous difficulty getting published at the end of her life. Or she might obsess about nineteenth-century Black sculptor Meta Vaux Warrick Fuller, who exhibited in Paris in 1900, but soon after found herself sinking under the creative quicksands of racism and childcare. That is, instead of discovering a soothing explanation for Rolanda's humiliating incapacity to be as persistently successful as Michelangelo or Pollock or Miguel Covarrubias, this intrepid investigator will instead have stumbled upon a troubling pattern of WOCA alienation and dispossession.

Exasperated, the WOCA will begin to search in panicked earnest for affirming clues to the Mystery of Rosa Rolanda's Disappearing Career, such as might be found in Rolanda's spastic reaction to Covarrubias's infant mistress, the danseuse and model Rocío Sagaón. After all, Rolanda once waved a gun in Sagaón's face and also dragged her around a room by the hair. The only problem is the sexism of this explanation for Rolanda's abandonment of her talent, because we are not convinced that women artists are really that fragile: even if your girlfriend dumped you once you hit your hard-bitten mid-thirties, your current boyfriend doesn't think that your sexual assault adds a special frisson to your lovemaking, and you had to go on Xanax after that dickhead strangled you in your Lyft, you're going to still keep making art if you're a Great Female Artist, right?

The answer seems to be a resounding *yes*, as history proves that Great Artists make fantastic art even when they're lunatics: Francis Bacon was manic as a wombat but at the age of eighty-eight made *Study of a Bull*, which is a haunting masterpiece of cool soft grays. Edward Munch was hella depressed and he made 1,789 artworks, the last of which, *Self-Portrait with a Pastel Stick*, was dated 1943, a year before he died at eighty. And then, well—Vincent van Gogh had some problems also.

Thus, the WOCA who's stressing out over Rosa Rolanda and wants to understand why, in the end, Rolanda was defeated, will have to look to other, more complicated etiologies of artistic washout, such as neoliberalism or sexism or racism or additional seemingly uncombatable social structures that keep art monopolists like the Metropolitan Museum in business and WOCAs in the margins of art history.

All of this is to say that maybe something bad happened to Rosa Rolanda that caused her to stop making art. Just by way of hypothesis, did Rolanda's gallerist beat her up in the back seat of a Lyft when she was riding home jubilant and champagne-drunk after her West Hollywood table read? And since then she's been "healing" by doing random Wikipedia searches and can't make art anymore? Or maybe her dealer required her to rewrite her mobile opera to star a Heroic Strong Brown Woman who cohered with the "dominantly realist styles of *mexicanidad*," and that stereotyping killed her inspiration? Or did the fact that Haidar came back from pregnancy leave at Snapchat, and ousted our hero from her only real source of income, finally drive her to meds that made performing impossible?

No, indeed, the mostly nonexistent Rosa Rolanda records remaining to us provide no proofs that Rolanda quit making art for the same horrible reasons as did the author of this unauthorized Metmuseum.org posting. Since only supremely famous Anglo artists like Philip Roth or Daniel Day-Lewis or Alice Munro or the amazing though ultimately indigent Lee Lozano announce their retirements to the *New York Times*, it's hard to know what makes a WOCA drop out unless there's a police report or a medical record or a renegade web confessional like this one. While the UN estimated in 2017 that between 35 and 70 percent of women worldwide have experienced physical abuse or rape, the effects of this quirk of human nature on WOCA art production has never been studied. And while Oxfam announced findings in 2017 that the majority of the world's poor are women ("600 million are in the most insecure and precarious forms of work"), its relief workers were so busy exploiting the women of Haiti that they didn't say how those stats affect WOCAs' Guggenheim applications. As to white supremacy's capacity to mutilate a woman artist of color's "vision," that would be super hard to quantify, and anyway, nobody really wants to talk about it because their bitterness is already turning into bipolarism without the additional aggravation. Which is probably why Rosa Rolanda never gave an interview where she said, "This shit is fucked and I quit," and we don't know the reason why she disappeared from the art world.

The WOCA who is flipping out about the possibility of continuing to make art should probably just purchase another Frida Kahlo magnet and put it on her fridge, and not read this unendorsed essay about Rosa Rolanda on Metmuseum.org. And she *really* shouldn't look at the studies that offer infuriating indications of why WOCAs might forgo art for paid work like nursing or prostitution, or shrivel away in front of their TVs while high on a little Oxy. Like, in 1991, the sociologist Joanna Stohs came out with a study titled *Moving beyond Women's Career Choices: Factors Associated with Career Continuity among Female Former Art Students*, where she concluded scientifically that "women artists" are totally screwed. Also, in 2015, a Scottish MBA named Emma Flynn published a thesis where she observed that if you don't have a gallery you might as well be dead. And in June of 2016, CUNY's Guttman College put out a paper finding that 80.5 percent of the artists represented by New York galleries were white, 30 percent of them were female, 8.8 percent were Black, and that Latinx people account for 1.2 percent, though they didn't do a WOCA breakdown. In 2005, the NEA did a gender-arts study that found that women artists mostly work part time, and earn $0.75 for every male dollar—but then the NEA failed to take race or ethnicity into account and so yet again we don't know how these depressing deets apply to WOCAs. On the writing side, in 2016 the Writers Guild of America-West estimated that US "women" television writers get about 29 percent of the jobs, and that "minorities" can be happy with 13.7 percent. And there was a 2011 Poetry Foundation study about minority women literati that culminated with a quote from a Filipina poet named Barbara Jane Reyes, who said succinctly that WOC authors are "having a very hard time."

As the reader can see, the Greek tragical storm cycle that is the fate of many WOCAs has escaped documentation, except in glimmers of doom discovered between the lines of these fancy studies. But if you're still curious, you could perform your own study here, on Metmuseum.com, by using the search function that we've helpfully provided in the upper right-hand corner. For example, if you type in "Rosa Rolanda," you'll find that Metmuseum.com replies, "No results found for 'Rosa Rolanda.' Showing 4 results for 'Rosa Roland.' " And then it inexplicably sends you to a picture of Buffalo Bill Cody and Members of His Wild West Show and also to one of a little silver camel tchotchke from 1400s Peru. If you type in "Latina," you'll dredge up a seventeenth-century etching of the German army and a picture of a little silver medal that somebody named E. Deblois received in nineteenth-century Portland, Maine. If you type in "Black Woman" you'll find a Watteau of a white woman fondling her breast and a Picasso sketch of a screaming creature of indeterminate race.

The Metropolitan Museum possesses two million works of art. It owns way more than 182 Picassos (I stopped counting) and maybe nine Richard Princes. It lays claim to ~33 Willem de Koonings and 5 Joan Mitchells. It holds somewhere around 32 Jackson Pollocks, 11 Lee Krasners, and one Mickalene Thomas (though they don't show you what the Thomas looks like on the website).

All of this is not to say that WOCAs are trees in the forest and no one hears them when they fall. WOCAs/WXCAs somehow have continued to exist and create. And thank God. There's Tracey Emin and Astrid Hadad and Lisa Teasley. There's Vaginal Davis and Faith Ringgold and Michele Serros and Senga Nengudi and Kara Walker and Laura Aguilar. There's old Frida Kahlo and Tania Bruguera and Ruth Asawa and Joy Harjo and Elsie Allen and Meta Vaux Warrick Fuller. There's Marta Minujín and Yayoi Kusama and Cui Xiuwen and Young Joon Kwak and Carmina Escobar and Zora Neale Hurston and Carrie Mae Weems and Julie Mehretu. There's Angela Seo and Nao Bustamante and Toba Khedoori and Ana Teresa Fernández and Jamie Okuma and Jae Jarrell and Paz Errázuriz, Charlene Teters, Yoko Ono, He Xiangning, Dindga McCannon, María Evelia Marmolejo, Graciela Iturbide, Josephine Myers-Wapp, Annie Pootoogook, and Darlene Ahuna. There's Holly Mititquq Nordlum and Mónica Mayer and Anita Endrezze. There's Beverly Buchanan and Emma Amos, Barbara Chase-Riboud, and Tona Brown.

And, for a time, there was Rosa Rolanda.

Autorretrato (1952) remains Rolanda's best work, its unique perfection found in the contrast between the sanguine beauty of the subject and the scary dancers swarming through her hair. The clock ticking in the right-hand corner sends chills to your bowels, as do the little skulls floating through the air. Still, this small output is not enough to satisfy the ravenous Rolanda fan, because Rolanda should have spent her last decades building upon her earlier rayographs and gouaches, her self-portraits, and even her meh orchids, and enjoyed a late glory filled with take-no-prisoners paintings and photographs. Yes! She should have been like Lee Bontecou, who at the age of seventy-two presided over the Hammer Museum like a queen during her rambling 2003 retrospective, or grizzled Louise Bourgeois, who accessed foundries, assistants, gophers, and lackeys, not to mention hundreds of tons of expensive steel and bronze, to make giant spiders that later sold for upwards of $24 million.

Unlike Picasso, Sargent, Covarrubias, Bontecou, Bourgeois, Van Gogh, and Leonardo da Vinci, Rosa Rolanda died of unspecified causes, though my guess is that she got killed by rage. She passed away in 1970, which was lucky, because she just missed Linda Nochlin's famous essay, "Why Have There Been No Great Women Artists?," which came out in 1971. "The fact of the matter is that there have been no supremely great women artists, as far as we know, although there have been many interesting and very good ones who remain insufficiently investigated or appreciated," Nochlin wrote, but of course Nochlin was wrong, may she rest in peace. The question was and remains not why there have been no great female artists, but rather why so many great women artists of color stop making their art. I will tell you for free that WOCAs don't quit because hosting elaborately catered parties like Rosa Rolanda did, or "healing" while writing copy for Metmuseum .org like I am doing, is so great. Parties, healing, and Metmuseum.org suck and make you want to kill somebody. Art is everything, and if you are an artist it is your life, so the trick is to find yourself making it into the WOCA

Hall of Fame listed above by somehow *doing your work*. Because there are even worse things than turning out like Rosa Rolanda, which is becoming a PTSD web copyeditor doodling abstracts onto your jeans and sabotaging your paycheck by writing essays like this in order to avoid going completely fucking crazy.

CHAPTER TWENTY-TWO THE DISEASE OF THE LEARNED

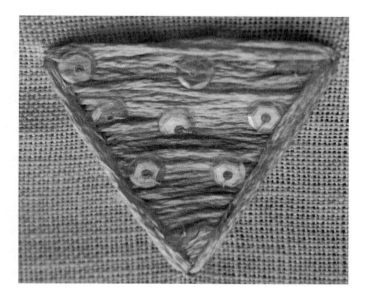

[Below, the reader will find my answer to the question *What is the statute of limitations for sexual assault?* I posted it on Quora, August 8, 2019. This essay/screed/FYI references *I've Got It All* (2000), which is a photograph of the British/Turkish artist Tracey Emin. The image shows Emin wearing a patchwork dress and sitting on the floor with her long legs splayed out. Emin looks down at her crotch. With her hands, she either catches a bounteous wad of pound notes and coins miraculously flowing out of her body or thriftily stuffs them into her vagina.

My accompanying textile illustration is titled *I've Got It All (variation)/we can form the idea of a golden mountain, and from thence conclude that such a mountain may actually exist* (2019) (silk thread and sequins on undyed linen).]

"I'm sorry," I yelled. It was September 18, 2018, and I struggled in the back-seat of a Lyft with my gallerist, Craig. The car hurtled us down LA's La Brea Avenue after the successful table read of my all-wymyn mobile opera, *Texit*. "I'm sorry, but I just can't. I'm with somebody—"

Craig hit me on my jaw with his open hand. He spat on my collarbone and my right shoulder. He slapped at my thighs and groin, so that the skin beneath my clothes turned hot from the violent friction.

"I would," I cried out. "But I can't."

"What the fuck is happening back there?" the Lyft driver said.

I have known Craig Wallace for two months and three days, ever since meeting him at a Snapchat/Murakami pop-up pre–soft opening in DTLA in June 2018. Our relationship was professional and previously involved no other physical contact than mandatory LA creative class hugging. Craig has dark hair and brown eyes. He is a white, thirty-six-year-old Yale grad. He has a slim build. He's around 5'9", and about 150 lb. No facial hair, no tattoos. That night, he wore a black shirt, black pants, black shoes, and a large, steel Omega Seamaster watch. He is handsome, with a dimple in his right cheek.

As for myself, I wore a pale-pink silk dress printed with mini black up-fists and a cotton XL men's daffodil-yellow Nordstrom sweater, the latter of which floated around my torso like a preppy ghost.

Craig punched me in the chest and dug his thumbs into my throat. He grabbed my sweater with both hands and ripped a hole through its chest. He tore the sweater off my head, cutting my left wrist with his sharp steel watch. He threw the sweater toward the windshield. Then he spat at the driver.

The driver was in his fifties and wore aluminum-rimmed glasses. He was white and bald. His voice boomeranged off the windshield when he braked at a red light and bellowed: "Cut that shit out!"

"Oh God," I said. "Craig, don't."

The driver reached into the back seat and struck Craig on the left cheek with the heel of his right hand. Craig sat back down immediately and stopped hitting me. He looked at the headrest in front of him, as if I weren't there.

"Why'd you do that?" I whispered.

Craig glared out of the car window. I put my hand over my mouth.

"You think you've got it all, don't you?" he rasped.

Craig opened the door of the Lyft and ran out into the traffic.

The driver and I watched as he scrambled haltingly in front of honking cars, reached the sidewalk, and sprinted east until he disappeared.

It took thirty-eight minutes for the Lyft driver to redirect our route to my studio apartment in Palms. I wiped the spit off of my throat and mechanically processed details like the bloody divot in my wrist and the driver's porpoise-blue glass frames, which flashed from the rearview mirror as he growled: "Sweetheart, you've got to call the police on that asshole. Don't you go thinking this was your fault!" He scowled at me over his shoulder when I wouldn't reply. We finally reached my address, on Overland, off the 10. He was still talking: "Listen to me. I know. Girls like you can't take that kind of behavior from anyone." I lurched out of the car. From the footwell, I grabbed my Ewa Partum tote printed with little lipstick labias, but forgot to retrieve my sweater. I stiff-legged it up the dry lawn fronting my stuccoed complex and unlatched the metal gate. I trudged up a small progress of steel steps. I rattled the key into my front door. I turned on all the lights and groped for my bed.

At the time, I'd painted my studio ebony and onyx, in honor of Goya's *Black Paintings*. On the eastside-facing wall, next to my silver microwave and mustard-colored hotplate, I'd hung hairy monster masks that I had made out of coconuts and acrylic wigs in homage to Cocteau's *Beauty and the Beast*. I sat on a pillow lopsidedly and tugged my phone out of my purse. I called my boyfriend, Brandon Chu, who was waiting for Craig and me to arrive at downtown's Standard Hotel. We had booked a suite to celebrate my premiere, and on the phone I could hear that my temporary Snapchat colleagues and my few weird artist-acquaintances had already arrived and were partying awkwardly together.

"Amanda," Brandon shouted, over a complicated Detroit Dubstep track. "Where are you guys? Everyone's here."

"I'm *here*," I murmured. My name is Amanda Ruiz. I am Chicana, 5'6", 132 lb., thirty-nine years old, and bisexual. I have muscular calves, large brown eyes, and no identifying marks beyond a persistently baffled facial expression. I am/was a conceptual/performance artist who attended RISD and once taught at Cornell. I cope(d) with starvation wages by writing ad copy for arts institutions, briefly doing social media marketing until Haidar came back, and continuing to congratulate myself on my 2009 Franklin Furnace and 2018 Slamdance Sparky. At the moment, though, it felt like a cosmic computer had deleted most of my CV, which retained only one obscene entry. I rolled up my torn skirt and saw that my thighs bore red bruises, which looked like paintings of miniature raw lamb chops.

"Here, where?" Brandon said. "What are you doing?"

"I'm think I'm busy experimenting with some pretty clichéd emotional states." I gently poked at the lamb chop on my right thigh.

"What?"

"Do you have a gun?" I looked down at my reddened chest. This is when I realized I was crying.

"What's going on?"

"I'm at home," I said. "Craig just beat me up."

*

When Brandon finally reached my apartment, I still sat on the bed. Brandon is Chinese-Peruvian-American. He went to UCLA law, and has black hair and coffee bean–colored matador eyes. He is 5'10", 172 lb., thirty-five years old, and has a copyright symbol tattooed on his left anklebone. He also has extremely high, very beautiful cheekbones, which make him look aerodynamic. I met him at Ralphs five months before, in March 2018.

He ran over to the bed and dabbed his fingers on my left wrist, which bore the cut from where Craig tore off my sweater and hurt me with his watch. "Is this from him?"

"I think he wanted to have sex." I lay down on top of my black goosedown comforter and sneezed. I didn't mention the spitting. "Who has sex like that?"

"I'm going to fucking kill him."

I raised my eyebrows at him. "Actually, I wanted to talk to you about that."

"About what?"

"What would happen if I killed him?" I asked. "Or, I don't know, maimed him?"

Brandon shook his head. "You can't kill him."

I blinked rapidly. "He said, 'You think you've got it all.' What does that mean?"

"It means he's a dick."

"The show was standing room." I twitched my fingers at my side as if I mimicked flight. "He owes me one hundred and thirteen dollars. And I lost my dad's sweater." I stared at the coconut heads on the wall. "My dad's dead."

"Oh, honey. I'm so sorry."

I curled my body around Brandon's legs. "I want you to go disfigure Craig, on the face. OK? I'm just kidding. Could you, though? I'm too tired to do it."

"Let's call the police." A stress bubble of spit formed on Brandon's lips. "You weren't doing anything wrong. You didn't deserve this."

I looked up at my apartment's white ceiling, which was bifurcated by a huge reddish water stain that made it look like an antigravitational crime scene. "I know I didn't do anything wrong."

"Amanda," Brandon said.

"Umrgh, I'm not going to talk about this anymore." I rolled over on my other side and pulled the comforter over my shoulder.

"We have to call the police," he said. "We should do it now, to get in a fresh report. Your injuries aren't actually that severe."

"Shut up, please," I said.

"Baby." He stroked my hair. "It'll be OK, I'll tell them what happened."

I extracted Brandon's hand from my head. "Either get Baby a nice Glock or let Baby go to sleep."

"Oh, Jesus," he said.

And then I did go to sleep, and I never found out what Craig meant when he said I had it all, and my bruises faded, and Brandon didn't get me a gun, and he didn't kill or disfigure Craig, and I didn't kill or disfigure Craig, either.

*

What I did do was look at my phone. I did that for about one year.

*

September 19, 2018, 3:45 a.m. PST

Good day! Your Lyft driver of 9/18/2018, 10:45 p.m. PST has sent you the following message!

Amanda, this is Mitch your driver from last nite. I hope you are alright. I have your sweater and will bring it to you. I didn't get your apartment number so please reply with your address.

*

"Hey, Siri, apparently I've got it all, but I think I lost it somewhere, so find it for me."

Checking my sources. OK, I found this on the web for 'I've Got It All.' Take a look:

It was mid-November '18, eight and a half weeks after Craig mauled me in the Lyft. Brandon and I sat in my studio's dining room/foyer. We hunkered at my particle-board dining table, which was covered with a red Guatemalan weaving that I'd embroidered with portraits of Hillary Clinton alternately laughing and screaming. Brandon wore a blue-and-white striped shirt and black jeans. His long, bare feet had wrinkly soles, like butterscotch brownies. While I chattered to my phone, he had placed his laptop on the table and opened its screen to a complicated-looking page.

"I need you to concentrate on what I'm trying to tell you," he said.

I held the phone up to him. "These algorithms are spooky, man, look at the weird stuff Siri sent me." My screen showed an image of a brunette woman in a multihued dress sitting on the ground. She parted her legs, amassing a big pile of glittery coins and paper bills around her crotch. She appeared to be either ejecting bank out of her birth canal or stuffing her life savings into her vagina.

"That's super cool, right?" I said.

"Can you stop messing with that for a second?" Brandon had texted me obsessively about legal research all night long and the shadows under his eyes were reaching peak inkiness. "I'm showing you the California Code. Your case is getting weaker by the second—but if you report now we might still be able to get this, misdemeanor sexual battery. Most likely with no jail time. The law gives you a year to complain before the statute of limitations kicks in, and I'll be your witness. So he'll probably get convicted. He'll have to pay a fine of . . ." Brandon squinted at the screen. "$2,000."

My head jerked back. "$2,000?"

"If he qualifies as your boss, it could be $3,000."

"What's the extra thousand for?"

Brandon's eyebags glimmered at me. "The abuse of power."

My iPhone, in its bumpy black case, looked like a grenade. I tried to twiddle it between my fingers, but just dropped it. "Such a bargain."

"Yeah, but he'd be registered as a sex offender." Brandon pointed at his screen. "His employers would see it on the web. Women would see it. It'd be a way of you getting control of this situation."

I placed my ring finger on my left eyelid, my thumb on the right eyelid, and mushed them down until I saw double. "If I could get control of this situation, it wouldn't end with me getting paid two grand. There'd be more rioting. Defenestration."

Drops of sweat appeared on Brandon's eyebrows. "Oh, you don't get the money."

My phone had landed next to my feet, which were bare except for stripy violet polish. I picked it up and raised it to my mouth. "Hey, Siri, how do you stop your body from feeling like it's breaking into pieces?"

OK, I found this on the web for 'How do you stop your body from feeling like it's breaking into pieces.' Take a look.

"Why haven't you called this in?" Brandon cradled his forehead in his right hand. "Do you blame yourself? Do you think you led him on, or something?"

"If crying and saying 'no' is super seductive, then yeah." I poked at my phone. The picture of the woman with the gold vagina had disappeared, and Siri sent me to a page about Sir Isaac Newton.

Brandon kept talking. "Then what's going on? You're not getting out of the house—you're not eating. You wouldn't go to the doctor. You've stopped showing up at Snapchat. You're not even making art anymore—"

"Haidar came back and so they let me go—and I *am* making art." I brandished my phone at him again, so the glowing rectangle of light zigzagged in front of his face. "I'm a conceptualist, remember? I'm trying to figure out the connections."

"What do you mean, connections?" Brandon glanced back at his computer and sniffed.

"Oh, between—like—the patriarchy and what it means to fucking know anything." I wore red-and-white polka-dot pajama shorts cut high up on my leg so that they revealed my now-invisible injuries. I stared down at my thighs as my nose started to drip. "There has to be a pattern to all of this, right? There's got to be a way of making things fit."

Brandon looked worried. "Fit?"

My throat bobbled. "There's got to be some kind of communication between the nature of objective reality and having the shitty luck of being born *this*." I flapped my hands at my body. "It's like, you think you're in a Lyft, but what you're really in is a truth factory, where everything you ever believed in is getting destroyed and recycled into a fucking nightmare and the only way to make it stop is to search for gaps in the man-facts called human history—so that you can see where there's a crack, where the things you knew before fell in. And I'm just trying to find them using Google."

Raising both hands, Brandon placed his fingers on his eyes, like I had been doing. Psychologists call this "mirroring." It's empathetic. Except, it looked as if he held up imaginary virtual reality goggles and peered through them in the hopes that they would make me resemble a normal girlfriend. This idea made me start laughing in an explosion of snot and tears.

"Am I making you hot right now?" I asked.

Brandon's eyes turned bunny pink. "It's not that I don't understand, or I guess, I don't understand, but I want to understand." He coughed. "I want to understand what . . . you understand . . ." Brandon turned back to his computer and touched its keyboard, as if it could help him.

I nodded as Brandon talked. I wanted to be empathetic, too, because trying to comprehend misdemeanor female sexual damage couldn't be easy for him. Except, at the same time, I also started looking at my phone again. It still showed that page on Isaac Newton, which turned out to be theoretically dense and interesting. I did this until Brandon made a wheezing sound. I noticed that he was staring at me and waiting for me to say something.

I shrugged. "If you were going to understand, you'd have to get a personality transplant that made 'I'm fine' and 'sorry' a permanent part of your vocabulary and would probably give you brain damage."

Brandon slumped in front of his laptop. He crushed his eyebrows together, thinking private thoughts. He let out a long breath.

"I don't think that's very helpful," he said.

*

From my research, I learned that Isaac Newton had a nervous breakdown, too. You can read all about it on Wikipedia, which sends you to Google Books, which directs you to scholarly articles published in paywall academic journals. So then you have to hack into JSTOR and SAGE, using the I.D. that you borrow from an assistant librarian at UCLA whom you emailed with a fake accusation about unpaid parking ticket fines sent from an account you rigged to look like it came from the Chancellor's office. The whole thing is incredibly labor-intensive, and by the time you finally comb through back issues of the *Royal Society Journal of the History of Science* and *Mental Health and Social Inclusion*, your boyfriend's not really texting you back, your career's in shreds, and three months have passed.

Isaac Newton had a nervous breakdown that lasted from 1692 to 1693. Before and after, he invented many important theories that changed the course of science. For example, in *Philosophiæ Naturalis Principia Mathematica* (1687), Newton articulated his third law of motion. This rule holds that when one body imposes force upon a second body, that second body will not fall apart or submit cravenly, but rather will exert a force that is equal in degree, and opposite in direction, to the first body.

And then, in *Opticks* (1704), Newton theorized that God had designed universal "ultimate particles," which were bodies that remained indestructible even in the face of crushing violence. Newton believed that heat (caused by friction) was made of such unbreakable atoms. These supreme forms could not be overcome through physical resistance or bargaining or false consciousness or procrastination.

Newton's two theories were beautiful because they depicted a universe whose laws imposed order. But they were eventually disproved. Newton's theory about heat being made of unbreakable particles was debunked in the mid-1850s by scientists Rudolf Clausius and Ludwig Boltzmann. They proved that heat is energy that can be dissipated and redistributed into the atmosphere in random molecular arrangements.

Newton's third law of motion was disproved by me in the backseat of a Lyft on September 18, 2018. Again, in *Philosophiæ Naturalis Principia Mathematica*, Newton propounded that when one body imposes force upon a second body, that second body will exert a force that is equal in degree, and opposite in direction, to the first body. But in the backseat of that Lyft, when Craig exerted his force on my body, my body was not equal in degree or opposed effectively to the force exerted by his body.

"I would if I could," I'd bleated. "But I can't."

I think that Newton knew all along that the universe lacked his theories' coherence. Once he realized that bodies were destructible, he developed an understandable case of schizophrenia with paranoid delusions. His mania took the form of radical insomnia, which caused him to writhe melancholically for weeks on end.

Newton took refuge from these agonies by studying alchemy. He sought the Philosopher's Stone, which would convert base metals into gold and make humans immortal. Newton even developed a recipe for the elixir of life, which involved mixing mercury with "oil of Vitriol" and a lot of wine. He drank it. Newton also subjected metals to taste tests, and often sucked on slugs of gold, lead, and mercury. Mercury, his notes say, is *strong, sourish, ungrateful.*

These practices probably didn't do his mental health any favors.

*

February 2, 2019, 4:16 a.m. PST

Good day! Your Lyft driver of 9/18/2018, 10:45 p.m. PST has sent you the following message!

Dear Amanda, this is Mitch Lowell, your Lyft driver who has your sweater. I havent heard back from you. I am happy to bring your sweater to you. I hope you are ok.

*

"Of course, I can only dominate you if you consent," I told Brandon.

We stood naked in my studio's bed area. It was early February. After having a popcorn-tossing panic attack during a New Year's feminist-critical screening of Woody Allen's *Manhattan* at MOCA, I'd decided that my apartment's Goya-black color story was "not helping." So I'd repainted it lilac, threw away the hairy Cocteau sculptures and replaced them by wall-mounting a Colt 9mm fake submachine gun that I'd bought on eBay years earlier for a defunct performance, and purchased a Catwoman comforter. The *punctus* of the room, however, was the stack of papers cascading all over the floor. In December, I had downloaded the treatises written by the eighteenth-century Scottish philosopher David Hume and his many commentators, printed them out at the UCLA library from my phone, and then studied them agitatedly in bed.

I had not seen Brandon in nineteen days. Now he filled the atmosphere with his soapy scent and almond-oiled nudity. His knobbly bare feet stepped over a few pages of Hume's *A Treatise on Human Nature* (1739–40), which I had marked in red with *YES* and *!!!* He tried to free his left foot from a leaf but it just stuck to his right foot. "What is all this again?"

I tidied some papers by kicking at them. "It's David Hume. Isaac Newton was just too bossy."

He looked at me sideways, a little sadly. "Huh?"

"Newton's *Weltanschauung*, it's just so rigid. 'Heat's an unbreakable particle.' Give me a break. It better not be." I gestured at my chest and thighs, where I could sometimes still feel the burn of Craig's hands. But I didn't know how to put this in words. So I said, "But Hume says there's a lot of reality that goes on right up here." I tapped at my temple. "Ain't that the truth."

Brandon gazed into my eyes like a harassed llama. "Babe, I don't know what you're saying."

"That's OK." I kissed him, putting some muscle into it. "I don't care."

We kissed some more for a little while. Then I grasped hold of Brandon's left wrist and delicately folded it up between his shoulder blades. I stuck my leg between his thighs and nudged my hip so that he had to balance on his right leg.

He tottered and laughed nervously. "Right, so you wanted to . . . ?"

I hugged him. "It's not a big deal. It's like what we do regularly but just reversed." I moved into a demonstration of a femme-top scenario involving some gentle obscenities and choreographed wrestling. "It's just that, from previous experience, I know it can help to rewrite what happened."

Brandon said, "Uhhhh." He glanced at the papers on the floor. "Are you talking about reality again?"

"Kind of." I hugged him tighter and gave him a few seconds to say, "You dominating me sexually is a great idea." When that didn't happen, I kissed him briskly between his pectorals. "It's totally fine. We can just have regular sex."

Brandon nodded energetically. "OK"

I led Brandon over to my bed, cleared off the papers, and we kissed lavishly with our tongues. I kept my eyes open the whole time. I observed Brandon's lashes flinch as he squeezed his eyes shut. We jumped onto the bed and gave each other oral sex, one after the other. Then we had a 69. After that, I got on my back. He penetrated me. Then I got on top. I rode him for a while. I watched us move around. When he flipped my legs over my head I flashed onto the woman with the more than $2,000 worth of gold coins coming out of her vagina. At that moment, my soul, which I realized suddenly had heft and substance, lifted out from my body and floated around the ceiling.

From its high perch, soul-me told physical-me to stop remembering everything all the time. Physical-me, still wriggling on the bed, explained how that was impossible. Soul-me then told physical-me that Brandon would ditch me soon if I didn't get my shit together. Physical-me retorted that instead of always defining myself by my relationships I should instead press criminal charges against Craig before time ran out. Even if David Hume says that most of reality is manufactured out of debatable contingencies, Brandon had explained that the California Penal Code's one-year statute of limitations remained an unnegotiable *a priori* rule like the laws of motion and universal heliocentrism. Soul-me testily reminded physical-me that if I filed a complaint I would have to speak to law enforcement officials, who were bastards, as physical-me would recall from my last experience. Physical-me acknowledged that my previous experiment with trusting the authorities had been a failure. Soul-me commiserated and said that the only solution was an intersectional gender revolution that would unseat this unbelievable presidential administration and usher all subordinated people into a new state of socialist wymynist liberty.

"Amanda?" Brandon said.

"Hey!" I said. Sex was over. Brandon and I lay back on my Catwoman comforter and wrapped our arms and legs around each other. We breathed in and out and didn't speak. I could tell from Brandon's chest-rhythms that he wasn't falling asleep. He grunted out a long, wet cough-sigh. I patted him on the hand and ground my teeth.

"I know," I finally said.

"I don't know what to do."

"There's nothing to do." I smeared my tears into the comforter. "You're the best."

"You know that what happened's not your fault, right?"

I lay there with my face smushed into the bed. "Yes."

"Then I don't understand why you're taking this *so hard*," Brandon said.

I made a soft tut-tut-tutting sound. "Because he didn't rape me."

"Uh huh."

I didn't answer.

Tenderly, he asked: "Did something happen to you before?"

I waited several minutes. "Yes." I stared at the white papers that drifted across my floor like misplaced clouds. "As a child I learned that I am capable of pure and infinite love, but then I turned eighteen and got forcibly 'sodomized' by a guy named Ned McClintock, whom I met in a teller's line in a downtown Wells Fargo. The police told me that my case was weak because I'd been drunk, didn't have any visible injuries, and didn't remember enough physical details. So after that I rejected the hegemony and made art into my God, which led me to produce immigration-rights mobile operas for Craig. And that's why I guess I'm just all fucked up again."

Brandon hiked himself up on his elbow. He peered down at me with a pale, frightened face, which had been ink-stained on the right side of his nose by the David Hume print-outs.

"Are you being serious?"

*

From my Google research, I have learned that David Hume also had a nervous breakdown.

In the first quarter of the eighteenth century, the future father of Empiricism was a manic, moon-faced teenager who spent his days in constant reading. He developed a ghoulish obsession with Isaac Newton, among other authors. Newton inspired Hume to refine his mind so exquisitely that he, too, could someday fathom heavenly subtleties. "I was continually fortifying myself with Reflections against Death, & Poverty, & Shame, & Pain, & all the other Calamities of Life," he would later explain to his physician in a letter dated 1734.

Predictably, Hume developed an extra-crispy generalized anxiety disorder: I "ruin'd my Health, tho' I was not sensible of it," he wrote.

In his medical correspondence, Hume admits that his illness manifested in hyper-salivation and lethargy. His local surgeon diagnosed him as suffering from a curious malady called "The Disease of the Learned," and treated his spittle and death obsession with "anti-hysteric pills" and pints of claret wine. These tranquilizers relieved Hume of his afflictive erudition and he once more ventured into society.

David Hume was amazing because he made his terrible experience with madness "fit." In his 1734 letter, Hume rendered a famous description of the fruits of his emotional collapse: "There seem'd to be open'd up to me a new Scene of Thought, which transported me beyond Measure, & made me, with an Ardor natural to young men, throw up every other Pleasure or Business to apply entirely to it."

In Hume's *A Treatise of Human Nature*, mostly written at the tail end of his twenties, he revealed that this breakthrough inspired him to launch an attack on Newton's grand theory: Hume divided the universe into two realms, and relegated Newton's reign to the inferior kingdom. He posited that Newton's small list of unbreakable *a priori* laws (such the laws of motion's governance over bodies) regulated only the rarest statements of irrefutable logic, which he described as fundamental *Relations of Ideas*.

Other than these few Newtonian infallibilities, Hume said, the remainder of the galaxy found itself liberated from the burden of absolutes. In this huge category bristled a pack of frangible facts—what he called *Matters of Fact*—which can be contested and revised. So, for example, statements like "I was not raped," or "I am fucked up" can be verified only *a posteriori*: Such matter-of-fact assertions must be proved by checking, not by referencing abstract principles.

This bifurcation between indissoluble natural laws and the fragile foundation of human consciousness has been called *Hume's Fork*.

Despite Hume's early experience with the Disease of the Learned, he remained an optimist. It would take centuries for philosophers like Arthur Schopenhauer and Albert Camus to detect distressing intimations within the Humean fork. But in *A Treatise*, Hume reassured his readers that epistemological contingency did not mean that life is meaningless. Rather, he said, it creates lots of great opportunities. The "reality" of almost every experience depends solely upon the elastic creativity of human perception.

"Nothing we imagine is absolutely impossible," he wrote, somewhat wildly, in a passage that I believe is a paean to his alchemy-mad hero, Isaac Newton. "We can form the idea of a golden mountain, and from thence conclude that such a mountain may actually exist."

*

"You don't want to have sex anymore," Brandon said.

"I do want to have sex," I said. It was Saturday, July 27, 2019, around 2 p.m. We had actually just had sex. We lay weary in my bed, surrounded by walls I'd lacquered hospital-white a month before. The apartment was cleansed of all my David Hume papers, which I'd replaced with one large painting made on the Fourth of July. The artwork hung above my bed's headboard. It starred the girl with the gold coin–dispensing vagina.

After I had been laid off from Snapchat, and then also fired from the Metropolitan Museum's Ministry of Truth, I decided to make an installation based on the photograph Siri had sent me in November '18. Last spring, I learned that the picture titled *I've Got It All* (2000) featured a Turkish-British artist named Tracey Emin. My 68" × 8'8" acrylic copy glittered with gold-foil chocolate coin wrappers I'd glued into a little mountain between the girl's spread legs. I hadn't done a perfect job adhering the coins, though. Several of the foils had popped off during our efforts at intercourse.

As Brandon looked at me with exhausted eyes, I plucked one of the bright bits from his dark hair.

"I think things would have turned out better if we'd just called the police," he said. His naked chest radiated heat that cooked me unpleasantly as we had twined together but was manageable now.

I sat up with my back against the bed's headboard, and flopped my legs over his hip. "What would be better, the sex?"

Brandon pressed his lower lip with his right thumb. "You know I'm talking about everything."

I closed my eyes. "Everything is fine."

"I don't get why you didn't take this seriously—especially since so many women have been really complaining about all of these assholes—"

Between my next two heartbeats, I flashed back to when I was eighteen years old and my father had brought me to the police station post–Ned McClintock. A tall, blue-eyed officer had given me the once-over and said, *So, you got in a fight with your boyfriend?* My dad replied, *You treat my daughter with respect, motherfucker, or I punch you in the face.*

"Like Christine Blasey Ford?" I asked in a monotone.

He shook his head. "Ugh. I don't know. Anyway, it's too late now."

"It hasn't been a year yet."

He popped his jaw. "I'm not talking about the law."

"Listen." I slid my hand beneath the sheet and pressed it lightly onto Brandon's belly. A physical pain thudded under my left breastbone. "I know it's been really difficult."

He tucked his chin into his chest and stared at his feet.

I said, "It's just that from before, I know that when you go through the system, then you can really get addicted to Ambien." I glared at the ghost-puppet shape of my hand touching him beneath the sheet.

"I can't do this anymore if we don't get past it." Brandon's eyes turned glossy and tears blossomed. They spilled down his cheeks. "Oh, oh."

I sprang forward and kissed him feverishly all over his face.

"It's too much," he cried. His shoulders shook and his mouth curled down into a grimace that I'd never seen before.

"I promise I'll tell the police!" I yelped, hugging him and kissing him in a panic. Woman tears are everyday garbage but man tears are magic. They made the pain in my chest shoot up my throat like a missile and then detonate shame throughout my body. I held Brandon in both arms and rocked him, while sweating a disgusting miasma down my breasts and belly. "Don't be sad," I whispered into his hot ear. "I'll take care of it, I swear."

*

August 4, 2019, 6:58 p.m. PST
Mitch, this is Amanda Ruiz, the woman with the yellow sweater. I am sorry it has taken so long to reply to your messages. I was hoping that we could meet on Wednesday, around 4 pm at my house. My apartment number is 3B.

*

Did Tracey Emin have a nervous breakdown?

The great British-Turkish artist Tracey Emin was raped at the age of thirteen, by a boy she calls "Steve Worrell" in her 1994 memoir *Exploration of the Soul*. That night, it was New Year's Eve. Emin walked through her hometown of Margate, England, toward Top Spot, the local disco. Young Emin planned to greet 1977 by bopping with her friends to cool hits like *Play That Funky Music White Boy* by Wild Cherry and *You Should Be Dancing* by the Bee Gees.

Emin took an alley shortcut to Top Spot, and ran into Steve Worrell. In *Exploration of the Soul*, she declines to describe him in much detail, or maybe she just couldn't because when you get raped your mind dies. She says only that he "pulled my skirt up . . . I said, 'No, get off, please.' He pulled me down the alley and pushed me to the ground."

Afterwards, Emin ran home and told her mother. But Pamela Cashin, a working-class white woman, did not call the police, possibly because Emin was biracial, not-rich, and lived in a bigoted society. Cashin's silent shelving of the assault hid the only evidence that would have proved Emin's blamelessness. Without proof of her virtue, Margate's men, who were "less than human," commenced treating Emin like a "slag," as she later reported in her 1995 video *Why I Never Became a Dancer*.

Emin began making art about her rape in the 1990s. Her projects took the form of shrill complaints embroidered onto blankets and abject self-portraiture. Art-world success quickly followed. At thirty-three, Charles Saatchi signed her, and she starred in the Royal Academy's blockbuster

1997 *Sensation* exhibit. Simultaneously, she garnered a reputation for in-stability. Part of Emin's crazy lady image stemmed from her drunken televi-sion appearances, like when she boozily yelled that she wanted to be with her mother on a '97 BBC show about the death of painting. But Emin's art assured her notoriety: In 1997, she made a quilt emblazoned with the words *PSYCO SLUT* [*sic*]. In 1999, she stitched a banner with the phrases *They Were the Ugly Cunts* and *No Fucking Way*. And in 2000, she produced the self-portrait photograph *I've Got It All*, which shows Emin wearing a multi-colored Vivienne Westwood dress and catching the golden massif of money from her vagina as she sits splay-legged on the ground.

Tracey Emin's art seems insane because she is a genius like other En-lightenment maniacs. At thirteen, she learned that Newton's universal third law of motion did not apply to women. When Steve Worrell attacked her in 1977, she discovered that her body was unequal to his body: her mother did not report her rape to the police, while the men of Margate called her "slag." She realized that a different First Principle ruled her fate, and this lesson infected her with the Disease of the Learned. Emin's erratic behavior and alcoholism arose from the revelation that being a woman of color was an objective relation of ideas, not a debatable matter of fact. The Humean fork sorted Emin into the reject pile because she was born female and brown to the low-income Pamela Cashin, which transformed her into an immutable slut.

And yet Emin managed to break this natural law. She did so by reporting on her sexual abuse through her art.

That is, when alcoholic and unrepaired Tracey Emin took a picture of herself with a precious vagina made out of pound notes and shiny coins, she "rewrote" Newtonian physics by performing the miracle Hume described in *A Treatise on Human Nature*: "We can form the idea of a golden moun-tain, and from thence conclude that such a mountain may actually exist."

*

I opened my door to Mitch Lowell on Wednesday, August 7, 2019, at 1:11 p.m., forty-two days before the statute of limitations on my misdemeanor sexual assault complaint would toll. I wore a black cotton dress with baggy side pockets, the left one of which held my phone. His green-blue eyes glimmered from behind his metallic glasses frames. His face was teardrop-shaped. He wore a linen-looking blue shirt with short sleeves and pearl-ized buttons, a brown belt with a silver clasp, and ironed blue jeans that he'd rolled up at the hems. I don't remember his shoes. He had a tonsured baldness, and buzzed, barely visible brown hair skirting the base of his skull. His skin looked dry, and deep dents creviced his forehead. He held my father's folded yellow sweater, which he gave to me. I unfolded the sweater. The rip in the chest had been carefully stitched back together with yellow thread.

I looked at him, raising my eyebrows.

"Just patched it up," he said.

"Thank you," I gasped.

I let him into the apartment. He sat at the table covered by the Guatemalan fabric embroidered with bipolar Hillary Clintons. I put the sweater on the table. I went to the mustard kitchenette and grabbed a teakettle from the burner and put it under my faucet and filled it. To the side of my "stove" stood a cabinet whose top shelf contained white cups, plates, and a blue teapot. I kept dry goods on the lower shelves. I extracted the teapot and cups and a box of organic red rooibos teabags. I made the tea and gave it to Mitch and sat down across from him at the table.

"Thank you," he said.

I didn't reply. I drank my tea.

Mitch didn't seem to like the silence. He sat with a very straight back and peered at the fake Colt submachine stuck up by my front door. A murky lemon-scented cologne emanated from his skin. He picked up his cup and put it back down. "I've been driving Lyft and Uber for about three years." He shifted in his seat. "I'm a film editor for the studios, but the technology changed and so—I'm just doing what I got to do."

I didn't know how to respond to that. "Do you like driving for Lyft?"

Mitch's mouth clenched. "What happened to you that night is not the worst thing I've seen." He stared at me without blinking. "That one got under my skin, though. I've been worrying about you for months. That guy beat you up pretty bad."

"I found it unpleasant," I agreed.

"You're a beautiful girl." Mitch flushed carmine and widened his eyes. "I hope you called the cops! I wanted to break his neck."

"I felt the same way," I laughed.

"Did you call the police?"

"I'm going to." I reached down and touched the phone in my left pocket.

Mitch pressed his fuzzy eyebrows together. "You should have done it that night. That's what I was trying to tell you. Because girls, you know, girls like you, they just freeze up like rabbits. That's why I've been trying to help."

"I could do it now." I dug the phone from my pocket and placed it on the table. I pushed its on/off button so that the icons displayed. I touched the phone icon and the keypad appeared. "I told my boyfriend I would today."

Mitch slammed his fist on the table, so the teacups rattled. "When I was young, you know what my friends and I would have done if some runt laid hands on one of our girls? We wouldn't have to call the police. We'd teach him manners with a lead pipe."

"OK," I said.

Mitch shrugged, and smiled a little. "Hey, sorry. I'm a man. It's my instinct."

"All right," I said.

"It's just, I saw you. You didn't do anything bad. Don't blame yourself. You kept yourself to yourself. And you weren't drunk—the girls I've seen in my car, wasted and half naked? Begging for a problem. Not you. And that guy? Fucking animal."

I stared at the phone. I started to feel hot again, in my chest. "Yeah."

He pointed at the phone. "You should call the police on him, I'll tell them what happened. They'll believe you."

"That's probably right." I flicked at the phone with my finger so that it budged into my teacup. The sweater was still on the table; its familiar yellow weave shone by the teapot.

"I'll help you," Mitch said again. After a few seconds, he began to drum his fingers on the table.

"My father helped me once," I finally said. I grabbed hold of the sweater, shook it loose, and tugged it over my head. I pulled the left sleeve over my wrist. "We had our problems. But if I could call anybody, it'd be him."

Mitch looked at me and didn't say anything.

Our tea was cooling. I took a sip. On the wall, my painting shed another gold foil. My phone started ringing, and flashed Brandon's name and shiny, smiling face.

"Who's that?" Mitch asked, craning his neck so he could see.

I reached over and rejected the call, and then clicked the iPhone's button so it went black. I scooped it from the table and dropped it back into my pocket.

"Isaac Newton," I said.

CHAPTER TWENTY-THREE **THIS IS BAD**

[I made and photographed these drawings in order to Snapchat them to Xōchitl Hernández on September 30, 2019. But then I just put them in a drawer and didn't send them. The drawings are graphite and colored pencil on Japanese paper. They find their inspiration in Hilma af Klint's watercolor-and-text *Parsifal Series* (1916).]

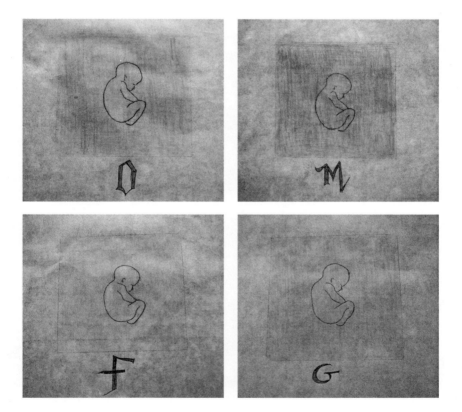

History

Tuesday, October 1, 2019
3:32 PM RU846 developments
4:16 PM woman means what
5:43 PM Aliza Shvarts freaked out Yale deans w self
induced
Tuesday, December 22, 2019
8:22 AM Bjork single mom
9:03 AM Bjork rich how much
11:45 AM Spore life cycle
5:16 PM Iris Van Herpen single breed

CHAPTER TWENTY-FOUR **THE SUCKING ONE**

[This is a Wiktionary edit that I posted for the entry on the etymology of "Female," which Wiktionary editors rejected as containing content that was "not suited for an encyclopedia" after a supermajority vote on October 1, 2019.]

female

1. Belonging to the sex which typically produces eggs (ova) . . .

Etymology

Borrowed from {{io|en|feminine}}, from {{m|la|fēmina||woman}}, from base word {{io|ine-pro|Proto-Indo-European *d^heh_1-m̥n-eh_2||who sucks}}. Related also to {{fētus}} and {{felare||la|to suck}} through Sanskrit धयति {{suck}}.

[edit]

Editing female (section)

In academic year 2007–8, twenty-two-year-old Yale art student and radical etymologist Aliza Shvarts deconstructed the alarming Proto-Indo-European base word of "female" by self-administering many possible pregnancies and then aborting them. Shvarts offered her project to her professors as a senior thesis, announcing that it consisted of two elements: The first component was a series of videos showing her cramping in various Connecticut motel bathtubs as a result of ingesting unnamed abortifacients. The second feature was an *objet* compiled out of Saran Wrap, Vaseline, and blood that she collected from her procedures.

Shvarts's rebellion constituted an offense against international linguistics but it did not qualify as a crime under the Connecticut Penal Code: In 1971's *Abele v. Markele*, federal judge Edward J. Lumbard liberated females from their jurisprudential if not etymological dilemma by striking down an 1860s state statute that penalized self-induction with a five-year prison sentence. "The Connecticut anti-abortion laws take from women the power to determine whether or not to have a child," Lumbard proclaimed. "In 1860, when these statutes were enacted in their present form, women had few rights. Since then, however, their status in our society has changed dramatically."

Had it? While Shvarts could not be arrested, manacled, tried, and incarcerated for putting daylight between her body and its putative *d^heh_1-$\underset{\circ}{m}n$-eh_2||who sucks derivation, she was punished: her classmates swarmed the university's Beinecke Plaza and cheered while sophomore John Behan, the leader of Choose Life at Yale, declared that "CLAY and the entire Yale community, I think, are appalled at what was a serious lapse in taste on the part of the student and the Yale art department." Days later, Wanda Franz, president of the National Right to Life Committee, appeared on Fox News and described Shvarts as a depraved serial killer. Panicking Yale deans thereafter commanded that Shvarts appear before them, and then issued a press release claiming that Shvarts had confessed that she had committed a fraud. "Had these acts been real, they would have violated basic ethical standards and raised serious mental and physical health concerns," spokeswoman Helaine S. Klasky wrote on April 17, 2008.

Shvarts responded by composing an essay in the *Yale Daily News*, where she explained that she had only told the Yale administrators that she could not be sure if she had become pregnant or not. She continued her assault on lexical patriarchy by observing that the reality of her pregnancies was "a matter of reading." She later clarified that her endurances should be called "miscarriages" rather than abortions because miscarriages are woman-defined occasions that unfurl outside of hospitals. The term "miscarriages," she allowed, also proved the most apt name for her art as it consisted in her mis-carrying her own body and culture as a matter of intent.

The repercussions continued apace: On April 18, the *Wall Street Journal*'s James Taratano conjectured that Shvarts was actually a secret double-agent language preservationist: "Could it be that Aliza Shvarts is an opponent of abortion who has staged a hoax aimed at embarrassing those who support or countenance abortion?" Taratano asked hopefully. On April 23, next to a front-page article whose banner headline erroneously asserted *Hillary Comes Up Big*, the *New Haven Register* reported that Yale "banned" Shvarts's art project unless and until she admitted in writing that her provocation was a "fiction." In the end, Shvarts declined to sacrifice her degree on the sacred altar of feminist hermeneutics and tendered another project in lieu of her videos and blood cube. Repeated web scourings, however, do not disclose what that enterprise might have been.

Today, Shvarts pursues her PhD in performance studies at NYU. Avid YouTube searches reveal that in the winter of 2009 she submitted a seminar final that featured her sitting on the floor splay-legged while wrapping a gift and simultaneously airing a blurry vaginal video with a creepy voice-over. And in March 2017, she gave a forty-minute speech about capitalism, Ad

Reinhardt, the Rothko Chapel, and "difficult art" in New York's blue chip Dominique Lévy gallery. These flights of fancy were both cerebral and a little boring. They certainly cannot match Shvarts's early efforts to extirpate the root meanings of "female." But then, what can?

Aliza Shvarts's abortion art demonstrated that federal judge Edward J. Lumbard was a nice person and an adorable airhead who was mistaken when he thought that he could give women "power": more than thirty years after *Abele v. Markele*, the female Yale senior trying to swap out the Proto-Indo-European "she who sucks" base word for a "she who seeks extreme freedom" neologism would find herself proscribed and branded as a mentally ill mass murderer.

The struggle, moreover, continues today: contemporary word artists who find themselves staring Shvartslike at their Accuhome Pregnancy Urine Midstream Testing Kit wand will similarly face a cabal of grammars that conspire to drag them back to their identity's putative origins. Such woefully inseminated conceptualists who sit in their beds shivering at the prospect of facing down an abortion and attempt to self-soothe with a brief interlude of feminist web paleographical research will find their hopes disappointed. Indeed, these haggard critical-lexicographers will discover that the basal origins of the word "female" link that term irreparably to "fetus." For both "female" and "fetus" are born out of not only the dreadful "*$d^{h}e$-$h_1(y)$-" but also the Sanskrit suck-phrase "धयति." Moreover, धयति is cognate with the Latin *fellō*, which then skids into *felare*, thus offering the extra word-origin whammy of "fellatio."

What is the sucking one to do? If the anarcho-philologist happens to be eleven weeks pregnant, she may just want to pause her enquiries for a moment to soak her e-*O.E.D.* in her tears. As the confused linguist collapses on the floor of her in-arrears apartment, she will sense within the region of her belly button an entity that is as strange as the language that she studies, as it may be erased (with a couple of doses of RU-486) and yet not really disappear. The gravid if harmless wretch (*qua* Johnson) will weep undecodable morphemes for a while, unless and until she draws strength from the crazily brave life-example of Aliza Shvarts. Then, this thesaural revolutionary will duly remind herself that she is not only pregnant, and reputedly female, but also a proud bisexual Chicanx pescatarian who is actually a great fan of *felare* as long as it is consensual and mutually affirming.

The pregnant Wiktionary editor's reassertion of her existential nonsuckingness does not mean that she will stop crying immediately, and about an hour of sobbingly paging through W. W. Skeat's *The Etymological Dictionary of the English Language* may yet still pass. Yet Aliza Shvarts's rebellious philology continues to offer its heart-lifting promise: Black people, Latinx people, trans people, queer people, and/or women people have been terminating and adopting words for a long time, the desperate etymologist will recall. How all of this may help out with the abortion decision remains unclear, but she hereby resolves that she *may change her social status dramatically* by inventing her own name, even if that transgression may be branded lapsed taste by John Behan or a sign of mass-murdering mental illness by Wanda Franz or Helaine S. Klasky. In honor of Aliza Shvarts and Judge Edward J. Lumbard, she decides on not a noun but rather a verb— *secliber*, which is a portmanteau of *secan*, the Old English term for "search for; pursue; long for, wish for" and *liber*, Latin for both "book" and "free." So *secliber* means one who Shvartsishly searches for freedom.

After a little bit more research, this woman, this bookworm, this *secliber*, who agrees with Aliza Shvarts that life is a matter of reading, will discover that it is not very difficult to mis-carry the Wiktionary's etymological explanation for "female." After all, we must always remember, and never forget, that the vast majority of Wikipedia editors are rich white college-educated men.

Perhaps this is why, when sister *seclibers* click on Wiktionary's entry for *$d^h eh_1$-mn-eh_2*, they will discover no real proof that women have been linguistically fated since antiquity to provide mouth and breast for men and children.

Instead, Wiktionary very helpfully says: "Wiktionary does not yet have a reconstruction page for Proto-Indo-European/$d^h eh_1$-mn-eh_2." And a tireless ransacking of Google only turns up references back to the original non-citation, in the endless loops of mob rule and false confirmation that in today's world qualify as knowledge.

CHAPTER TWENTY-FIVE YEAH GETTING A JOB IS PROBABLY A GOOD IDEA

[Text from Francesca Maroni, who is a marketing VP at Snapchat, Inc., and was my boss when I temped there before Haidar came back from her pregnancy leave. Francesca sent me the message on December 12, 2019.]

Hey mandy a permanent spot
opened up in mrktng r u interested
in applying

[Text from Francesca Maroni, marketing VP at Snapchat, Inc., sent on December 15, 2019.]

Mandy u in? Submit application
asap

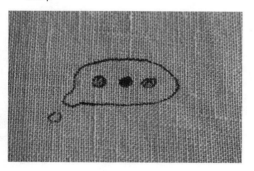

CHAPTER TWENTY-SIX BJÖRK'S KIDS SEEM OK

[This YouTube of Björk singing "Sacrifice" in Paris in 2013 features her dancing around in a curious dress. I posted my comment on the video on December 27, 2019.]

Amandapanda 1 minute ago

I am not sure if pregnancy intensifies female rationality or renders it temporarily kaput. As I sit in my bedroom watching YouTube videos of the singer Björk and ponder my future, I'm divided on the issue. Finding myself thirty-nine years old, destitute of both my girlfriend and now my boyfriend, reduced to using eviction notices as tissues, and somehow still harboring artistic ambition, I have to rely on my ability to calculate with mathematical precision various pros and cons when deciding whether to terminate my "condition." Under California law, I have one or two weeks left, and after that I will have to take matters into my own hands, an unreliable and even potentially mortally dangerous prospect. I worry that I am not thinking clearly.

As my ex-lover Xóchitl well knows, I have never considered motherhood before, a vocation for which I seemed ineligible as a consequence of my devotion to the arts. When I line up this binomial on my computer screen, the brutal Boolean algebra of the situation = abortion 1, child 0: Abortion true, child false. After all, I martyred the love of my life in order to assign the greatest value to the variable of my work, always my beautiful work, which required from me every single sacrifice. And my offerings on that altar allowed me opportunities to do projects in Japan, Mexico, LA, and New York. I screened a film at Slamdance and I taught at Cornell. I won a Sparky and I residenced at Yaddo and MacDowell. I made my calculations, and I made my decisions, so that I could be the next Joseph Beuys, Marina Abramović, or Marcel Duchamp.

Yet now, such questionable logic is overtaken by a delirious vision of a red beating heart filled with love, which has fixated me for the past two weeks. This red beating heart of love does not belong to the fetus but rather to its host, that is, to me. This numinous love courses out of me or perhaps I should say deeper into me. It flows into the seahorse floating within my torso as I write this. This love pulses out of me like blood drops from a wound, and I cannot shrug off the giddy trepidation that Fate or my aging biology calls upon me to nourish my tiny vampire with it until I die.

So you see that I cannot quite understand whether this pregnancy has made me crazy or whether my newfound commitment to self-abnegating love, even with its consequent hazards both personal and professional, are symptoms of an infant intelligence that I should not ignore.

Still, I've got to decide.

*

In spring 2013, the singer Björk performed a stop on her Biophilia tour before an audience in the Zénith de Paris theater, in the 19th arrondissement. The then-forty-seven-year-old avant-garde singer-songwriter appeared in the massive stadium and sang a series of dirges that prayed for technology to reunite human beings with nature, a theme that Björk also illustrated with her choice of costume: she wore a frizzy red wig and a bulbous, off-white dress fashioned of lustrous laser-cut acrylic jersey. This stiff yet undulating armature enveloped her body in what appears to be a collection of cocoons or navels or sand dunes or anthills. So attired, she wailed the symbolist lyrics of songs like "Sacrifice," which you can play by clicking the arrow above:

> *Why this sacrifice?*
> *Now she regrets the whole thing,*
> *A delayed reaction.*

As Björk sang these lyrics, which could signify either an anthropomorphically warming earth or a disappointed woman, the dress glimmered and protruded on her awkwardly dancing body. The gown, painstakingly crafted by the Dutch designer Iris van Herpen in a 3D manufacturing process that took four months, promoted the fantasy that the audience wasn't just enjoying a mere concert performed by an international pop superstar but rather was witnessing the rousings of a human being who had reached an extreme stage of evolution. According to interviews that van Herpen gave to the fashion press, she built the garment while inspired by the lifecycles of bacilli, vermin, lice, and termites. During the show, the dress's gorgeously creepy biomorphic allusions fused with Björk's lyrical performance. The act presented the crowd with a complex collaboration that drew upon the forceful personalities of the two women artists. Both art forms—the songs, the dress—overlapped and merged until they formed a miraculous composite that sang in different, occasionally clashing, registers about the contest between love and death.

> *Build a bridge to her.*
> *Initiate a touch*
> *Before it's too late.*

Björk's lyrics expressed the possibilities of hope and ardor in the face of the apocalypse. Meanwhile, van Herpen's gown glistened like a carapace. The dress raised a skeptical eyebrow at Björk's amorous optimism and seemed with its lumps and whorls to confirm the implacable progress of nature, which creates and destroys with terrifying disregard for the human beings it often crushes.

This collaboration and simultaneous competition between the songs and the costume proved a remarkably successful form of aesthetic mutualism. Many artists who work together do not discover such a triumphal resolution to their differences. For example, Mark Rothko found working with Philip Johnson on the Houston Rothko Chapel traumatic. He committed suicide before the chapel was finished. Salvador Dali and Luis Buñuel worked together on *Un Chien Andalou*, but now Buñuel is the one who gets most of the credit.

Björk and van Herpen's quarrelsome harmony, on the other hand, is delightful precisely because of its dueling messages of faith versus practicality, sympathy versus harsh disinterest.

*

Iris van Herpen designed Björk's dress with the lifecycles of bacilli in mind.

Bacilli develop through a process called *sporulation*. Bacilli not yet differentiated malinger as vegetative cells, and these begin the process of division when they detect certain peptides on their surfaces. The vegetative cells gather nuclear material into filaments, and their plasmatic membrane invaginates, forming a septum. The septum then curves around an immature spore, which develops a double membrane made of the mother cell in a process called *engulfment*. The spore thereafter grows a cortex called a *spore coat*, which makes it resistant to heat and solvents. Lysis enzymes then disrupt the mother cell, and the mature spore is released.

What I am describing here is natural subtraction. 1−0=1. That is, that the now-invalid mother cell dies while the new spore escapes. *Lysis* refers to cell disintegration that occurs when the membrane ruptures. *Lysis* comes from the ancient Greek word *luein*, which means "loosen."

In a 2007 article published in the *Journal of Bacteriology*, Doctors Shigeo Hosoya, Zuolei Lu, Yousuke Ozaki, Michio Takeuchi, and Tsutomu Sato described this stage of spore formation as unfolding when the "mother cell engulfs the future daughter cell and eventually actively lyses prior to release of the spore."

They called this the "mother cell death process."

*

On the Biophilia tour, why didn't Iris van Herpen's dress engulf the singer Björk and actively lyse?

Why didn't Björk find her singing disrupted by Iris van Herpen's spore coat, and begin to asphyxiate from artistically suicidal enzymes?

That is, why did these two beings work together so well and not realize a deadly binary, like Philip Johnson and Mark Rothko, or Luis Buñuel and Salvador Dali? Why could both be true, and one not demand the falseness of the other?

*

When I found out I was pregnant in September, I had been recently sexually assaulted by my gallerist, laid off at Snapchat, fired from the Metropolitan Museum, broken up with by my lawyer boyfriend, and started a part-time gig as a salesgirl at Blick's, the art-supply store.

In the days before I discovered that I was with child I had just finished piecing back together a shattered performance art piece about white fragility called *Texit*, which had been mauled by my gallerist's edits. On the afternoon I took my pregnancy test, I began making Texit's costume, based on a design that I had created back in 2014, when I was on my eleventh version of the script. Texit's livery involved a lot of blue spandex and a red cape made out of fine Japanese Kozogami paper that I had stolen from Blick's.

I am a Chicana bisexual performance artist and writer. My life has been about my work. When I saw the two vertical pink lines on my pregnancy test, however, I (once again) ceased my labors on *Texit*.

I am three months late on my rent. I only still live here because, under California law, landlords can't personally physically evict indigent tenants but have to file a lawsuit and wait until the sheriff's office finally shows up to drag the penniless wretch out. I am eating a lot of peanut butter. I'm going to maybe apply for a job that's opened up at Snapchat but for some reason have not done so yet. I have not yet told Brandon, my former boyfriend, about the pregnancy or asked him for money. I do not plan on doing so, either.

I have spent these weeks doing four things:

1) Working at Blick's.
2) Trying to fill out an application for a permanent job at Snapchat but more just staring into space.
3) Crying.
4) Writing this essay and another one that I've already posted on Wiktionary.

*

In five goddamn minutes I am going to get my act together.

*

Björk Guðmundsdóttir is a single mother. She also holds international renown as a pop-art singer-songwriter. She first achieved fame as the front-woman for the band the Sugarcubes, whose biggest hit was the 1987 single "Birthday." Björk's voice sounds weird and warbly and childlike. She has elf eyes and a snub nose. She left the Sugarcubes in the 1990s and embarked upon an almost grotesquely successful solo career, which spans IDM, tri-hop, classical, and electronic musical styles. She dresses crazy in Iris van Herpen bacilli frocks and also wears sexy costumes shaped like swans. She is so famous that in 2015 the Museum of Modern Art in New York held a poorly received retrospective of her work, a show that displayed mainly her music videos.

Björk is a genius. But in 1986, she gave birth to a son named Sindri Eldon Thórsson. Sindri's father was Björk's husband at the time, a guitarist named Þór Eldon. Björk divorced Eldon in 1988. In 2000, she became romantically involved with the artist Matthew Barney, and in 2002 bore their daughter, whom they named Ísadóra "Doa" Bjarkardóttir Barney. Björk and Barney broke up in 2013, the same year as Björk's *Biophilia* tour. Björk felt so devastated about their estrangement that she wrote a savagely grief-struck album called *Vulnicura*. *Vulnicura* forms a portmanteau of the Latin words for "wound" and "cure," and so means "cure for wounds." The album is really just about the breakup with Matthew Barney, a relationship that had caught on fire and burned down in a bubbling mass of blood and ash.

From *Vulnicura*'s "History of Touches":

> *I wake you up in the night*
> *Feeling this is our last time together*
> *Therefore sensing all the moments*
> *We've been together.*

Still, all of this warbling about lovers leaving is not that interesting. Off they go, the men, the women—look at their backsides as they run away. It's not their best angle. Go ahead, *sense all the moments,* but then go to the bathroom and splash some water on your face.

No, what fascinates is Björk herself. I find myself fixated particularly on the question of how Björk managed as a single mother to continue making avant-garde work. The babies did not initiate in Björk an artistic mother death process. In 2001, Björk put out a single called "Mother Heroic" where she *did* sing *Oh, thou that bowest thy ecstatic face / Thy perfect sorrows are the world's to keep,* indicating that parenthood kicked her ass. And in 2015 Matthew Barney sued Björk in the Brooklyn Supreme Court, alleging that Björk unhealthily monopolized their daughter, Doa. As he testified: "Björk's self-focused mindset . . . flows, in part, from her belief that as Doa's mother, she has far greater rights than I do as Doa's father."

Yet meanwhile, as Björk clutched her daughter to her hip, she also starred in the badly received show at MoMA and screamed *I wake you up in the night / Feeling this is our last time together* to packed houses in New York, Manchester, Rome, and Lyon on the Vulnicura tour. That same year she additionally released three new videos ("Black Lake," "Family," and "Mouth Mantra"), and an all-string acoustic vinyl of *Vulnicura,* which engaged a viola organista designed in the fifteenth century by Leonardo da Vinci. She also created an app for her single "Stonemilker" (featuring another grim mothering motif), was nominated for a Grammy, and graced *Time* magazine's "100 Most Influential People in the World" issue. The newspapers do not report the outcome of the Barney litigation. But in 2016, Björk remained sufficiently artistically liberated that she debuted *Björk Digital,* a virtual reality show that as of this writing travels the globe. She also DJ'd parties in Australia and Tokyo.

Björk's son is now thirty-three years old and the leader of his own musical act called Sindri Eldon and the Ways, which is an execrable impersonation of the band Green Day and features Sindri's abysmal nasal singing and insipid guitar playing. *Breaking up is hard to do / But growing up is harder* is the type of stuff Sindri caterwauls into his microphone. Sindri's videos and interviews reveal him as healthy and annoying. He sports a full, glossy beard, indicating that his B12 levels are high; he has obviously not been starved as a result of Björk's artistic single-motherdom. Sindri once told the *Reykjavik Grapevine* that he counted himself a far superior lyricist and songwriter than his mother. So, Sindri is frustrated and blames the distaff side as men are wont to do. He is apparently married, though, so perhaps Björk shouldn't be blamed for infecting Sindri with an incurable Hamlet syndrome. All in all, old Sindri appears to be tottering toward adulthood in much the same baffled fashion as many other millennials, which is to say, he is doing just fine.

Doa Bjarkardóttir Barney is eighteen years old. She possesses a Twitter account that lists her home as Brooklyn, where her dad is. So maybe there's some Björk-directed anger there. Before she protected her account, curious observers could see that Doa possessed eleven followers and that she liked to post funny fish-eye selfies of herself. She also Tweeted pictures of dogs and of television shows. From this small archive, creepy stalkers/potential artist-mothers doing due diligence could conclude that she has healthy cognitive function. Google Images research reveals that every once in a while paparazzi take pictures of Björk ambling around Iceland hand-in-hand with Doa, so at least they get along well enough to take walks together and physically touch.

It's too soon to tell if Björk's art and possessive personality did any damage to her daughter. I realize that this is a sexist question, but I don't care. I am pregnant and I want to know.

The kid seems normal enough.

*

As I sit here writing this, I feel nauseated but am trying to ignore it. I am also distracted by a pile of blue and red materials that sits on the work table in the southwest corner of my bedroom. The day I found out I was pregnant, I neatly folded the blue spandex superhero suit and the red Kozogami paper super-Texit cape and placed them there. I have not touched them since.

When I first began developing *Texit*, I would sit at my desk and write out messy, wonderful drafts of the spoken-word elements and the dancing sections of the show. I plotted out how to break the fourth wall and I even designed the lighting, which was inspired by Abe Feder's 1930's plans for the WPA Federal Theater. I would sit almost perfectly still at my Prius's dashboard and write for eight, ten, hours at a time, only taking breaks to drink water and to pee. I would create, drink, and pee. Create, drink, and pee.

I was very "happy," which for an artist means that you are *doing the work*. It doesn't actually mean that you are what other human beings call happy, which is some sort of emotional state defined by laughing and smiling.

Making art is strange. An artist must trust her outcast nature and not let economics dull her instincts. She must also remain sufficiently remote from personal concerns that she feels free enough to imagine and to execute. I mean, right? I do not know how Björk managed to drop apps and vinyls and get a MoMA show and make the *Time* 100 list while hoarding children.

Is it because Björk is rich? On Google it says that Björk's net worth is 45 million dollars, which is exactly 45 million more dollars than I have.

Is it because Iceland has subsidized childcare and six months of guaranteed parental leave?

I am from the United States, which speaks for itself.

Still, other women have been able to simultaneously make art and children without the $45 million and the being from Iceland.

Who again? Karen Finley did it. Toni Morrison had kids. And Sally Mann and Lorna Simpson. Mickalene Thomas.

But let us not forget old Sylvia Plath, who activated an atom bomb's worth of lysis enzymes on herself when Ted Hughes left her to raise their two children on her own.

*

Iris van Herpen made the shimmering bacillus-themed dress that Björk wore when she took the stage in Paris. The dress enveloped or invaginated Björk but contributed to the performance and did not self-destruct.

Van Herpen is a Dutch designer, aged thirty-four as I write this. She is tall and rangy with long dark-blond hair. Her face droops and her wide blue eyes gaze into photographers' lenses with an abstracted expression. She has a boyfriend, named Salvador Breed, who works as a sound artist. In 2015, the *New York Times* wrote a profile of van Herpen and illustrated the article with a picture of her and Breed. In the photograph, Breed clings to Van Herpen and nuzzles his face into her neck. Van Herpen stares into the great beyond with a slightly disgusted expression. If a meddling wizard froze van Herpen and Breed in those positions and then dragged them apart, Breed would appear to be hugging a ghost and Van Herpen would look as if she were enjoying a solitary moment on a park bench after awakening from an enervating Klonopin high.

As far as I can tell from rigorous Google searches, van Herpen does not have any children. She did not breed, or has not yet bred, with Breed.

Van Herpen graduated from the ArtEZ Institute of the Arts Arnhem, in the eastern Netherlands, in 2006. A year later, at the age of twenty-three, she founded her label. Van Herpen quickly grew famous for designing biomorphic science-y outfits that have graced the frames of not only Björk but also Tilda Swinton, Daphne Guinness, and Scarlett Johannsson, who are all artists or arty and mothers, as well as incredibly rich.

From the first, van Herpen made bizarre dresses that looked like fossils or spaceships. People liked this, but she did not climb toward fashion superstardom until 2010, when she began using 3D printing to make her clothes. Van Herpen was the first designer to bring this technological element into fashion, designing polymer dresses that look like giant dragon mouths and trilobite exoskeletons, or in the case of the Biophilia costume, like anthills and bacilli. *Time* magazine listed her 3D dresses as one of the fifty best inventions of 2011. Van Herpen attempted a ready-to-wear line but remains most famous for couture. Van Herpen presented at the London and Amsterdam and Paris Fashion Weeks. In 2014 she won the ANDAM Fashion Award and in 2015 she won the Marie-Claire Prix de la Mode. Her work headlined at the Palais de Tokyo in Paris and the Victoria & Albert in London. In 2012, the Groninger Museum in the Netherlands gave her a solo exhibition, and in 2016, one of her 3D dresses stood next to couture by Yves St. Laurent, Karl Lagerfeld, and Coco Chanel in the Metropolitan Museum of Art's *Manus × Machina* show.

When interviewed, Iris van Herpen does not talk a lot about her boyfriend or her personal plans regarding children. In 2013, however, she did tell Susanne Madsen of *Dazed* magazine that she loved skydiving. "Skydiving is the most special feeling you can have," she said.

Iris van Herpen is an artist and knows that she must remain free.

*

In the video "Sacrifice," Björk stands beneath a spotlight and sings *Build a bridge to her* while Iris van Herpen's dress flashes like a wasp's nest around her body.

Björk and Iris van Herpen do not activate murderous enzymes against themselves or each other during this interaction. Instead, the singer and the dress debate each other. Their main disagreement seems to be about the ability of the human race to feel and give love during the ghastly age of the Anthropocene. Björk insists that such human love remains possible, but the dress suggests that Björk perseveres only because she is a predator, as all humans are predators who seek the tragic paradox of sporification and survival.

Through their work, these two women also initiate a conversation about loneliness and art. When Björk sings about *building a bridge* she claims that the female artist doesn't have to be isolated. She can be connected with the rest of the world. Meanwhile, van Herpen's dress, which encases Björk like armor or a habitat, suggests something quite different: the artist may long for love but, alas, can exist only in the self-sustaining microcosm that is her work.

The observer, however, may note excitedly that both ideas persist despite their contradictions. In Björk's and van Herpen's universe, Johnson does not have to kill Rothko and Buñuel spares Dali. There is no horrid Boolean loosening. There are, instead: Morrison, Finlay, Thomas, Simpson, and Mann. Life flourishes in the struggle between love and the pitiless labor of creation.

"Sacrifice" suggests a dazzling idea: the affectionate cannibal, who is also an artist, need not fear subtraction. The red beating heart filled with love + art = a possibility.

*

This is what I mean by wondering whether pregnancy elevates reason or renders a formerly rational person totally nutty.

Perhaps I should not be getting family planning and career advice from YouTube.

My body swells like a fruit. I look to the southwest corner of my bedroom and wonder how the superhero Texit costume would look on me at eight months. Pretty good, I think.

If I went back to work at Snapchat and, realistically, accepted a year off from art, I might be able to manage it.

Snapchat salary = $65K before tax. Hours = ~ 60. Hours in a week = 168. Hours spent sleeping = 49. 45? 40?

Rent = $30K. Childcare in Los Angeles, approx. annual cost = ~ $14.5K

*

What if you have a child and take a year off from art and then discover you can't do it anymore?

Mother cell death? Now she regrets the whole thing, a delayed reaction.

Or maybe you just make the art, even if you can't. You sing about love and bridges at the same time that you wear the terrifying dress.

Art 1, Child 0.

Art 0, Child 1.

Art 1, Child 1.

*

Art 1, Child 1.

The real problem is the money.

History

Monday, December 14, 2020
10:50 PM How long go without sleep without die
12:46 PM baby no stop crying what do
Wednesday, December 30, 2020
10:43 AM Mothers work/life how to survive
11:48 PM Joseph Beuys triangle symbolism
Friday, April 1, 2022
3:39 PM Toba Khedoori MacDowell Genius grant why how
9:14 PM Xōchitl Hernández news
Saturday, August 20, 2022
2:16 PM Claude Cahun fighting Nazis
12:59 PM Processing grief father how

CHAPTER TWENTY-SEVEN **THE CRY-IT-OUT METHOD**

[I posted this Comment to the YouTube video of *I Like America and America Likes Me* by Joseph Beuys on December 30, 2020. This video shows Joseph Beuys's famous three-day-long interaction with a coyote in a New York art gallery. It was filmed in 1974.]

I had hoped that I could make art after having a baby but now understand the hopefully temporary impossibility of this goal. My eight-month-old son Mauricio lies before me in his crib, finally sleeping with the questionable aid of the "fade" method. The scent of milk perfumes my life. My mind fills with visions of his infinitesimal hands and his furious Nixonian face. I am in love with my son. I love him. I don't think it's very good for my work. My work might be dead. As I stand over Mauricio's bassinet and breathe him into me (I am thumb-typing this Comment on my phone), I can feel my formerly stringent aesthetic standards crumble. I used to spend my days worrying about Wittgenstein and curatorial ethics and art world economics and faux art institutional point-of-viewlessness. Today I entertain mostly globular thoughts, framed by threadbare conceits like *don't die, are you still breathing*, and *when will this pandemic ever end*.

I am a performance artist, or I was. Right now I am a single mother. A single mother does not make art by loving in a frenzy, cleaning up shit, and working at all hours in her closet/makeshift home office/bunker. Does she? A single mother does not make art by freaking out about childcare and sore breasts and pumping milk and cracked nipples. A single mother does not make art by surviving the wail-struck darkness. Right? Instead, she wrestles with her laptop in bed and, after recovering from her periodic panic attacks, she writes memos on how to extract maximal money from Snap's, that is, her employer's, March $175M re-upped joint venture with NBCUniversal. She does this only so that her son will have food, shelter, medical care, a nanny, and savings that will hopefully vanish into one of Los Angeles's better private schools. The single mother does this. This is not art. It doesn't feel anything like art. And because the single mother does not make her art by raising her infant son, her actions are merely that, actions, not "Actions." Her output remains unreviewed, ungranted, unworkshopped, and undocumented, except for when she records it online in the form of furious, unread Comments to YouTube videos or Instagrams or Facebook status updates or Reddit posts or rejected Wikipedia entries.

A long time back, I used to dematerialize the art object by running naked through the streets of Tokyo while singing a shape-note song titled *NED McCLINTOCK SHOULD BE IN JAIL*. In a childless and protracted youth that I can no longer really remember except for that time when Xóchitl crushed my soul, I also produced a mangled table read of a script about an emotionally vulnerable alt-right insurrectionist named Texit. In terms of a full-scale production, I got so far as to purchase a fake Colt 9mm submachine gun from eBay and later half-completed a blue, red-caped costume with "Texit" spelled out on the chest in sequins.

Now the fake 9mm submachine and Texit costume languish at the bottom of my closet and I have traded emotional vulnerability for a "norm" job. I run naked through my apartment after my life-vandalizing son, and dematerialize myself by breastfeeding, rushing to doctor visits, kissing, screaming my guts out at Black Lives Matter protests, washing everybody's hands, and unsleeping.

Some would say that my laborious devotion qualifies as art. In 1917, Baroness Elsa von Freytag-Loringhoven tried to teach us that all life is a product of the artist's willpower and intention by walking around in glamorous outfits and co-inventing a urinal as an art product. In 1979, the Croatian performance artist Sanja Iveković masturbated as performance art, calling her piece *Triangle* in honor of her vagina and the ergonomics of state surveillance. The contemporary conceptualist Mierle Laderman Ukeles argues that cleaning is art and that landfills are social sculptures, and grew famous for artistically vacuuming and also shaking the hand of every sanitation worker in New York. A feminist performance artist named Jill Miller drives around Pittsburgh in a "Milk Truck" with a giant pink papier mâché breast stuck to its roof, wherein she provides safe harbor for new mothers who text her when they get kicked out of restaurants for trying to breastfeed. In 2016, Guggenheim/Hugo Boss fellow and auto-ethnographic artist Simone Leigh occupied New York's New Museum's top floor with a BIPOC-centered alternative medical space called a "Waiting Room" that had care sessions, including acupuncture workshops and guided meditation classes. And in 2011's *Birth of Baby X*, performance artist Marni Kotak gave birth to her son in Brooklyn's Microscope Gallery, which earned her the 2012–13 Franklin Furnace Fund Award (three years

156

after mine). In the minds of these very resourceful women, the art and caring fuse into one thing.

But taking care of and loving my son does not feel like performance art to me.

Art requires a distance, an artifice, an audience, a purpose apart. My critique concerns more than capitalism. Even if the artist gifts her work to the sacred space untroubled by money markets, she creates an energy for an audience. Creating an energy for an audience requires her to see herself with the eyes of others, and mandates that she package the work for those others' consumption.

But I do not want to create a consumable out of my adoration of my son. My love exists for him alone.

My art must come in other forms.

But I am too scared and too tired to make anything.

*

In 1974 the god who was the German performance artist Joseph Beuys decided that he would cure America, in the creation of an action that would balm the wounds caused by the American frontiersman's genocide of Native Americans. Beuys planned on achieving this miracle by flying to New York and living with a coyote in a cell for three days. Beuys and his assistants would provide food, shelter, companionship, a place to urinate and defecate, and spiritual counsel to the coyote. The coyote represented Native Americans, and the copies of the *Wall Street Journal* that Beuys's assistants brought in every day for the coyote to pee on represented the United States and its capitalism.

Beuys called the performance *I Like America and America Likes Me.*

Using a peeing coyote as a stand-in for murdered Indigenous people proved one of Beuys's most impudent ideas, not the least because he joined the Hitler Youth in 1936, volunteered for the Luftwaffe in 1941, and fought either so viciously or ineptly on the Western Front that he took wounds five times. Beuys also battled in the Crimea, acting as a rear-gunner on a Stuka dive-bomber, which crashed into the Front in the effort to wrest it back from Stalin. When Beuys later began making artwork, one of his most memorable actions entailed his telling falsehoods about the rescue party who salvaged him from his Stuka wreckage. Beuys said that after he plummeted to the earth, his broken and burned body found salvation in a tribe of Tatars, who covered his skin in milk and animal fats and then wrapped him in layers of felt. "Had it not been for the Tartars [*arch.*], I would not be alive today," he told an interviewer in 1978, explaining why many of his works contained the elements of felt and tallow, and why he himself often donned a felt suit. But the Tatar story proved a complete fiction, as rescue-party Germans reported discovering Beuys alone in the snow, without a nomad in sight. Also, Stalin had begun cleansing the Crimea of the Tatar tribes, so they would not have been in the area at that time.

Who was this fantasist and Hitler lackey to rehabilitate America and its Native victims? Nobody, a lot of people would answer. But Beuys possessed a fanatical trust in himself, a self-regard that all great artists, it seems, must cling to—if not to create objectively great work, then at least in order to persuade history-blind gallery owners to give them white cubes for coyotes to pee in, and for teams of assistants to help them pull off their performances.

On May 21, Beuys arrived in New York on a flight from West Germany. He spent his journey wrapped head-to-toe in a felt cloak and with his eyes shut so that he would not see any part of America until he reached the art space. An assistant helped him carry several items: Beuys brought with him a crooked staff, two large pieces of felt, a pair of gloves, a mystical diagram, and a musical triangle with its metal beater. A white ambulance transported Beuys from the John F. Kennedy airport to impresario René Block's gallery on 409 West Broadway, in Soho. Here, the coyote, captured from the wild by yet another stalwart assistant, waited for him in a wire-netted pen set up in the building.

Beuys did not think that his art consisted of *taking care* of the coyote. He did not lay down the *Wall Street Journal* in the same spirit that Simone Leigh orchestrated an acupuncture class on the top floor of the New Museum. Beuys did not clean up the coyote's poop, thinking that he concretized conceptualism like Mierle Laderman Ukeles did when she vacuumed her house. When he brought the coyote into the gallery from the wild he did not say *voilà!* like Marni Kotak did when she brought her own son into the Microscope Art Gallery from the wild space of her womb. Beuys did not say, "My life and my art are one." He had something more fancy in mind, fancy like the embellishments he told about the Tatars.

Beuys entered the René Block Gallery bundled up in one of his felt blankets, with the crooked staff poking up from his head. In a corner sat a pallet of straw that both Beuys and the coyote would sleep on, and strewn around lay the bundles of the *Wall Street Journal*. Assistants placed in the pen one dog bowl full of meat and another with water. The second piece of felt lumped on the floor as an additional place to rest or sleep. The gallery featured two large rectangular windows, from which light cascaded into the shadowy room.

As the reader can see from the YouTube to which this Comment attaches, one of Beuys's minions filmed the Beuys-coyote encounter, and the tape shows the poor canine skittering nervously as Beuys first appeared to him on Day #1. Beuys entered the space, moving smoothly like an apparition. Beuys did not look human because he wore a thick felt poncho that extended from his knees all the way up to his skull, and out of the top emerged the crooked staff. Beuys began bowing and squatting in front of the coyote in an incomprehensible ritual dance. The coyote stared at him, and Beuys stared back from an opening in the felt where his eyes peeped through. The coyote pranced around with anxiety as Beuys rhythmically continued to bow and squat and walk around like an alien priest. Beuys occasionally held up a diagram that illustrated with a triangle and lightning bolts the New Agey and racist musings of fin de siècle Austrian occultist Rudolf Steiner, who believed that Culture, Economy, and the State together could combine into a perfect polygonic social organism. Beuys believed he spiritually mended the Native Americans/coyote and the murderous white Americans with his dancing and his mystical Steiner drawing. Sometimes, Beuys would also take out his metal triangle and ring it with the beater. *Ding, ding*, it went. *Ding, ding, ding.*

The coyote continued jumping around for the first two, then three days. But after that, it grew curious about its new prison mate. It walked up to Beuys and pulled on his felt cloak with its teeth. The coyote then ran to its food bowl and kicked it all around, and looked back at Beuys to see if Beuys observed its antics. Beuys continued bowing and banging on the triangle while wrapped up in the felt and crowned with the crooked staff head. The coyote eventually relaxed, and rested at Beuys's feet, occasionally jumping on him and tugging on the cloak some more.

I first saw *I Like America and America Likes Me* in 2001, when I attended RISD to obtain my BFA. At the time, I thought that I "got it." I fanatically admired how Beuys released the shamanistic powers of the performance artist, who could direct energy through embodied practices that would exorcise the old bloodstained ghosts of power, history, hierarchy, and gender. I knew, tangentially, that Beuys married (Eva Wurmbach) and even had two children (Wenzel and Jessyka), but these facts seemed peripheral to me. I saw Beuys as a singular creature who used the triangle in his art to capture ancient, chthonic forces that would set his audience on a path toward liberation and aesthetic transcendence. In works such as *I Like America*, I believed that Beuys created a new, secular religion and invented a fresh mode of living.

That is to say, I had no idea what *I Like America and America Likes Me* was about. But as it turned out, neither did Joseph Beuys.

Mauricio's father is Brandon Chu, who pays me $2,284 a month in child support. Since I pay my child care worker, Fred Muñoz, a Los Angeles living wage, I am monthly out-of-pocket $1,094 on that score alone. I possess sole custody, since both Brandon and I wanted it that way. Brandon sees Mauricio four times a month, but he has a new girlfriend now, Seraphina, and they plan to get married and create their own family, which I support.

I never wanted to be pregnant or have children until I did become pregnant and have a child. Now I apparently resemble many other women (Xōchitl) in my desire to be a mother always, a passion that eclipses anything else. Except that I also want to make art more than anything else, too.

Mauricio is mine, and separates me from art. As of this morning, he weighs nineteen pounds and three ounces. His delicate egg head radiates with copious, very soft black hair, and he inherited his father's eyes and my dark skin. He looks at me with a vast emotional intelligence that reveals itself in the furrow of his forehead and the way that he watches me like a judgmental Druid as I move about our house, cooking him vegetable mash and cleaning up vomit and pasty food bits. He observes me with the affected neuralgia of James Baldwin as I try to slither away from his nursery in order to get him to sleep. Before the weekly shopping trip, he stares menacingly at me and/or his now live-in nanny, Fred the charitable Dominican American nurse's assistant from Glendora, before he bursts into tears. Both Fred and I agree that Mauricio has developed certain sophisticated judgments about the arrangements of society that he will share with us when he can finally speak.

The most perfect arrangement would be that neither you nor Fred ever leave my side, I suspect that he will say. *I find it tragic when either of you go away.*

Again, this is not art. I am worried that my art has drifted away from me so far that I can only see it as a small point on a cosmic graph, an infinitesimally tiny point glimmering in opposition to two large points that cluster close together.

Like Beuys's art in *I Like America and America Likes Me*, my life can be described in terms of a triangle.

Euclid first explained triangles in mid third century B.C.E. He taught us that an isosceles triangle displays two sides of equivalent length and bears congruent base angles. Euclid called his proposition *pons asinorum*, or the "bridge of donkeys," to convey his distaste for people who couldn't understand it.

A line, on the other hand, does not boast an angle. It consists of only two points. Euclid defined lines as "lengths without breadth," and Plato described them as "extremities of a surface." In the nineteenth century, the *Encyclopaedia Britannica* defined a line as the "path of a moving point."

Much of the time I worry that I am a line. On those depleted days, I cannot discern art on my graph at all. It seems as if the extremity of my surface extends only between Mauricio and me. I exist as pure length without breadth. I walk on a path that moves only toward him.

X   X
Me   Mauricio

But that's not really true. I am an artist, and that means that art remains around here, *somewhere*. I will admit, though, that my muse retreated from me years ago. The blame for my performance artist block cannot rest with Mauricio alone. My breakup movie screened three years ago, and I streaked through Tokyo the week that Barack Obama first debated Mitt Romney. Since Xōchitl dumped me in 2016, my economic disorganization, job changes, and emotional kaputness rendered me incapable of doing much but sabotaging my paying gigs by posting Marxist-feminist screeds onto employer websites. Since that embarrassing period, I spend my spare time writing strange Comments like these on the internet. My baby provides only the most satisfying of several distractions that long ago suspended my full artistic practice.

Still, the art cannot be gone. It must somehow endure in my life.

As such, I cannot be a line. I am a triangle, like the metal triangle that Joseph Beuys banged at the coyote in 1974.

Recall the isosceles triangles and its two equivalent lengths and congruent angles. That is the *pons asinorum* that I walk daily. Mauricio and I stand in very close, equidistant proximity, while art marks a spot millions of miles away. As such, the two sides of the triangle match and the base angles mirror one another:

X
Me

                                                                    X
                                                                    Art

X
Mauricio

Joseph Beuys believed that *I Like America* also organized around the form of an isosceles triangle. When he finished his performance, he grandly told an interviewer: "I believe I made contact with the psychological trauma point of the United States' energy constellation; the whole American trauma with the Indian, the Red man . . . you could say that reckoning has to be made with the coyote, and only then can the trauma be lifted."

Beuys believed, wrongly, that three points defined *I Like America and America Likes Me*. According to Beuys's mistaken mathematics, the coyote constituted the first "trauma" point. Art designated the second point. The third point exists as Beuys himself, the "I." Beuys felt very close to art, but not so close that he felt that he, as a caregiver, existed as art, the way that Mierle Laderman Ukeles, Jill Miller, Simone Leigh, and Marni Kotak made their cleaning, safehousing, medical healing, and birthwork art. Beuys worked as a showman, and had to add a separate element, a contrivance, like that created by the artificial Tatar story. I think his breathtakingly un-warranted Messiah complex might explain his insistence on decoupaging his coyote care with arty stuff: saviors are heroic, and so have to "do some-thing." Something, that is, besides nurturing their families and communi-ties or safeguarding breastfeeding moms or sanitizing the entire house ev-ery day or playing with rapidly domesticating animals.

Joseph Beuys's spiritually vaudevillian streak clarifies why he put on the cloak and made a head out of a crooked staff, and danced weirdly. It also confirms that he believed that art formed one point, and his "I" formed another. The coyote manifested its point at a farther remove, since it repre-sented The Wild and also The Red Man, according to Joseph Beuys.

Beuys thus thought that he created in *I Like America and America Likes Me* a perfect isosceles triangle:

X
Beuys

X
Coyote

X
Art

*

I thought the same thing for a long time, too.

But I now know that Beuys and I made an interpretive error.

Beuys did not make contact with the Red Man, or force a reckoning with American genocidal trauma by flapping a Steiner diagram in front of the coyote or beating on a metal triangle. These hoped-for residues of *I Like America and America Likes Me* proved so totally unsuccessful that they did not exist. The inventor of the Tatar fiction could not heal American genocidal memory through the racist act of anthropomorphizing Native Americans into coyotes. This is why the felt cloak was nothing. The crooked staff that stuck out of it like a head was nothing. The *Wall Street Journal*s were nothing, except good for pee soakage. The Rudolf Steiner diagram was nothing. The music made by the beating of the triangle was nothing. All of these elements may be withheld from *I Like America* and fed instead to Euclid's donkey.

I Like America and America Likes Me is actually something, though. It succeeds as art, though not as the art that Beuys imagined he made. *I Like America*'s art exists in Beuys's caring for another creature. No meaning prevailed in the work apart from Beuys being with the coyote. He made the leap that I refuse to take with Mauricio, but that others after him, such as Mierle Laderman Ukeles and Jill Miller and Simone Leigh and Marni Kotak, accomplished with so much greater audacity than even Beuys himself.

In *I Like America*, Beuys merged with his art, because his art enacted love. He only tended to an animal, as does a zookeeper or a pet parent or a dogsitter.

X   X
Beuys/Art   Coyote

*

Joseph Beuys stood in the René Block Gallery with the coyote, invisible except for his felt cloak and the crooked staff that stuck out above his head, and bowed at the beast like an ersatz medicine man. The coyote looked at him for a while, and then walked over to one of the gallery's rectangular windows to gaze at the street outside. Beuys continued to genuflect and crouch. The coyote grew bored of staring out of the window and ran back to Beuys and bit playfully at the felt cloak. Beuys bobbed around some more. The coyote wagged its tail and jumped on Joseph Beuys. Then the coyote ran behind Beuys and snapped playfully at his bottom, so that Beuys stopped dancing. Beuys turned around to look at the coyote, unsure what to do.

Recall that Joseph Beuys brought with him a pair of gloves. As this YouTube reveals, on day four or day five, Joseph Beuys stopped bowing and crouching and started just throwing the gloves at the coyote like he would a tennis ball. Fetch! The coyote chased after the gloves, wagging its tail. Joseph Beuys threw them again. Then the coyote jumped on Beuys and pulled at his cloak some more, so that the game continued. Beuys patiently obliged the coyote, who perhaps did not like to be imprisoned in René Block's art gallery, but did like Joseph Beuys.

That is why Joseph Beuys called his action *I Like America and America Likes Me*.

*

Fred Muñoz, Mauricio's nanny, sometimes stands next to me as I look down at Mauricio when he sleeps in his crib. He'll typically do this if I start crying.

"You're a good mother," Fred will say.

"No, I'm not," I'll answer.

Fred comes from a family of eight brothers and sisters. Fred trained as a nurse's aide at West Los Angeles College, which maintains a very fine program. Fred worked in USC's pediatric oncology ward for twelve years but then burned out. He now works for me and also sleeps in the living room since he found out his roommate and sister were exposed. He stands five feet, seven inches, and is forty-one years old. Fred's fur-brown eyes glisten with specks of leaf green. Fred cracked a molar that he needs to get fixed. Fred knows how to deal with diaper rash and reverse cycling and even problems with letdown. He understands how to reassure worn-out women.

I'll hold Mauricio in my arms and close my eyes and cry for a while until I feel better. Mauricio feels like primordial life, breathing and wriggling. I attend to Mauricio's perfect skin with a combination of cocoa butter, shea butter, and cornstarch. I breastfeed every two hours. I don't sleep very much at night.

"You're a good mother, Amanda," he says again. "You're catching on just fine."

"Thank you Fred," I'll say.

It doesn't really get a lot more interesting than that at my house these days, unless you count the minute movements that I track in Mauricio's face when he looks at me or when he naps. The other OK moments come when I write these Comments to YouTube videos or Reddit feeds or Facebook posts or when I post on Instagram, or send people emails.

*

When Joseph Beuys made *I Like America and America Likes Me*, he was a line but erroneously believed that he was a triangle.

Joseph Beuys unintentionally invented what I call *care art*, that is, art that takes the form of caring for another being or, perhaps, yourself. When Sanja Iveković masturbated as art, she took care of herself. When Mierle Laderman Ukeles artistically vacuumed, she took care of herself and her family. When Jill Miller performatively dashes around Pittsburgh providing a breastfeeding space, she takes care of discriminated-against moms. When Simone Leigh created a Guggenheim-y alternative medical care establishment out of the top floor of the New Museum, she offered the community healing. And when Marni Kotak gave birth to her son in the Microscope Gallery, she enacted that crucial stage of care that takes the form of nourishing a baby within the body and then pushing it out into the scary world.

These women took up Beuys's challenge and achieved what he could not. They did not need to dress up in felt or wave around a manifesto. They realized Euclid's "breadthless line" and manufactured work that proved indistinguishable from their own laborious acts of goodwill. Very little artifice exists in the space between the artist and the art. These women added nothing superfluous but the intention that art exist in and through their care.

X
Giving a damn/Art

*

As I write this (it has taken me three days to get this down, and I'm now working at the desk in my bedroom), Mauricio cries out from the nursery. My entire body stiffens with something like pain, but Fred told me that I need to start consistently sleep training my son even though it seems like the world is falling apart. Sleep training may take three different forms: 1) the "cry-it-out method," where the baby wails itself to sleep; 2) the "no tears" method, where the parent staggers into the nursery every time the baby cries; and 3) the "fade" method, where the parent sits on the floor with the baby shrieking in his crib and then silently crawls away when the kid finally drops off.

"Cry it out," Fred always says, raising his eyebrows at me.

At this moment I sit in front of my computer and weep as my son cries. I look at the closet where my artificial gun and blue and-red Texit costume lie buried beneath some coats and books and whatever else I squashed in there.

I could take the fake 9mm Colt that I intended to use in *Texit*, virtually commandeer the Gagosian's Insta feed, and then livestream myself "fading"/crawling around Mauricio's bassinet and call it art. Or I could let Mauricio unrelievedly cry in the bassinet and call it art. Or I could run over to the bassinet every time he cries and call it art. I could sit at the feet of the bassinet and cry and call it art, and when my boss calls me repeatedly on my iPhone I could hold up the phone for the audience and bawl over said boss's ringtone, which is an excerpt from Yoko Ono's 1973 anthem "Angry Young Woman."

But I am not a line, I am an isosceles triangle, like Joseph Beuys wanted to be. I am possessive of my son and also a fancy egomaniac like Joseph Beuys, and so I need to "add something." What I am really trying to convey in this perfervid Comment about Joseph Beuys and his coyote is this: despite the current catastrophe and my overwhelming responsibilities, I remain an artist in search of a style, in search of inspiration, in search of an offramp to this donkey bridge down which I trudge and amble. My only "creative time" comes when I write these interminable Comments and post and spellcheck them and noodle with the syntax and then check to see if I get any hearts or likes or shares.

Still, writing is not my art, because I am a performance artist with a social practice that I built over the last twenty years. I do not want to be a writer, since writers exchange color, sound, speech, the stage, the street, and thus the now-much-missed feel and touch of other human beings for this haunted craft of word design.

On YouTube, the coyote wags and nips, while Joseph Beuys, the husband and father, basks in the delightful illusion that felt blankets and lunatic dancing make him an art shaman who can heal the world. His unhinged self-confidence, freedom from public health terrors, and apparently robust circadian rhythms made everything easy.

But I am struggling.

CHAPTER TWENTY-EIGHT OWN YOUR EMOTION

[Subreddit on Toba Khedoori's *Untitled (Table and Chair)* (1999), which I posted on April 3, 2022. *Table and Chair* is a painting of a table and chair that float in nothingness.]

My girlfriend Xōchitl broke up with me because we had incompatible life goals. Xōchitl wanted to have a baby with me, and I wanted to travel like an astronaut to the farthest reaches of consciousness.

"You can still have a family and travel to the farthest reaches of whatever," Xōchitl insisted, as she rapidly chopped onions and parsley in the eat-in kitchen of our artsy Los Feliz apartment. We collected Navajo rugs and hand-thrown vases, and in the breakfast nook we had hung a framed poster of Toba Khedoori's painting *Untitled (Table and Chair)* (1999). This was six years ago, in 2016, after we had returned from New York because I'd just been fired from my Guggenheim residency for posting a pirate Glenn Ligon didactic.

"I don't think so." I'd been drinking a glass of pinot grigio by the sink. "How are we going to take care of a baby when you're filming me dying in Mexico?"

Xōchitl's eyelids quivered. "I told you, we're not doing that."

"But I just got the NEA!"

"You're not dying. Trust me. You're a thirty-six-year-old woman in good health. You're statistically likely to survive until you're eighty-six point two. I'll film you then."

"I don't mean *dying*. I mean capital D *Dying*. Like we're all always Dying. Plus, I'll be doing a liquid fast so I'll get really empty and pure. It'll be amazing. I'll be the Chicana Zarathustra."

Xōchitl stared at the onions and sucked in her bottom lip. "It's called a *Messiah complex*, Amanda," she said.

Xōchitl had domesticated me like a poodle with the rewards of her short, thick legs and wide mouth full of very straight, slightly coffee-stained teeth. Her brindle-colored hair ascended from her head to form a distracted pterodactyl that flew behind her while she stomped around our walnut-paneled kitchen.

As a serious actuary, a Fellow, Xōchitl spent eight years toiling at Munger & Hanley after passing a brutally escalating level of Herculean labors that apexed in a four-hour stochastic calculus and game theory massacre called Exam 9. At the time of our argument, she was thirty-seven years old. We had met at the Hammer five years before, and she had flambéed my sangfroid on our first date by removing a stray eyelash from my cheek while chatting about something called "Brownian motion."

"Brownian motion helps actuaries predict chaotic events," she'd told me. "It's a way to, you know, see around the corners of mysteries—like the probabilities of getting decapitated in a car accident or dying from septicemia, and stuff."

I fell in love with her because of her wacky theories. When Xōchitl taught me about the Stratonovich integral, or read to me from *The Science and Secrets of Wheat Trading*, my brain felt like it leaned sideways, and I could fathom the world from a new and thrilling angle.

Now it was different. Xōchitl gave me side-eye as I attempted to rekindle "the fire" by doing a flirty bang-bang with my hips. The wine slopped a little out of my glass. "Honey Bunny, if we put the kid thing on hold, what are the chances of you breaking up with me?"

She kept chopping the onions, ferociously. But then she started laughing. "Forty-two percent."

"No!" I danced some more around the kitchen. "Look—we'll just go to Mexico, have a couple margaritas, and then I'll starve myself and look into the void, see if there's anything there."

Xōchitl looked up at me and squinted. "*Then* we'll have a baby."

"Yes." I nodded, not sure if I was lying. I had wanted to put off the procreation thing for about seven more years—I was going to go to MacDowell, start up production on *Texit* right after Mexico, and then supposedly do lots of other stuff. But Xōchitl kept getting mad. I looked helplessly around the kitchen, fixating on the cardamom jar in the spice cabinet. "A bay-*bee*. A small person who's completely dependent on you." I started to sweat. "How does that work?"

"Do you swear?" Xōchitl asked.

I tried a joke by placing my hand over my heart: "I will, to the best of my ability, preserve, protect, and defend the Constitution of the United States." But, wrong audience. I immediately corrected with: "Yes, yes, yes."

Xōchitl's face glistened with sudden rapture. Using her professional talents, she began to plot out our nonexistent daughter's future. "She'll do Spanish at Yale, and get a Master's in logic, and then go to business school." She stopped chopping the onions and counted the forecast laurels on her fingers. "And she'll have four children, and speak Mandarin. And she'll be a good person and also run marathons."

"OK," I said.

*

As I have mentioned, Toba Khedoori's painting *Untitled (Table and Chair)* (1999) decorated Xōchitl's and my breakfast nook when we lived together. In this work, MacArthur "Genius" Grant winner Khedoori renders her subjects with faint beige oils and obsessive accuracy, revealing the eponymous two pieces of furniture that stray in a vastness of pale and unmarked paper.

Art patrons can only guess why Toba Khedoori painted a picture of a table and chair floating in light brown emptiness. Khedoori will not tell us because she does not do interviews. Almost no information about her may be gleaned from web searches, except for basics like her Iraqi-Australian origins and 1964 birth. She moved to Los Angeles in 1990 and attended UCLA. Her career accelerated in her early twenties because of her precociously nihilist use of negative space. For Khedoori, "using negative space" means painting objects like brick walls and stadiums and hearth fires in the centers of huge blank pieces of waxed paper. Khedoori leaves her margins massive and entirely vacated, except when she stains them deep black. David Zwirner represents her in New York and Regan Projects does so in LA. She has an identical twin sister named Rachel, a sculptor who makes installations out of lots of cracked mirrors and wire and has not won a MacArthur.

Khedoori appears attractive, huge-eyed, and alienated in one of the two photographs of her that are available online, both posted by the MacArthur Foundation. The first photograph reveals Khedoori staring up at the viewer as she sits on a paint-splattered scaffold. She wears miniature gold hoops in her earlobes, what appear to be Saucony running shoes on her small feet, and has masses of dark wavy hair that she ties back at the nape of her neck. In the other photograph, Khedoori glares mournfully, half hidden behind a white pillar. When the MacArthur Foundation awarded Khedoori their famous grant in 2002, its judges described her fin de siècle "nothing" drawings as "quiet, reticent works [that] . . . convey a sense of mystery and invit[e] the viewer to speculate on their meaning while appreciating their serene beauty."

What this means is, the MacArthur folks don't know precisely why Toba Khedoori sets her figures adrift within the cold and unpopulated cosmos either.

It took me a long time to learn what Xōchitl knew passionately when we first met. She graduated *summa* from both Choate and Wellesley, and her mother founded a white-shoe law firm in Boston. I dropped out of the Rhode Island School of Design; my mother died from an overdose, and my father would expire from multiple myeloma. Xōchitl wore long plaid shorts and sandals and said it was OK to drive a Volvo instead of a Prius. I had piercings and bossy vegan tendencies. I thought all of this meant that Xōchitl was the fatal bourgeois whom I had been sent from outer space to save. "I can't help it," she'd say, laughing into my neck. "I think everything we need is right here."

"This?" I'd say, waving my hand around. "This is nothing. I have plans for us, kid. Travel, prizes, Klaus Biesenbach texting us for brunch in Kiev, and maybe not being broke all the time—"

"I got money," Xōchitl said. "*We* have money."

I shook my head. "You have no idea how good things are going to get."

I'd lead her to our minimalist bedroom, where I'd take off all of her clothes. That was *my* room. Xōchitl had filled the den and living room with wicker, superconceptual paintings, and big soft sofas. The bedroom remained empty and white, except for our California king and a little table and chair that I'd bought at Goodwill in the 2000s.

I'd spread her out naked on the bed while she smiled at me. Her body glowed, empty of marks and scars, like negative space that I would fill with objective reality and fire. Her eyes threw sparks amid the shadow of her dappled hair.

"Come here," she'd say.

I have a son now. He's two years old. Mauricio. Xōchitl's seen his picture on Instagram and hearted it. About four months ago, she also sent me a message:

How's it going? she asked.

I miss you, I replied.

She didn't react to that. Instead, she wrote: *Your son's beautiful.*

How's Greta and your daughter, I wrote back, sobbing.

Good. How's your work?

What, I wrote, *at Snapchat? It's fine.*

YOUR WORK, she answered.

I'm not an artist anymore, I typed out.

But I read those things you're writing online.
That's nothing, I said.
Nothing's nothing, Amanda, she argued with me, as usual.
I printed out that exchange and keep it in a drawer. I never look at it.

*

The hours following my first date with Xōchitl were spent dreamily meditating upon her thoughts on decapitation and Brownian motion. I swiftly looked up the doctrine and learned that its discoverer had also believed that "nothing's nothing." The few photographs I found of Robert Brown revealed that he was a slim, large-eyed Scotsman with dapper muttonchop sideburns and a cleft chin. His placid appearance belied the obsessions that made him a father of stochastic process theory, a branch of mathematics that finds patterns within random activity, that is, in chaos.

Brown became Keeper of the British Museum's Herbarium in the 1820s, after fleeing the profession of medicine as well as sanctioned romantic entanglements. For much of his youth, Brown had embarked upon the life of an adventurer-botanist who collected "new" specimens in places like the Desertas Islands, Madeira, and the Cape of Good Hope. In a long career full of conquest and tribulation, Brown counted his 1801 voyage to New Holland (now Australia) on the dilapidated HMS *Investigator* as his most far-reaching, and devastating, expedition.

In the seventeenth and eighteenth centuries, young Europeans regularly dashed across the seas to discover the mysteries—the Somethings—that in those years remained hidden in maps whose void-struck sparseness bears a startling resemblance to the advanced minimalism of Toba Khedoori.

Brown, like other imperialists whose ambitions for subject matter would claim so many "dark continents," expectantly navigated southeast. He took with him an avid twenty-something companion named Peter Good, who functioned as the *Investigator*'s on-board horticulturalist. The two enthusiasts stalwartly sailed the dangerous seas for several months but then made a fateful stop at the sun-blasted mountains of Timor. There, Good contracted dysentery, an affliction that quickly culled much of the *Investigator*'s crew. Brown attended to the boy with his own ration of water and bunya nuts that he roasted in campfire coals. He also nursed Good with his slim stock of medicines and covered up the patient's shivering form with his own blankets and coat. Still, the victim grew weaker every day, and soon could barely lift his head. Upon reaching Port Jackson, Brown and the other survivors carried the barely breathing Good to Sydney in the hopes that colony doctors could help. But Good died upon arrival, on June 12, 1803.

171

Good's death exposed Brown to the problem of negative space, which turned out to be far more horrifying than the gratifying emptiness promised by Continental cartographers. I suspect that the trauma stayed with him the rest of his days. Brown would later spend long years in search of proof that "nothing was nothing," embarking upon experiments that might uncover a natural law that assured him something always persists.

This passion led to his greatest achievements.

*

In 2016, Xōchitl and I went to Mexico so that I could Die. My brush with annihilation would be metaphorically artistic and educational, though, not literal and awful like poor Peter Good's and Robert Brown's.

It was shortly after our kitchen argument in Los Feliz. I brought Xōchitl to the rural village of Cabo Corrientes. We lived in this idyll of stones, lichen, scorpions, and snakes for three months, squatting in a beach hut that had no running water, and electricity whose predictability remained inaccessible to even the most tested of actuaries. I said that the experience would help Xōchitl Grow and Reach beyond Herself. I also explained that the physical suffering brought on by this ordeal would deepen my practice as an artist, and because she accompanied me on the Journey she would also in some ways be sort of like an artist.

"I'm not an artist," Xōchitl said, as she constructed a desalination system out of plastic tubs, aluminum foil, and copper tubing. She was topless and wore Levi's cut offs. She had tied her hair back with red string. Her face peeled from sunburn. "Artists are insane."

I carefully taught Xōchitl that artists are not insane by describing for her the long performance art tradition of undergoing bodily mortification in order to See What Was Out There. I gave her a seminar on Chris Burden's 1974 performance of *Trans-Fixed*, when the artist had himself crucified to a Volkswagen Beetle so that the pain could bring him revelation. I explained that the title of the action referred both to its literal Christlike enactment (since the term comes from the Latin root word for *pierced through*) and also its contemporary meaning of being fixated by an idea or an image—like Moses, Jesus, and Muhammad were transfixed by the excruciating presence of Yahweh and Allah.

"Please stop talking right now," Xōchitl said, while brushing her teeth in our cabin, using salt that she had to harvest from the ocean because I did not want to interrupt the purity of our experience by using any products manufactured by conglomerates.

When Xōchitl several weeks later began eating Snickers candy bars in front of me, I also gave her a mini-colloquium on Marina Abramović's 1974 performance of *Rhythm 5*, where the artist constructed a large, hollow, five-pointed wooden star. Abramović lay down in the middle of the star and set it on fire with gasoline and matches. When she lost consciousness because the fire ate up all the oxygen in the star's center, she had to be saved by an audience member. I expounded on how the five-pointed symbol superficially represents communism (Abramović is from the former Yugoslavia) but bears a deeper and older relation to the pentagram, which illustrates the four elements and the *quintessence*, and thus symbolizes the ouroboros that the artist accessed as she passed out of the corporeal phase and into a parallel consciousness where things like Snickers, which are made out of corn syrup, do not and cannot exist.

"I more like the art where people don't maybe croak," Xōchitl responded, looking at me from beneath her bangs with eyes that I now recognize harbored a deepening distrust.

I won't go into the rest of the tutorials on aesthetic self-annulment—the discussions of Vito Acconci's *Seedbed*, where Acconci embodied Pan by masturbating eight hours a day for three weeks, or of how Tehching Hsieh discovered his personal divinity by locking himself in a cage and going mute for one year, or about Ragnar Kjartansson's movie *God*, which shows him repeating the phrase "Sorrow Conquers Happiness" so relentlessly that he loses his voice. Suffice it to say that I thought I had prepared Xōchitl for our Process. We spent the summer and fall reading, meditating, and foraging for our food in an admittedly misguided homage to Thoreau. Finally, I felt ready to begin my fast. I would do it with the purpose of removing all possible worldly obstacles between my subjectivity and Reality. By thus killing the "I," I would hopefully glimpse the Something that persists beyond the scrims of Nothing that we layer onto existence with the meaningless rituals animating late capitalism and its opiate propagandas that we call negative liberty and popular culture.

"It's time to go *home*," Xōchitl said, wearing a Choate sweatshirt and pounding on the desalination device, which was getting leaky. "You've been tripping since May. I've got to get back to work. And, you know, get pregnant, like you promised."

"Honey Bunny, now it's time for me to starve myself." I gestured meaningfully at my body. "I'm going to self-mortify, and you're going to film it."

"Is this what you're going to be like when we finally have kids?" Xōchitl pulled on a hank of her hair. She examined her ends, narrowing her large, leaf-shaped eyes as she looked for splits. "I gotta get out of here. I'm not filming anything."

I titled my video *Ain't Nobody Leaving* (2017) to memorialize a conversation that Xōchitl and I had on the seventh day of the action. The movie shows me stranded on a beach empty of all human artifacts except for our cabin/shed/seagull nest. I sit cross-legged and face the lettuce-colored ocean. The long piece of black hair that hangs from the left side of my head half-covers my face, fluttering slightly in the sea breeze. At the beginning of the video, my expression possesses the vulnerable serenity of Beyoncé in "Halo" but later takes on the addled hostility of Gary Busey on *Late Night*. The other side of my scalp sprouts a grown-out *ombre* buzz. My eyes remain mostly closed throughout. My breasts are extremely small, with disproportionately large dark nipples. My bristling bush denotes seventies' freethinking. I wear a frosting of zinc oxide across my nose that progressively smears around my face like misapplied conglomerate toothpaste. I actually don't even look that thin.

I'm not eating so that I can empty myself out and Connect to the Source, I say into the camera, in between rhythmic bouts of *ujjayi* breathing that I quickly abandon. Other times, I say, *I'm really hungry and I can't believe that you are eating that sandwich in front of me right now.* And: *I'm starting to get really clear that there's nothing after death, just more death.* And: *What does love even mean.*

A mint-green Klean Kanteen props up in my lap. I drink from it every half hour, because you dehydrate surprisingly fast when you don't eat anything. Periodically I also get up to pee out the water, and the camera shows the sand kicking up from my bare, slightly splayed feet as I serpentine across the shore to our shed's guano-spattered back forty.

Xōchitl had sat before me, also cross-legged, but forgoing sympathetic nudity in favor of a white dress with blue embroidery. She clutched her strong brown hands around a wad of recycled decomposable paper towels printed with strawberries. She'd use the towels to wipe the sea mist off of the lens of my NEX-FS100, which she'd fixed to a Benro tripod mount stuck in the sand perilously close to the high-tide line. She filmed nonstop like Warhol's *Empire*. She never appears on camera, but I will probably go to my deathbed haunted by the ineradicable memory of her wide-jawed and increasingly demonic face framed by moss-green waves. Offscreen, you can hear her talking.

What I think that you need to really "process" is that I have been sneezing out bugs here for over two months so that you could finally get clear about where you stand in our relationship. Our DYNAMIC. Our PATHOLOGY, if you like. I have been supporting you for five years because I love you. LOVE. It does mean something. To me. It means everything to me. But it's not worth this.

Because there's no movement here. There's no forward drive, as far as I can tell. From you—there's no motion.

Brownian motion, I mutter.

What?

Brownian motion, you were talking about that when we first started dating and you were studying for your CAS 1. That probability test.

Are you hallucinating?

Brownian motion sounds like Own Your Emotion if you pronounce it weird, I say.

Exactly, she says.

A few minutes pass. Then she says: *I'm leaving you, Amanda.*

Ain't nobody leaving, I reply.

Ain't Nobody Leaving premiered at 2018's Slamdance festival. It got a standing ovation and I took a bow in front of about eighty people while wearing a navy-blue Uniqlo onesie and high on half a Xanax. I won the Spirit of Slamdance prize in a surprise upset that had me beating Bogdhan Zoblocca's poignant gorefest *Z myru po nytsi—golomu sorochka*, which is about two Ukrainian brothers serially killing protesters during the Orange Revolution and which, despite its loss, later got picked up by the Independent Film Channel for $800,000. I had traveled to the stony wastes of Utah alone to receive my bronze dog "Sparky" statue, which is what I got instead of $800,000, plus also $1,200 in credit for legal services from the Pierce Law Group that I later sold to a Brutalist named Marsha Gleiberman for $420. Xōchitl did not attend as my plus one because breaking up with me, fleeing California, and buying a prewar two-bedroom on the Upper West Side ate up her free time. Thus the Xanax.

I then showed *Ain't* at the Atlanta, Tallgrass, Berlin, and IndieLisboa film festivals. I got food poisoning in Portugal and a stress rash that I thought was cancer in Kruezberg. I also stayed for two months at the MacDowell Colony in Peterborough, New Hampshire, where I did zero artwork but did *not* have an affair with Marsha even though she showed up in my cabin naked except for seersucker overalls and hoisting a magnum of pinot.

My performance art inspiration dried up when Xōchitl left and my dad died. Early in my career, before I fully realized the life/death distinction that money negotiates, I had resisted capitalism by refusing to get a dealer. So I did not have to worry about David Zwirner or Regan Projects bothering me about my productivity. Instead, I watched the bottom fall out of my life while writing web copy for the uniformly unforgiving art world behemoth The Whitney/Max Mara.

My affect became what I would like to call "experimental." Back in 2011, for example, I occupied MOCA's Laura Aguilar listing with an anarcho-lesbian manifesta about Latina visibility. I later also hijacked the Guggenheim website with a gospel on child-freedom that did not turn out to be compatible with full-time employment, housing stability, or personal happiness.

I now found myself returning to my controversial habits. I annotated Thomas "Painter of Light" Kinkade's painting of a rustic castle with unpunctuated primary screams. I also had a sketchy episode where I dematerialized the art object far too forcefully at LACMA by collapsing into ceaseless hysterical giggles while trying to write a review of an egregiously curated Agnes Martin exhibition. But without a larger arts practice in which to suspend these gestures, they seemed less like metacriticisms and more like just regular mistakes that a depressed demi-employed person might indulge in when trying to get over a bad breakup and father *mortem*.

I also squandered a titanic amount of time on social media. The web is the existential vape of our age, and when I wasn't running remotely amok for Max Mara, I smoked up all my talent by writing Comments, photo-sharing, a little bit of hacking, IM, augmented reality, face filtering, tweeting, pinning, YouTube hypnosis, LinkedIn creeping, Facebook blocking, Tinder unmatching, Instagram poetry dawdling, likes, emojis, Periscope haiku, bitching on Foursquare, art criticism on Yik-Yak, journaling on Wikipedia, Snapchat obscenity, Reporting Abuse, Asking Inappropriate Questions on eBay, getting my reviews rejected by Yelp, and posting increasingly Sylvia Plathian subreddit confessions, the likes of which you are reading right here.

And I taught a winter semester Embodied Performance workshop at Cornell during a polar vortex that turned the sky apocalypse black, which caused me eventually to lie down sobbing on my rented apartment's sisal-covered floor until I passed out.

*

How did Robert Brown deal with his own bereavement? More productively than I. In the aftermath of Peter Good's death in Sydney, Brown's journals confirm that he stayed behind in Australia for eighteen months. He busied himself with naming herbs and topographic features in honor of his friend, and making gloomy notes about the dried-out husks of spore-bearing mosses that he found embedded in the mountainsides: "Within the tropic, unless at very great heights, cryptogamous plants appear to form hardly one fifth of the whole number of species," he observed in scratchy jottings posthumously published in *The Miscellaneous Botanical Works of Robert Brown*, Vol. 27 (1866).

Brown never made an open confession of his feelings about Peter Good's death. Only a few clues give us a sense of the depth of his despair over that negation that gaped where Good once stood. For example, Brown baptized a delicately yellow-blossomed genus of the pea family *Goodia*, and a slightly wild-looking red spindled shrub *Grevillea goodii*. But perhaps the best indication of Brown's sorrow may be discerned in his behavior twenty-four years subsequent to Good's extinction, when Brown performed experiments on the British Museum's collection of flora and made his monumental discovery.

In 1827, the fifty-four-year-old Brown stood in the basement murk of the British Museum's Herbarium, brooding through the lens of his bronze Leitz microscope and picking through his extensive collection of dried herbs and flowers. In the weeks previous, he had made a startling observation of molecular motion surrounding the pollen of the living pink fairy flower, which danced in chaotic choreography when trapped in a drop of water. Brown theorized warily that this intense activity might be produced by *pneuma*, known to the ancient Greeks as "breath," or the source of all life. If so, he calculated, such antics would not appear in dead specimens. He now applied himself to discovering whether some revenant of that energy might also emanate from a lifeless plant.

Carefully, he selected the remains of an Australian moss, which he had collected in the dark days following Good's demise. The moss was dry, brown, and furry. Using a pair of tweezers, Brown extracted several spores from its crispy husk. He floated the dead particles in a drop of water, placed it on a slide, and looked at it through his Leitz's lens.

The spores moved. In unpredictable patterns.

In his 1828 treatise, *On the Existence of Active Molecules*, he wrote excitedly that the particles had "equally vivid Motion on immersion in water" despite the fact that the Australian moss "had been dried upwards of one hundred years . . . I now therefore expected to find these molecules in all organic bodies: and accordingly on examining the various animal and vegetable tissues, whether living or dead, they were always found to exist."

Brown's glimpse into the mysteries of existence raised a thousand more questions than it answered, and I find it easy to get caught up in his ardor. I think he must have been plagued by a desperate hope: if Something, indeed, always Moved, that is, *always existed*, could that mean that earthly goods persisted past death? And if so, what shape did Something wrench out of Nothingness, what did its agitated mandala signify, and what could it become?

*

An alert follower of Toba Khedoori will recognize that she possesses a much less romantic engagement with Nothing than did Robert Brown. Khedoori makes most of her works on parchment paper, which bears the raw color of closed eyelids. In one painting, however, she depicts a square-shaped fire and sets it in an abundance of pure blackness. If the observer is in a delusionally good mood, she might think that it looks like the campfires that Robert Brown built to fend off the starless and serpent-hissing night while he tried to save Peter Good's life.

Khedoori makes her drawings of empty chairs or brick walls or fires and hangs them in the off-center of her *horror vacui*. As I've already noted, the artist remains silent as to her motives. However, when Xōchitl broke up with me and I began to squat in a savagely minimal sub-sublet in Palms, I looked up *Table and Chair* on Artsy. While the painting had hung in Xōchitl's and my breakfast nook, I had lazily interpreted it as an affirmation of existence. But now, as I stared at the image on my phone, I discerned no Brownian consolations, no signs of life. I understood instead that in the work, Khedoori refers you to the remorseless exit that surrounds each person, and the planet.

*

After my screening of *Ain't Nobody Leaving* at Slamdance, the hairy, humped human error that we call 2018 began to rampage across the earth. I still squatted in the apartment in Palms and dealt with the presidency by listening to the shrieky tunes of Diamanda Galás until late at night, which permitted me to survive on rage.

Upon getting fired from the museums for my unauthorized postings and catalepsy, I optimized my "work week" by contracting carpal tunnel on social media. I cannot say that I either enjoyed writing or found in it a valid substitute for performance art. I feared very greatly that all of my woebegone exposition just amounted to nothing. Occasionally, when I could make my words fit together with the precise angst that buoys *Ain't Nobody Leaving*, I *did* experience a nearly physical satisfaction, like that which arrives when you gobble three Snickers after a long fast. The feeling always evaporated, though. I could not stand that my text remained locked in digital space, when it should have been doing something meaningful like getting sprayed illegally on Wall Street or being declaimed by me as I stood

178

naked and painted in primary colors while starring at the Edinburgh Fringe Festival.

But I kept at it. On my lentil-crusted phone, I wrote increasingly elaborate Instagram and Vimeo and Wikipedia essays on subjects like video artist Sanja Iveković's masturbation protocols and the grouchy process of "crispation" coined by French philosopher Gabriel Marcel. I'm not sure if this period qualified as Bargaining or Anger. All I know is that I found it far more amusing to worry about my ability to describe concisely Mickalene Thomas's various real estate holdings than, say, remember Xōchitl's beautiful Satan face while she'd yelled at me on the beach at Cabo Corrientes. Xōchitl's memory could do nothing but infect me with emotional septicemia, as she now lived full-time in New York—dating a Mount Sinai gynecologist for Christ's sake and announcing her pregnancy on Facebook.

I would look around my room, at my white-painted walls with their small smudges and cracks. They looked like the map of an empty and innocent world soon to meet its conquerors. Depending on the arrangement of my furniture, sometimes my pinewood Ikea chair would find itself stranded against the wall, framed by the pale paint that transformed it into a triggeringly minimalist symbol of isolation.

I spent months perfecting this depression delivery system until I finally met a lawyer named Brandon and began to engage in copious sexual intercourse with him. I also attained respectable work at an internet firm whose pathologies meshed with my own. Except for a yearlong interlude where I went crazy again after a gallerist/failed rapist ruined all of my hopes, these felicities released me from my melancholy and for a brief interregnum "love" and "a norm career" began doodling themselves into the wide wastes of my mental margins. Eventually, however, I realized that this graffiti was easily washed off with one or two frenzied conversations with my boyfriend about my how my personal emotional style was not very "helpful," and an increasing anxiety that my performance block had enlarged into a Gibraltar that I would never overcome again.

Once more, I would find myself back in my room, looking at the white emptiness, the chair, and listening to shrieky Diamanda as I tapped, tapped, tapped into my phone.

But something was different now.

From within the supposed inertia idling inside of me, I could feel some kind of mobility, a species of difficult-to-map energy.

I found myself filled with Brownian motion, if you will.

This Motion first expressed itself as a slight nausea, and a desire for sleep more powerful than any irritation over my entropic work ethic. My tiny breasts grew plumper, and then sore. My cheeks turned full and springy to the touch. My hair grew lustrous. I tasted metal on my tongue and became enraged by a constant craving for apples.

I went to CVS; peed on my stick.

I was pregnant.

*

Robert Brown did more than just discover Brownian motion. In 1833, he named the cell nucleus, drawing upon the Latin word *nuculeus*, which signifies the fertile "kernel" or "seed." I like to think that Brown's identification of Motion and his dubbing of the nucleus sprang from the same faith, which holds that even in the midst of seeming nothingness there exists secret, potential life. In any case, Brown spent the rest of *his* life dining out on these achievements. He died in London's Soho in 1858.

Scientists could not determine the significance of Brownian motion for a long time. It appeared to them incomprehensible, without pattern or source, like life itself can seem sometimes. Seventy-eight years would have to pass in the wake of Brown's revelation before we could understand it.

In 1905, Albert Einstein took up Brown's observation. Being Einstein, he quickly understood that the ghost of Peter Good had not been responsible for shocking Australian moss spores into so much confusion under the Leitz lens in 1827. Rather, Einstein determined that water molecules surrounding the spores had impelled the seemingly trackless movement Brown detected.

Einstein, however, was of Brown's same cast of mind, because he also had an appetite for discovering the Something that existed within apparent zilch. Einstein studied the anarchic bombardments of atoms that characterize Brownian motion and developed an exquisitely complicated theorem for predicting the particles' travel patterns. Fast forward a little over a century, and we find Brownian motion used to prophesize a host of eternal returns, such as the life cycles of fractals, the gravitational whirligigging of black holes, and, more importantly from Xōchitl's point of view, the seasons of the stock market and the hidden richness of human mortality, which—to paraphrase Robert Brown—"will always be found to exist."

*

My son Mauricio does not care about Brownian motion or Toba Khedoori. Mauricio has wide brown eyes and looks a great deal like his absconded father, Brandon. He wriggles on his blanket, a wild life-force of soft skin and screams. Mauricio loves his nanny and me. My son also likes bananas and to look at birds.

Mauricio is already full of everything.

It is my job not to fill him with me.

So I do not whisper my secrets in his ear when I bathe him or put him down for sleep. I only want him to feel happy and well fed.

I do not say, *I was selfish with Xōchitl and that's why she left me. I wish I could do it over again. I love her indestructibly every single day.*

A person must be raised with some emptiness that they can fill themselves or leave as is. That is, they must be raised in freedom.

*

Three years after Toba Khedoori won the MacArthur, she broke style. She began to paint smaller canvases and filled them in nearly or entirely.

Untitled (Clouds) (2005) holds a gray-and-white thundercloud that takes up two-thirds of the paper. *Untitled (black squares)* (2011–12) bears a multitude of tiny mother-of-pearl-hued squares, like a pixilation, or fine bathroom tile. A winter woodland occupies the entirety of *Untitled (branches I)* (2011–12), and a leafy branch crowds *Untitled (leaves/branches)* (2011–12).

One might imagine that spiritually modified crops grew suddenly in her work. Khedoori spent the first two decades of her career floating in outer space, only to return to earth with a harvest of country walks and technological strangeness.

The whole time she had been painting the void, had she secretly planted nuclei in her margins? Those vibrating kernels and seeds? Or had she only discovered them later, when she realized that her early style was dead?

*

When I decided that I would have a child, I became incredibly organized. I signed on for permanent employment at Snapchat, paid my bills, and moved into a larger apartment in Glendale. I abandoned *Texit* completely and started writing well-researched memos for my supervisors at Snapchat, where I labor in Santa Monica, not counting the year when I "worked from home" in order to avoid the plague. The memos are not poetic. I write them like a robot would, that is, a robot manufactured in the 1980s and not one of those empathetic robots that star in movies today. The memos detail market share and how to optimally capitalize on Snapchat's proprietary geofilters and paintbrush tool. The loss of my identity and my new raving cleanliness inspired me to throw away a lot of my belongings, a lot of shoes. I also trashed all of Xōchitl's clothes that I had stolen, and, tragically, a lot of my vintage porn.

When Mauricio turned one, I decided to relieve myself of the burden of my artistic history. I would delete the thousands of words that cluttered up my phone and laptop storage and in so doing psychologically close the circle, as it were.

Writing is easy to give up. The longer you stop writing, the more your essays seem ridiculous and badly made. You remember yourself sweating over your computer while crafting dialogue or refining grammar. You reflect on how the whole time you had been engaged in that costive process other people had knit sweaters, gone out to dinner, watched movies, and experienced satisfying fornication with humans other than themselves. Your narratives, moreover, which once seemed so originally profound, reveal themselves as barely dissimilar variants of potboilers that have been written by millions of wretches for the past few centuries.

Writing is also hard to give up. I could not just click on files and *delete all*. I had to see if my ideas were indeed so predictable and derivative. While the baby wailed, I opened up my YouTube essay on Joseph Beuys, my incandescent emails about Sanja Iveković, and my laughable screeds on the enviable child freedom of Jean Genet. I blinked into the wintergreen glow of my EliteBook, studying my rantings on colonialism and the art market industrial complex. I noticed my tendency toward the breathless run-on and the clingy semicolon. I perceived the thesaurus's deep influence. I clicked through, quickly at first, then with more patience, remembering with fondness how these efforts had carved some order out of the randomness of my Xōchitless life.

I printed out all of my essays, spread them out on my bed, and tried to see them with the ruthless eyes of an editor. I read them twice. I read them again.

Then I took out a pencil, and began to correct them.

CHAPTER TWENTY-NINE MAKE SOME-THING OUT OF IT

[August 21, 2022, Facebook posting of Claude Cahun's *Untitled* (1928) and *Untitled* (1928).]

The day after my father died I stood in the bedroom of his apartment and put on his XL yellow cotton sweater, and then stared at myself in the full-length mirror attached to the door of his bedroom. Throughout his fifties and sixties, Eddie Ruiz had worn an XL, though he stood only 5'9", as he had thrived at over 230 pounds before his symptoms hit. He built up his noble size working as an automotive service technician at Burbank Auto Tech for thirty years, and at Koreatown's Excel Auto Shop for twenty-three years before that. The mechanic's days shift between bouts of sedentary technical work executed with diagnostic computers and episodes of grappling with impact wrenches and tooth ratchets. From the resulting lack of aerobic exercise and periodic muscular stress, my father's body had blossomed into a round, hardened torso balanced upon two slender legs made half-hairless by the constant rubbing of his men's socks. Whenever he wore the yellow sweater, then, he resembled a Latino version of Belvoir Castle's giddily restored golden portrait of Henry VIII, which shows the king wearing a resplendent citron doublet, and echoes the lavish style of Hans Holbein the Younger.

Dad took care to present a clean and neat appearance outside of the garage. With his tortoiseshell spectacles and tweed caps, the latter of which covered his bald spot, he even tended toward the dapper. The XL yellow cotton sweater came originally from Nordstrom, but I had bought it for him on eBay six years before his death. He wore it when I came over for our weekly Friday dinners. He would sit at his black-painted oak dining-room table, glowing like a daffodil while swiftly eating the easy Bon Appétit pan-Asian stir-fry that I cooked him in his small kitchen. I had given him the sweater for Christmas in 2010, along with a box of butter cookies and a subscription to the *Atlantic Monthly*, the last of which was a pedantic mistake that I regretted later except that it gave me something to read on the evenings I stayed overnight.

When I offered him the sweater that Christmas morning, he had tugged it over his head immediately upon tearing it from its shining green wrapping. His brawny trapezius muscles stretched out the cotton weave and his stomach strained the garment at its waist. The sweater adhered snugly to his copious belly in a fetching way, which he modeled laughingly by the decorated pine tree as I took his photograph with my phone. Back in '10, there were no signs of the blood disease that would later shrink my father so effectively that he weighed only twenty more pounds than I did. As his doctors later told us, however, his hemoglobin began to deviate from its cyclically efficient production schedule as early as 2007. By 2016, he found himself captive at the Norris Cancer Center, eventually unable to remember the words not only for Nordstrom and sweater, but also for Christmas and tooth ratchet and yellow and me.

On December 24, at 1:34 in the afternoon, my father died of multiple myeloma on Norris's third floor, room 311. Multiple myeloma is a blood cancer. As a consequence of his obstreperous outward denials of personal vulnerability, Dad did not visit a physician to get a blood panel until two months before his demise. Such a test would have revealed the drop in his red-cell count years before he first showed signs of illness. Medical professionals respond to these declines with alacrity and would have likely treated his condition with a bone marrow transplant. Such a protocol provides no guarantees, but does allow the patient a slight chance of survival.

Apparently my father had been noticing for the past two years his decreasing capacity to haul semi-truck Michelins and tighten lug nuts. But he had shouldered these warnings quietly, discerning in them the signs of our family's seemingly inescapable fate—we came from a line of ancestors extinguished early from car accidents, from breast cancer, from alcoholism, and, as in the case of my barely remembered mother, from drug overdose.

On December 25, twenty-three hours after the doctor pronounced him, I gazed silently at my father's vacant apartment. As I have mentioned, I entered his personal quarters. The bedroom had a beige wall-to-wall rug and a queen-size bed covered with a brown-and-orange quilt purchased in the 1990s from a Burbank garage sale. His closet featured rolling doors, painted white, which hid a small collection of jeans and flannel shirts, along with a neat row of sneakers, work boots, and cowboy boots. By the east wall stood a small walnut dresser with five drawers that contained his underwear, socks, white T-shirts, and three pastel sweaters. The sweaters huddled together inside the second top drawer. I turned from my father's bed toward the dresser, opened the second drawer, and selected the yellow sweater. I slipped it over my head. I moved over to the bedroom's door, which bore the full-length mirror on its interior side. I closed the door. I sat on the ground, cross-legged, and stared at myself in the glass.

The mirror returned to me the spectacle of my strange, shattered face and my flattened hair. I examined the lineaments of the sweater billowing around me, noting how the radiant curves of the cotton resembled the vividly restored crimson drapery of Peter Paul Rubens's 1612 *The Entombment*. That picture is famous for Rubens's rendering of the intricate, though now heavily repainted, folds of a red robe worn by an Apostle who carries Christ's pallid body to its grave.

I glared at myself within the swirl of my father's huge clothing. And then, without quite understanding the significance of the gesture, I snapped a self-portrait. I did so by blinking my eyes shut and opening them back up, like the lens of a camera.

I am a forty-two-year-old Chicana artist, what one might call *una Conceptualista*. I do not paint like Hans Holbein the Younger or Peter Paul Rubens. Instead, I make odd films and race around cities yelling protest anthems. I have made art about rape culture, a controlling Bulgarian curator, the collapse of a six-year romance, the gender binary, and the racial panopticon. I have staged plays and cut myself while singing opera and fan-dancing. Before large audiences, I have disclosed the particulars of my orgasms, my intersectional Latinx queerness, my body confidence, my girlfriend Xōchitl's ice-hearted rejection of me, and my terrors of becoming an older woman within a misogynistic capitalist culture. For more than twenty years, I have relished transforming my personal pain into a discourse that I hope will enliven and not destroy the sensibilities of my audience. My maintenance of art's delicate balances, which finds me ricocheting between shock and uplift, translates my life into a renewably consumable object whose manufacture gives me a reason to persist. All of this is to say that I am a working, autocritical cultural producer and not a raving madwoman, because I have learned how to strike a bargain between truth and beauty.

I have never been able, however, to negotiate my father's death. The bitter facts of his disappearance measure to such a weight that they tip the scales of aesthetics into a landslide. Though it would be wonderful if I could trap my memories of my father into a bound and finished artifact, I have proven incapable of making art about what happened in Norris Cancer Hospital's Room 311 in December of 2016.

Taking that "photograph" of myself with my shuttering eyes was the closest I ever got.

*

In 1928, the thirty-four-year-old artist Claude Cahun memorialized her father's death by shaving her head, pulling on a man's corduroy suit, and sitting for an allusive self-portrait photograph shot by her lover, Marcel Moore, née Suzanne Malherbe. Cahun's father was the renowned and stylish French-Jewish journalist Maurice Schwob, who had taken a stance against the Dreyfus affair as the editor of the daily Nantes newspaper, *Le Phare de la Loire*. Though historians of Dreyfus defenses rank first in importance Émile Zola's *J'Accuse*, written for *Le Figaro*, scholars have documented rapturously how Schwob wrote such stinging governmental indictments that Cahun, then a child called Lucy, suffered sufficiently violent reprisals from her school classmates that her minders whisked her to a facility in England.

Very little information about Schwob and Cahun's relationship exists in the archives, whose offerings mainly survive in the form of bare dates, ambiguous writings, and photographs. We do know that Schwob's empathy for the despised did not, at first, extend perfectly to his daughter. He disapproved of her passion for Marcel/Suzanne, which had first kindled into a roaring flame at the enthusiastic age of fourteen. After an initial awkward period spent berating Cahun for her Sapphism as well as for her desire to become a writer, Schwob acceded after she grew ill and pale from grief. Schwob, a divorcé who curiously married Marcel's own mother in 1917 when Cahun was twenty-one years of age, entrusted his daughter to her stepsister. The girls thereafter nourished each other with their mutual love and grew into brave and passionate women who left Nantes to storm the artistic citadel of Paris in 1918.

While Schwob toiled in Nantes, Cahun and Moore became part of the luminous circle of surrealists—André Breton, Lise Deharme, Paul Éluard—and began to invent conceptualism. They did so by writing dense and confusing poetry, as well as shooting multiple photographs of Cahun, which displayed her inhabitation of multiple characters. These autofictional photographs, which are largely untitled, now form the heart of Cahun's fame. Cahun and Moore's first experiments show Cahun revealed as a golden Buddha (1920), as a lipsticked bodybuilder wearing a T-shirt that reads *I Am in Training Don't Kiss Me* (1927), as the letters *C* and *M* (1928), and as a scarred mime holding a mirrored ball (1927). These images remain as exciting and fresh as the day they were first developed, as they waged battle against the surrealists' and the larger world's homophobia with their celebrations of queer identity.

Schwob himself was no stranger to auto-portraiture, and since every self-portrait is an idealized and *ergo* fictionalized representation, he may qualify as the first person to have revealed to Cahun and Moore the protean force of this art form.

Schwob engineered a famous image of himself, which he produced in 1917. In the photograph, he sits in full profile, wearing a luxurious suit made of black corduroy or wool. The suit has a high collar. Schwob's head is shaved, and his clear-cut profile, with its generous nose and solid chin, reflects light gliding into the room from a nearby window. His left hand crosses over his right arm, and he tucks his fingers beneath his elbow. His eyes appear amused and kind. He bears a suggestion of a smile. The photograph glows with an intense chiaroscuro, its light edges picking out the delicate folds of the suit's fabric. Schwob's neck is sturdy and thick; his stomach expands toward the border of the photograph.

In 1928, Claude Cahun coped with her complicated sorrow at Schwob's passing by replicating this image down to its smallest detail.

*

In the last few weeks of my father's life, he received inpatient care at the USC Norris Comprehensive Cancer Center. Norris sits on the health sciences campus of the University of Southern California, close to downtown Los Angeles. His single room had been painted bright white and featured a small dormant television affixed to the wall opposite his narrow white bed. He lay on the bed without his glasses on. The room also possessed a small window that looked out onto a beige section of the USC campus. A rolling

IV attached to a machine that monitored his vital signs stood next to him. Various pipes and tubes connected to his left arm, which stuck out naked from under his blue-and-white checked hospital gown.

My father's bald head gleamed against his pillow, glittering with sweat. He had tilted brown eyes and a deep dimple in his chin. He looked at me in a hazy way, either from the drugs or because he had gone blind suddenly in one eye, his left eye. He made no elegiac mentions of my mother or of his long career in the automotive industry. He also refrained from complaining about my childlessly romantic predispositions, which he had exploded over periodically during the decades after I had come out to him as an artist and also as bi.

Instead, on the second day of his hospital stay, he reported that he could see the sixteenth-century court of Henry VIII in his blind eye, and me with his right eye. He also hallucinated eating and would move his hand from his chest up to his open mouth, as if he held a forkful of pan-Asian stir-fry. A few nights later, he explained that, while the physical book was not in his possession, in another dimension he was rereading Ernest Hemingway's novel *The Old Man and the Sea*, which he had first encountered when he was sixteen years old in Mexico.

"I forgot I even read it until just right now," he said.

The gentle and harried nurses would bustle into the room and wash his body with very light swipes of a sponge. Once, a blue-eyed RN with a floral tattoo on her neck prayed by his bedside while we silently abided her generosity. Both of us found this ritual exceptionally unnerving but could not bring ourselves to request that she stop.

My father's mental fog cleared with increasing rarity, and I had trouble attracting the attention of his sighted eye, the one that did not witness the cinquecento intrigues of Henry VIII's court. For the duration of his hospital stay, I wore elastic pink and black yoga clothes, which allowed me to clench my body into a fetal position while listening to his historical peregrinations. I curled up tightly in a greenish-beige leatherette chair that an orderly had placed close to him, and grasped his bed's metal railings. I would sometimes rest my forehead against my hands, pressing my cheek against the guardrails' cool steel. My father stared ahead and discussed with me how the miracle of his seeing the apostate Henry VIII and the argumentative Catholic Sir Thomas More in his blind eye meant that life did not end at death, and that he was either experiencing a previous existence or an anachronistic future career in interfaith arbitration that he would enjoy in heaven. I refrained from explaining that he was not witnessing the afterlife, but rather, that the Gothic establishing shots and codpieced costumes he observed in his blind eye were phantom reruns of the 1960 Columbia Pictures Saint Thomas biopic *A Man for All Seasons,* which we had watched together last summer on PBS.

Sometimes, though, he would stop talking about Henry VIII or Hemingway and focus on me in a manner that indicated a fresh lucidity. He would smile and shake his head.

"It's OK, Amanda," he'd say. "It's natural."

"Dad," I'd reply. Or, "Daddy."

Multiple myeloma kills its sufferers in a particularly cruel way, and if I am to write about my father's death I must spare you the details, and if I do not write the details, I cannot write about his death. I *can* provoke you with abstractions that hint at an MM patient's subsidence of dignity and consequent juddering panics. I could go into more specifics about how I will always be grateful to the producers of PBS for providing my father faith in providence while he suffered *in extremis.* I could also recount the antics of the stubby-legged, dark-haired, fun-loving male nurse whom I had to flirt with like a prostitute so that he would come back from his interminable "coffee breaks" and give my father morphine. I can say very plainly that the disease kills by the formation of cancer cells in the bone marrow. I could also mention that multiple myeloma possesses the alternative name of "Kahler's disease," as it was first documented by Dr. Otto Kahler, an Austrian physician who in 1889, in Prague, treated one Dr. Loos for fatigue and fractures.

But I cannot write about what actually happened to my father, Eddie Ruiz, during the last weeks of his life in December 2016. That event remains incommunicable except through strategies of candor that I fear would annihilate the reader's mind, or worse, be converted into a thrilling medical tell-all that people would read on planes or in bank queues (certainly not in hospital waiting rooms) in order to pass the time. Truly describing my father's death would lead to the quandary described by God in the book of Exodus, when he explained to Moses that "no one shall see me and live." God, like me, was a neurotic creative who understood that the inexorable truths of life and death could only very rarely be recited and still qualify as an artwork. Instead, such description would most likely exist as an obscenity and an act of soul-threatening treachery.

Because of the destruction that the truth wields upon art, most artists do not possess the mental strength required for reflecting the insuperabilities of human fate in their work. Toni Morrison once, in the great 1987 novel *Beloved,* grew close to reaching the sublime horror that exists at the juncture of truth and art, but at the last moment she deflected by distracting her readers with stark depiction and a ravishing use of color. Sylvia Plath expressed her own pain in poetry that occasionally used naked words, but her brutal talent did not protect her from self-slaughter. Franz Kafka explained how all human effort is meaningless and people are mere pawns in an absurd world order, but, even then, he left us with unfinished texts.

In my estimation, the New York photographer David Wojnarowicz reigns supreme of all the artists in the world who have dared to show the truth about human existence, namely through his 1987 photograph of his dead lover Peter Hujar. This black-and-white untitled image shows Hujar's expressive remains and transfixes the viewer with abject minutiae such as the droop of Hujar's lip and the downward tug of his eyelid. In so exposing his beloved, Wojnarowicz committed the dangerous act of offering Hujar's defenselessness to a hating world that would not yet admit that HIV was a human disease and not a "gay cancer." Wojnarowicz did pay for his valor, however. He grew into a controversial figure censored by the Smithsonian and castigated by Congressmen John Boehner and Eric Cantor. But Wojnarowicz may have also undergone a different type of penalty—perhaps, at certain moments of self-doubt, he feared that he betrayed Hujar in Hujar's most necessary moment of privacy. Hujar's dear body, awful in its disintegration, was forced to become something else than the everything it must have represented to Wojnarowicz. Wojnarowicz took the photograph of Hujar, published it, and then lost control of it as his lover's ransacked face spoke to some people very clearly about a kind of state-approved genocide, but for others simply counted among billions of other bibelots that are tagged for capitalists' consumption.

Wojnarowicz finds a defense to making Hujar "into something public" (to borrow from his 1989 essay "Postcards from America: X-Rays from Hell") in his bearing witness to HIV/AIDS during an era when Ronald Reagan would not even utter the words in mixed company. Wojnarowicz's gesture "serve[s] as another powerful dismantling tool," he wrote. But there are other deaths, what Simone de Beauvoir once described ironically as "very easy deaths," such as the demises of elderly people who succumb to heart disease or aneurism, osteoporosis or blood cancer, which do not carry such an exigency. Each person who so dies possesses the same story, which if actually transmitted to the art world would so gall critics, curators, collectors, and gallerists with the ferocity of the death process that it would not "dismantle" hegemony but only the artist's career. At the same time, if a narrator told the tale of a true human death, she would commit a perfidy upon the dead person, who cannot consent to having their infinite torment transformed into an *objet*, because consent is an ever-refreshable contract that may be signed only by a living person who may yet change their mind.

Consequently, most working artists, that is, those fabricators who cherish their livelihoods and sometimes even their relationships, convey half-truths about life and death while resorting to the same elegant indirections that Claude Cahun would rely upon when she imitated her father's 1917 self-portrait. In this way, they avoid the ethical risks run by David Wojnarowicz. Using beauty, fiction, abstraction, suggestion, myth, erasure, incompleteness, and autobiography, they avoid disclosing the intimate evidence of a dying person's agony. Yet, in withholding those facts, they transform human loss into a withstandable metonym that merchants may consign to consumers via market delivery systems.

That is, they make that person's death into something that it is not.

*

When Claude Cahun posed for her 1928 portrait, she mimed the content and style of her father's 1917 image. Color processing remained an exotic medium in the 1920s, used only by sophisticated first adopters of the technology. Cahun either did not employ it on account of its inaccessibility or because of the severity of her aesthetics. The resulting gelatin silver prints transfix us with their radiances of grays, inky darks, creams, and gleaming pearl shades. We know that Marcel Moore sat behind the camera during these sittings, of which Cahun scholars have estimated that there were two.

In the first image, Cahun sits in profile, her right side revealed to the viewer. The image is an upper-body shot. It reveals Cahun's face, shoulder, and the tips of her left fingers, which reach around to grasp her right arm in a gesture identical to her father's. The high collar of her man's suit grazes the base of her skull and her jawline. Cahun's shorn hair bristles to a half-inch length and shines with white or pale-yellow dye, possibly mimicking her father's signature baldness. Light flows in through a window, brightening Cahun's blandly unsmiling face and rendering the texture of her jacket visible. Her suit is made of fine pincord corduroy, and the intaglio of the fabric creates a geometric effect that well answers the gauziness of the light. The suit envelops Cahun's frame, and critics such as Angela Woodlee argue that the clothing Cahun wears in the portraits is the same as that worn by her father in his 1917 likeness.

The second image is a full-body shot. It discloses Cahun with a shaved head, sitting on the ground cross-legged. She wears the same corduroy suit. The picture's backdrop, which in the previous version only appeared as a dark shadow, is now broadcast as a sheet hung against a wall. This photograph shows a more intensely disconsolate Cahun: though her facial expression differs from the previous replica's by only a thread's breadth—a very slightly turned-down lip, a downcast eye just perceptibly more shadowed—it conveys to viewers a woman who has entered the deeper waters of grief. Her naked skull increases the sense of vulnerability. Whereas her father's nude head conveyed solidity in his 1917 *retrato*, the pencil-line lineaments of her parietal bones recall those of sleeping infants. The effect proves so moving that the viewer finds herself motivated to protect Cahun from her anguish.

This custodial arrogance on the part of the audience is itself quite interesting, because Cahun's display of fragility conceals a character stalwart enough that she would later fearlessly combat and sabotage the Nazis. Only when I researched Cahun's fortitude, habits of activism, liberationist dressing, and her difficult parental dynamics, did I realize that Cahun remained in control of her gifts even at these lowest moments of orphaning. Cahun and Moore's *Untitled* (1928) and *Untitled* (1928) may be heirlooms of wild daughter-love, but this passion has been sourced, framed, staged, captured, and printed with the cool premeditation that fine art requires.

Cahun's measured transformation of her father's loss constituted a betrayal of Maurice Schwob, because it found her calculating his deterioration instead of purely feeling it. The unfiltered afflictions that she once knew as Lucy, and the undocumented panic that she experienced upon witnessing her father's corpse, transmute into an icon as deftly manipulated as the retouched Holbein Henry or the refurbished Rubens Christ.

Still, no other real option existed for the artist. If Cahun had laid down and wept upon the floor, Marcel Moore probably would not have photographed this display of emotion. Cahun had to cut faith with her father in order to convert his death into a conceptualist masterpiece.

*

"I see castles and knights on horses," my father said, staring at me. "It's wonderful."

I looked into his left eye, his blind eye.

I did not see Thomas Cromwell plotting or the greensward of England.

I saw something that I cannot talk or write about.

*

As I describe my father, I can feel myself fictionalizing. He was not always the greatest person. But I will draw a line through that. I want to depict him as the Hans Holbein acolyte and centuries of avid restorers have illustrated Henry VIII—with precious indigo and superfluous gold paint.

*

Claude Cahun made a masterpiece out of her father's death, though her motivation for doing so remains the subject of speculation. Based on my own frantic personal experience, I think that she re-created him in order to "make something out if it." Such is the way of artists. If artists could not "make something out of it," then they would go completely crazy. For example, Simone de Beauvoir did not want to get institutionalized after her mother, Françoise Brasseur, died of cancer in 1963, and so she sketched the last six weeks of Brasseur's life in her gracefully minimalist *A Very Easy Death* (1964), which helped earn her the Jerusalem Prize in 1975 and the Austrian State Prize for European Literature in 1978.

Similarly, Ernest Hemingway feared correctly that his father's suicide would someday lure him into madness. He defended himself against that atrocity by creating the oedipal Robert Jordan in *For Whom the Bell Tolls* (1940), which helped pave his road to *The Old Man and the Sea* (1952) and the 1954 Nobel Prize.

Cahun also guarded against clinical depression with the creation of the 1928 portraits, but did not win such accolades as de Beauvoir and Hemingway enjoyed until after she died. In the 1920s, she and Moore became respected but marginal figures in Paris's surrealist circles. Later, the Gestapo destroyed most of their work when the Nazis invaded the Isle of Jersey, where Cahun and Moore had set up a household. Cahun's health deteriorated during World War II, when she and Moore were imprisoned separately for vandalizing the German army's barracks through ingenious conceptualist stratagems that bore the influence of Schwob's unstinting stance during the Dreyfus affair. Cahun, despairing over a German victory and her mistaken fears that Moore had already gone to her quietus, tried to kill herself in her cell several times. Even after the Allies liberated her and Moore, her health never recovered, and she died on Jersey in 1954. Marcel Moore endured until 1972.

Cahun's portraits, however, live on. In the 1990s she and Moore emerged from the shadows of history to become recognized as two of the most talented artists of midcentury Europe. The writer and curator François Leperlier initiated contemporary Cahun studies with his landmark 1992 publication of *Claude Cahun: L'écart et la metamorphose*. Yale University has acquired a cache of Cahun papers, and the Metropolitan Museum of Art purchased a Cahun/Moore gelatin silver print of a priapic puppet called *Le Père*. Cahun and Moore have also been collected or shown at arts institutions such as the Getty Museum and the Los Angeles Museum of the Holocaust.

The two 1928 portraits, in particular, enjoy a flourishing afterlife. The originals reside in dust-free archives located in the Jersey Heritage Trust on Jersey Isle, to which Cahun scholars make regular pilgrimages. A glamorous, platinum-haired UC Santa Barbara professor named Dr. Abigail Solomon-Godeau and an untraceable British expert named Roger Pilgrim have researched intently the two photographs' dates and conditions of making. Angela Woodlee, who wrote a dissertation on Cahun at the University of Georgia and now works at Christie's, has theorized that the portraits express Cahun's interests in Jewish identity and vampirism. The pictures also irradiate the web, where Pinterest pinners and Instagram aficionados post them so that their followers will know that they care about trans people, art, and women.

After having marched through almost six years of unproductive grief over my father, it is difficult for me to witness the fruits of Cahun's merciless art practice and remain untempted by it.

*

He died. I went to his house. I stood in his bedroom. I slipped on his yellow sweater. I closed the bedroom door. I sat on the floor. He was dead. I looked at myself in the mirror.

The glass enclosed me in the same borders as would a picture frame. The sweater swirled around my small-breasted torso, mimicking the riverine folds found in Baroque religious painting. When my father was alive, it had stretched out on his body like the girdle of Henry VIII, challenged by the girth created by rigorous wrenchwork and sedentary engine diagnostics. Now the sweater bagged so much that its neckhole fell over my left shoulder, revealing the pink spandex strap of my yoga top. The yellow cotton smelled of turmeric from the easy pan-Asian dinners I'd made, as well as the ineradicable motor oil that always graced the tips of Dad's rough fingers.

I stared at my own face. Like my father, my eyes are tilted and I have a dimple in my chin. But the skin around my eyes had faded into paperwhite, while the area around my mouth flushed hot fuchsia. I was thirty-six years old. I could see slender dents forming around my lips.

I closed my eyes and snapped my self-portrait. I still have the picture. The picture is also of Dad. If I print out that superimposed image in a story I will feel the discipline of artmaking strengthen me while it distances me from him. And what I will remember of his life and its ending will escape the heroism practiced by David Wojnarowicz, who insisted that we all see

Peter Hujar and somehow continue to live. Instead, my work will varnish my father's departure, like the too-bright touches of the restorer's brush alter the colors of Hans Holbein's Henry VIII and Rubens's *The Entombment*. Dad's death will shape-shift, like Cahun's self-portraits enlarge from the stents of Pinterest interpretations and Angela Woodlee's theories about vampirism. What I recall now and can't write down will be made surreal by word choice, by editing, by my father's dreams of Hemingway and Tudor knights, by the fiction that will be put down half-read, by my act of betrayal and its vanishing point of hope, and I will create the art that can only exist when you refuse to say what really happened.

History

Wednesday, May 3, 2023
4:15 PM Publishing creative nonfiction how
Friday, May 19, 2023
5:43 PM Three year old males energy levels how much
abnormal
6:19 PM Bad mothering would be defined as
Thursday, June 1, 2023
8:14 AM Marisa Merz why so successful
Wednesday, June 7, 2023
3:28 AM Sleep tips sleep drugs female mother
5:14 AM Can you take sleep drugs with three-year-old
6:17 AM Octahedrons what are they
Thursday, June 29, 2023
7:13 AM Literary journal what ones where
9:56 AM Literary journals pay?
5:14 PM Cimarron review
6:41 PM Paris Review
8:36 PM Santa Monica Review

CHAPTER THIRTY ARTE POVERA

[The *Santa Monica Review* does not publish its essays online.]

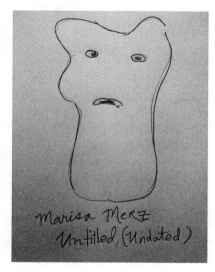

Marisa Merz
Untitled (Undated)

Multitasking Tuna

"Stop writing," my son Mauricio says.

We're in the kitchen, at our house in Glendale. It's April, Saturday. It's raining. Mauricio sits on a pillow/booster seat in our eating nook. He is massive at 37 pounds. His head bears the shape of a musk melon. His crazy eyes beam deadly gamma rays at me. It's a family resemblance. My hair detonates from my skull in a dark-brown puff and I have a caffeinated gaze, which resembles @pumpkintheracoon's when I look at Mauricio and a Rottweiler's when I look at anybody else.

"I'm not writing," I say. I am preparing us lunch at the kitchen island, which is cluttered with tuna fish cans, fruits and vegetables, a copy of *The Handbook of Clay Science*, an old iPad displaying a movie about emotional ponies, and a marketing report composed only of the title *NBC/Snap Celebrity Optimization in the Twilight of Authenticity Culture*. I'm not really cooking, though. I'm hunched over, mushing my thumbs into my iPhone. *Marsa messiah was a famous moth ant*. There's yogurt on the phone. "I'm just doing something for a second," I say.

"I'm hungry, Mama," Mauricio shouts.

"I'm making you lunch, just in a tiny second."

"No WRITING," Mauricio says.

"I'm not." I'm sweating hot under my armpits because spellcheck is an evil bourgeois morality system designed to destroy all literary creativity.

"Writing's bad," Mauricio says.

"Yes," I say.

"I hate writing," Mauricio says.

"Yeah, it's so gross." I eventually tap out the words *Marisa Merz was able to be a famous artist and a mother and not go crazy* into the Notes app on my phone.

Three-year-olds eat regular food, and with their own hands. This means that my own hands are now sometimes free. I can do anything with these free hands. I could use my hands to write a report on an incipient NBC-Universal/Snap merger that is due in two days to Francesca Maroni, my boss at Snapchat, Inc. Or, I could use my free hands to write an explosively creative nonfiction essay about an Italian sculptor named Marisa Merz. Or, I can use my hands to craft this tuna salad that my son and I will sit down and eat together.

"MAMA," my son shrieks wildly.

Yes! Yes! Yes!

Real tuna salad is made, not written about. The recipe requires opening a can of tuna-in-water and mashing it with whole fat yogurt, salt, and some herbs. If, like me, you are a working-mother-writer of color feeling *agida* because you're having trouble "fitting it all in," then you can replace your creative nonfiction work or horrible work-work with the equivocal satisfaction of tuna sculpture. This procedure mandates that you put down your iPhone and use those unencumbered hands to mash the tuna salad into the shape of, say, a mournful little cat-head, like *Untitled, Undated, 8*, an unfired clay figurine made in the 1980s by my would-be subject, Marisa Merz.

Tuna salad forms a good sculpture material. From my previous life as a full-time conceptual artist, I know that Chicken of the Sea possesses a smooth, pliable quality reminiscent of low-grade kaolinite clay, a material used commonly in the plastic arts. Like "disordered" kaolinite that has absorbed too much moisture, however, tuna salad can turn soft and unstable.

If I over-yogurt it, as apparently I have today, the Marisa Merz tuna cat-head will not stay upright on the plate. I form the dairy-fish into dissolving ears and a drooping muzzle, and it hovers in a liminal state between art and a concave blob.

There's tuna in my hair. I prop up the mushy sculpture with a snapped celery stick. I realize that a metaphor lurks within the practice of stabilizing a collapsing Marisa Merz mutant tuna cat-head for my three-year-old son. I decide not to chase the analogy down. Instead, I do an art mulligan by scraping the imploded head off the plate with my fingers. While Mauricio begins to fist-bash the eating nook table like a violent political protester, I slide the iPad on the kitchen island with my elbow, and somehow maneuver it between my right wrist and my left forearm. I carry the iPad to him and he immediately stares at the ponies emoting on its shiny screen. Then I go back to the kitchen island and make an armature out of a peeled and cored apple. I put that in the center of the dish. After that, I layer the tuna over the apple.

My lunch is leftover tuna and watching Mauricio lay waste to my work. He eats with a fierce face, like a mobster killing something. As he chews lavishly, monstrously, his huge luminously beautiful brown eyes stare at me with unblinking focus. I reach over to his plate and eat some of the apple armature, which sits within the tuna-head like brains. Mauricio stops chewing and stretches out his arms, like Jesus at the Olympics.

"AAAAAAAHHHHHHHH!" he roars. "AAAAHHHHHHGGHGHGH-GH!" He smiles and starts laughing. He's guffawing like someone has just said something so originally and shockingly funny that they deserve two Webbys. His teeth gleam inside of his soft red mouth: white bone, thick life.

Marsa Mooz wuz gryt at mulitksking I type into my iPhone, laughing, too. *Marisa Meerkat told the truth with her art aka transcenended the Patrick praty patriarchy.*

That's my productivity for the day.

The Biography of Marisa Merz

Marisa Merz was able to be a famous artist and a mother and not go crazy. Marisa Merz was great at multitasking. Marisa Merz told the truth with her art, which is to say, she somehow transcended the patriarchy.

I, too, can not go crazy and be great at multitasking and truth stuff by writing the essay on artist-mother Marisa Merz that I could not write yesterday. By harnessing my own personal will-to-power, I have transformed myself from an impoverished full-time Conceptual Artist into a marketing executive-writer-mother. This means that if I do not get murdered by my workload, I will be even more amazing than single hyphenate Marisa Merz because I will qualify as a mind-blowing double hyphenate. All I have to do is budget my time. Yes, all I have to do is force myself to write my delicately lyrical arts essay now, at three o'clock in the morning, this Monday morning, a work morning.

Marisa Merz was born in Turin, Italy, in 1926, and died there in 2019. Her father worked as a mechanic in Turin's Fiat plant. When I did research on Marisa Merz way back in the grim days of 2016, and then, again, last week, I could find little other background information on Marisa Merz. I did dig up a few pictures illustrating breathless reviews of her shows. These photographs reveal that Marisa Merz had red cheeks, small brown eyes, and brown hair. She wore horn-rimmed glasses. She gravitated toward oversized patterned house dresses and pilling pastel cardigans. She was one of the most celebrated artists in the cosmos.

Superstar mother-conceptualist Marisa Merz did not get famous for a long time, and when she did, she hated it. Most of her personal data remains inaccessible for creative nonfiction writers because she abhorred talking to the press and ran away whenever reporters tried to interview her. Google research *does* reveal the detail that in 1960 she married another artist named Mario Merz. A researcher who types "Mario Merz" rather than "Marisa Merz" into Google will not have any trouble discovering a tremendous amount of biographical information about this manly sculptor.

Mario Merz became one of the most noted members of the Arte Povera generation, a group of primarily male midcentury Italian artists who made their names by using "poor materials," meaning whatever detritus they could find lying around. Members of the Arte Povera movement rebelled against the art world, capitalism, and primary caregiving. Mario Merz participated in this uprising by assembling igloos out of glass, putty, metal, and, once, an antelope's head. He also stacked newspapers and called the resulting arrangement "poor art." He hung motorcycles upside down on gallery walls and called that poor art, too. Everybody in the art world that Mario Merz critiqued through his art supported him by clapping loudly and calling him a visionary, like Leonardo da Vinci. Mario Merz pounded his hairy chest and agreed with their assessment. Perhaps Mario Merz's incredible self-confidence came not just from the fact that he was a nonhyphenate but also from his membership in a higher Turinese caste than Marisa Merz's: his father worked as an engineer at the Fiat plant, making the designs that Marisa's father would later build. This paternal status may explain some of

Mario's aesthetic braggadocio, as well as the structural sophistication of his igloos and the motorcycle levitation.

Marisa Merz's art does not, at first, impress viewers with its grandeur or engineering. She began making sculptures in her house at the same time that she birthed and began to raise her and Mario's infant daughter, Beatrice. While Mario ran around an applauding Europe constructing built environments out of animal parts and Ducatis, Marisa Merz stood in her Turin kitchen and made apple and banana purées for their baby, born in 1960. Marisa Merz first concocted sculptures out of household materials, though she did not use food like I did yesterday. She employed even weirder substances, like aluminum HVAC ducts that she pulled from her home vents. She made silver squidlike constructions out of the ducts and hung them from the kitchen ceiling, stooping beneath them as she stirred soup. She also grabbed hold of copper wires she found in the garage and knit unraveling booties out of them. She put on the booties and slid around the house in them as an art performance. She drew blurry dogs and awkward-looking angels with pencil and pastels on random pieces of paper. She mushed up fragments of nylon and stuck them in between joined steel toothpicks, so they looked like fishing flies manufactured in an insane asylum.

As Beatrice grew older, Marisa Merz began searching out other "poor" art supplies, and graduated eventually to working with cheap kaolinite clay, known in geological circles as "disordered kaolinite" because of its distressed atomic composition. Out of this fascinating substance she created her greatest works. Among these is the little unfired cat-head sculpture, *Untitled, Undated, 8*, which would become part of her epic collection of zoomorphic figurines.

Marisa Merz's use of disordered kaolinite clay to make bizarre animal sculptures was a kind of provocation. It added an unspoken feminist element to the practice of Arte Povera. While Mario used motorcycles and taxidermy to ask the question *Who's got two thumbs and is awesome?*, Marisa Merz's art looks like accessories made by a bonkers hedgewitch who has started to make effigies out of the dirt that surrounds her.

Marisa Merz's gendered deploy of Arte Povera signaled her rightful place on art's Mount Olympus. She now presides on that divine peak alongside other geniuses, like the anonymous, that is, female, creator of the hanging-breasted Venus of Willendorf, and the cubist Quilters of Gee's Bend, who all used simple materials to express racialized and gendered belief systems and thus changed the symbolic order of the world.

As I sit here on my futon writing about Marisa Merz while listening to my son thrash in his bed down the hall, I want to be her so bad. I am exhausted and typing things that need a lot of editing, but I would like to make something authentic like Marisa Merz did, and, like her, I would like to change the world with the revelations of my art.

I know that Marisa Merz achieved these miracles because she could think for herself.

Not Thinking for Myself

I am driving to work and trying to think for myself.

It's 8:45 AM pee S tee in Los Angeles. I am in my Prius driving on the 101. I am dictating this section of my creative nonfiction essay on Marissa Mertz into my iPhone which is seated on a little dock attached to my dashboard and infected with spellcheck that I don't know how to disable. No need to honk sir I see you I am heading west to 523 ocean front walk I can't tell if ways is working. I work in Santa Monica California which is Snapchat's HQ. Since early 2020 I have cognitively disassociated full time as a marketing associate for the perpetually failing social media unicorn Snapchat which is hilarious really because my life up to now has been devoted to creating art that is by nature unmarketable. In other words I have imposter syndrome which is funny because Snapchat is the home of authenticity culture quote unquote a dumb marketing thing that has to do with expressing feelings and emotions on your phone. My being a fraud though has paid off because my salary has now reached $75200 which I find incredible get out of my fucking way because I have spent most of my existence being basically literally personally poor. Not that I ever see any of my income since the money promptly vanishes into my son Marie Seo as soon as it is paid into my vanguard account. That's right I'm on your tail bro why don't you freaking my vanguard balance account currently is $1293.

I am trying to think for myself as I dictate this portion of my literary non fiction my God which I intend to submit someday to a literary journal like the Paris review or the cinnamon review no that's not how you spell it or the shit paragraph break

OK

What I have learned about being a writer while taking care of a toddler and working constantly is that you can be a fake executive I RL but a real artist inside your mind. Whereas in your former life you were a full time Latina conceptualist and insanely dedicated your entire life to art now you can't do that. So you remain an artist by trying to hold your ideas quietly in your head somewhere close to the front of your brain where you can't forget them even when you can't work on them. You hoard all of the ephemerally high concept aesthetic connections you've made in like a side pocket of your cerebral cortex while you commute or make tuna or write memos about your company's shitty NBC deal. Because you worry that you're actually going to become a non hyphenate I RL marketing executive if you're not making art all the time. Right? So you do try to do it all the time. But you can't do it all the time because you are completely always screwed. So what you do is you try to think about your art all the time which is a way of thinking for yourself like Marissa Mertz did when she made that unfired cat head out of Calendar I play no KAOL I and I T clay

I have a ten forty five with Francesca that I totally forgot about

The Art of the Misfit

At some point in the mid-1980s, before Marisa Merz achieved the blockbuster fame that gilds her name today, she purchased an inexpensive hunk of kaolinite clay from her local art supplier. She carried it to her home studio and placed it on her worktable, next to a tangle of copper wires. She clipped a few strands of the copper filaments with a pair of shears and wove them into a round armature. She began shaping the clay around the copper sphere with her small, hard hands.

It was early morning. Down the hall, Marisa Merz could hear her daughter Beatrice rustling her bedcovers as the dawn brightened the air. On the other side of the house, Merz's husband Mario called out plaintively for *una tazza di caffè*. Marisa Merz remained at her worktable for a few moments longer. She shaped the clay around the copper sphere by patting the kaolinite, wetting it, and denting it with her thick fingers.

"Mama," Beatrice demanded from her bedroom. The girl was now in her twenties but still lived at home. "Come here."

"Yes, yes, one second," Marisa Merz replied.

"Marisa, just a little cup," Mario shouted. Suddenly, there came a loud crashing sound from the kitchen.

"I'm going to make it, stop it," Marisa Merz yelled back.

Marisa Merz remained in her workspace, staring at the clay lump she'd built over the netting. She shoved it softly into the proto-form of a primordial cat-head. She thumbed two indentations into its upper "face" for eyes. She poked a finger lower down to create a little gasping mouth.

Marisa Merz then stepped back and glared at her work. She studied it for several intense seconds.

But could Marisa Merz concentrate on her project? Don't artists need to focus unilaterally and consistently on their ventures in order to bring them to any kind of fruition?

No, to the first question. To the second question: We hope not.

Marisa Merz's family kept clamoring for coffee and breakfast. Mario continued making an alarming banging sound in the kitchen. So Marisa Merz took hold of a rag and draped it over the semi-sculpture, in order that the clay would not dry out. She picked up the nascent cat-head and stored it beneath her worktable, to keep it safe. Marisa Merz washed her hands in a little basin propped up against a nearby wall, and walked out of her studio. She proceeded into the kitchen and began to make espresso for her husband and daughter.

The nearly made, dented-eyed and slack-jawed cat-head sat under its rag beneath the worktable. It waited for its creator to return. Outside, the early dawn expanded into bright daylight. All across the city, Turinese opened their doors and yelled greetings to their neighbors. Children began to play in the street. Cars puttered up and down the highways. The church-tower clock banged out seven times.

The cat-head stared into the darkness of its little shroud. Although by all appearances this creature remained protected, it was actually in great danger. All of its quivering atoms existed on the borders of becoming and unbecoming. At that moment no one could say whether the proto cat-head would develop into a true work of art titled *Untitled*. The clay lump seemed just as likely to be accidentally destroyed by exposure to water and return to the earth as so much wet dirt.

But Marisa Merz's lugubrious cat-head did not dissolve into abject failure, like the work of innumerable other women whose dead dreams haunt the pages of art history. It is difficult to formulate in human language an explanation for why mom-conceptualist Marisa Merz managed to finish not only the cat-head but also so many other pieces of catastrophic art that she'd eventually win the Venice Biennale's 2013 Golden Lion and enjoy a supernova 2017 Hammer Museum retrospective. We *could* suggest that Marisa Merz succeeded at making both art and a family because she was *a great female artist*, but we fear that no one will understand what we are saying. If we explain shruggingly that Marisa Merz could "have it all" because she was a GFA, it's likely that we'll only confuse our reader. In his effort to conceptualize the hyphenated ontology of Marisa Merz, he might make the classic mistake of putting breasts on Michelangelo or a vagina on Picasso.

No, the key to understanding Marisa Merz is not to reformulate the biology of Picasso or Michelangelo or to otherwise assimilate her into the overwhelmingly white male historical tradition of "genius."

Instead, one must realize that Marisa Merz's is the *art of the misfit*.

The misfit: Otherwise known as the *disadattata* in Italian, feminine, singular. From the sixteenth-century verb *disadattare*, which meant "to un-fit," or "to disorder."

While Italian dictionaries do not admit this specifically, we know that the feminine singular misfit is a woman and a mother who is also an artist. She might also have a couple of other jobs and possibly be a racial minority. The *disadattata* feels *unfit* because she raises her child while constructing sculptures that straddle the line separating cat-heads from crud-lumps. If she lived in Turin, she made her art while Mario Merz bashed around the kitchen in a pretense of making coffee for himself but was really just trying to get some attention. If she lives in Los Angeles, she "writes" while honk-ingly driving down the 101 or while hiding from her boss in her workplace bathroom, whose stalls can double as residency studios.

Marisa Merz may have appeared like a petit bourgeois third-grade gram-mar teacher on account of the cardigans, but look closely at her sculptures and paintings and you'll see all of her fits miss. She cobbled "poor materi-als" into weirdo felines, unusable fishing flies, fake squids, invisible dog-paintings, and useless shoes. Her work is "the real thing" because it threat-ens constantly to fall apart. This instability constitutes the secret to Marisa Merz's success. In her hands, Arte Povera was a metonym for the mother-artist who is by nature a misfit.

The poor material is me, Marisa Merz's art says.

The Literary Composition of Kaolinite Clay

The kaolinite clay that Marisa Merz used to sculpt her cat-head known as *Untitled, Undated, 8* is formed out of degraded feldspar, a milky-white stone that comprises 60 percent of the earth's visible rock formations.

The feldspar group includes the moonstone, which symbolizes love and hope, and labradorite, which is a stone of protection. When hope and pro-tection dissolve due to the unstoppable processes of the earth, they turn into a hydrous-layer aluminum silicate formed out of two plates. Kaolin-ite is known as a 1:1 clay because of this two-plate structure. The soil sur-vives as a compromise between one plate made out of silica tetrahedrons, which look like wee pyramids, and another knit out of alumina octahe-drons, which resemble jacks. The two layers hitch together in a struggle for cohesion. Inevitably, the octahedral plate reigns supreme, as it proves the more rigid. The octahedrons' merciless nature requires the flexible tetrahe-dral plate to scavenge for space by arduously tilting and rotating. The tetra-hedrons must embrace liminality as they discover themselves mired within existential insecurity.

While the tetrahedral layer certainly aspires to adapt to the demands of the octahedrons with flawless equanimity, sometimes mistakes are made. These errors take the form of what clay scientists call "misfits," which occur when the tetrahedral layer fails to conform to nature's pitiless imperialism, or, perhaps, the tetrahedrons have simply failed to work hard enough to obtain 1:1 equipoise with the octahedrons. The precise etiology of misfiture remains a mystery yet to be resolved. Scientific scans reveal only that when the 1:1 plates fit imperfectly, the vulnerable tetrahedrons can curl into peaks and valleys. Such peak-valleys create a mangled atomic appearance and general incoherence. The resulting low-grade clay is dubbed "disordered kaolinite" by geologists. Since disordered kaolinite's tetrahedral layer exists in a hyphenated state of adaptation, it suffers from a metaphysical dilemma native to the genus *disadattata*: it never knows whether it is expressing its authentic self by succumbing to the octahedrons or whether the octahedrons are crushing it beyond recognition.

Adding to disordered kaolinite's distress is the fact that some model-minority tetrahedrons do manage to fit into the 1:1 organization with a fair amount of aplomb. When nature's harsh laws allow, or, rather, when the triumphal tetrahedrons engage their Nietzschean will-to-power to connect successfully with the octahedrons, a unicorn kaolinite emerges: its plates adjust into a series of perfect stacks. Photomicrographs of the precious stacks reveal kaolinite crystals so beautifully organized that they resemble delicate papers bound along a seam.

On account of this likeness, these unhindered plates are known also as "books."

My Little Pony

Today is Friday. I am at work, supposedly laboring at my desk on my overdue memo to my boss Francesca about how to NBC-ishly fix Snapchat, Inc.'s secular market *disadattamento*, a chronic financial disorder brought on by the company's insistence on marketing itself as "authentic," i.e., dedicated to IRL friendships rather than the fake celebrity culture so profitably engineered by our rival, Instagram, Inc.

I am not writing my overdue memo, though. I am instead sitting here in a Snapchat, Inc., toilet stall trying to be like undisordered kaolinite by producing a perfect book or, at the very least, a piece of minimally maladjusted creative nonfiction that could maybe get published by the *Paris Review* or the *Cimarron Review*, etc.

However, my son is here. Mauricio's preschool is getting retrofitted for solar and babysitting did not come through. This means that instead of manufacturing the brief I owe Francesca, or writing furtively about Marisa Merz, I have spent the last two hours preventing Mauricio from destroying my mostly male colleagues' cubicles. When Mauricio began marauding around the office earlier in the day, Snapchat's frat of brogrammers began communicating to me that they hate children via slow blinking and the drawling out of rhetorical questions like *Like, is this really conducive?* That's when I brought Mauricio out to the lobby. I attempted to pacify him on the vestibule's expensive Afghani carpet by wrapping my limbs around his wriggling body in a frantic swaddling gesture. But that didn't work.

"MOM I'M NOT GOING TO," Mauricio yelled, running around.

"OK, just come here," I said, spread-eagled on the carpet.

"YOU'RE GOING TO DO IT," he yelled some more.

"Yes, I'm going to do it," I replied. I had no idea what he was talking about. "Just come give me a hug for a second."

Beyond a blue-and-white-striped shirt that tugs over his round belly, and silver sweatpants that swim around his stocky legs, today Mauricio wears a dented and ripping Stetson cowboy hat crafted out of two Vons paper bags and Elmer's glue. I constructed this chapeau for him last weekend after he demanded it while watching a cartoon on his iPad. This cartoon was the unspeakably bad yet wildly popular animated television show called *My Little Pony*, which stars a character called "Apple Jack." Apple Jack is an empathetic female orange-colored Earth pony from the South, possibly the Ozarks. Apple Jack wears a Stetson constantly. While maintaining this signature look, Apple Jack loves nothing more than to work the apple harvest at her humble home, Sweet Apple Acres. Nevertheless, one day Apple Jack grew tempted by the lure of fancy faraway Manehattan, the home of hashtaggedly celebrity unicorn ponies who force hayseed Earth ponies to undergo makeovers. Apple Jack learned quickly that she did not "fit in" with the unicorn ponies, and manifested her robust individualism by continuing to sport the Stetson and then racing back home.

When my son mandated that he, too, wear a Stetson because he also did not "fit in," I felt the heavy cold hand of fear rest itself briefly upon my heart. Mauricio is the sort of child who lovingly hugs strange brogrammers, but, as we have all learned this morning, he also has no problem demolishing their laptops using a combination of spittle and fists. I fear that, like his mother, Mauricio is doomed to discover that he is a poor material fated to submit to the hegemony of octahedral unicorn ponies from

Manehattan. I would prefer that he remain forever innocent of these painful spiritual dilemmas.

Still, I made him the hat.

At the moment, I myself am wearing a moonstone ring and three-dollar men's olive cargo shorts. Before, when I brought Mauricio out to the Snapchat lobby, he sprinted circles around my carcass while twisting up his face and roaring. I "took a moment for myself" by blinking up at the ceiling with a slightly dead feeling, while fluorescents beamed down on my face. The brogrammers passed back and forth above me, creating an eclipse or strobe effect as their heads obscured the light. I closed my eyes.

I had, all morning, tried to keep my art thoughts in my head, but I could now feel them leaking out onto the Afghani carpet along with my soul and will to live. I wondered if I'm a good mother and decided no. Then I started worrying about the NBC propaganda that I have to write Francesca before she fires me for my missed deadline. I felt an overwhelming confusion about how I'm supposed to be a great female artist when really I am just a Chicana-burnout who had collapsed in the Snapchat, Inc., lobby as if deceased. With some bitterness, I brooded on the fact that while Marisa Merz learned how to align her crystals into perfect books, my own personal opus remains a fustercluck of unpublishably spellchecked cursing stored in iPhone Notes.

"MAMAMAMAMMA," Mauricio bassooned.

I opened my eyes. My darling son stood astride me, his Stetson haloed by the fluorescents. His cheeks puffed briefly as if he had to make a doo. He crouched and hurled himself upon my stomach like a police officer making an illegal arrest.

I grasped his ravening, fruit-scented body to me in a muzzle-hug.

Then I lifted him into the air with my hands and my bare feet.

Mauricio hovered above me, flying like a unicorn pony. His Stetson fell off as he looked down at me. His eyes drilled into mine, with deep, almost insane eye-contact.

"I love you," he said.

I could feel my literal, physical heart unsnap, like an opened coin purse. It hurt.

That moment was better than anything in my life. Even art.

"I think you're OK too," I managed to say.

Fifteen minutes later, though, I slipped off to the bathroom and began writing these very pages in the last toilet stall of Snapchat's bathroom.

I think a brogrammer named Gunter is watching Mauricio.

I just heard something crash.

NBCU/SNAP Goals: Celebrity Influencer Optimization in the Twilight of Authenticity Culture

To: Francesca Maroni, VP of Marketing
From: Amanda Ruiz
Re: Snapchat/NBC merger
Date: June 18, 2023

Dear Francesca,

This memo will explain how Snapchat's continual nosedive in market share (our Q1 earnings report revealed yet another a loss of >$2.2B) will find itself soon reversed by our much-publicized $14.2B merger with NBCUniversal. Actually, this memo will offer talking points on how you can compellingly, if probably falsely, assure NBCU's flailing CEO Allan Ides that his plan to engulf our company will draw attractive famous humans to both brands and stave off our collective Yahoo-like corporate death.

NBCU's plummeting fortunes can be ascribed to the irretrievable desuetude of television generally, but Snapchat's enduringly incipient doom owes to its strenuously cultivated anticapitalist "authenticity culture." "Authenticity culture" signifies Snapchat's commitment to trafficking in unpurchasable experiences captured in unstaged and vanishing photographs that one trades lovingly with friends. Said commitment does not, at first, seem like a terrible business plan. After all, "authenticity culture" bears an impressive heritage, touching on landmarks as diverse as orange Earth ponies, the savage communication habits of toddlers, and the marvelous Arte Povera of the Turinese conceptualist Marisa Merz.

The connection between Snapchat, Inc.'s authenticity and this litany of seemingly unrelated iconoclasts may seem tenuous, but a deeper look reveals that Snapchat's corporate ideology belongs in this august company: For example, consider how Marisa Merz's disordered kaolinite cat-head sculpture, *Untitled, Undated, 8*, formed part of a twentieth-century Italian art movement whose members made art out of "poor materials." In creating work that existed in the liminal space between precious *objets* and trash, Arte Povera artists like Marisa Merz rebelled against soul-corroding markets and in that way "kept it real."

Similarly, Snapchat's authenticity culture resists capitalism's anti-humanity by marketing "poor materials." Authenticity culture's poor materials are made of a different sort of refuse than Arte Povera's: Snapchat's garbage is composed of the aforementioned gratis and thus unvalued IRL human relationships, such as those captured in the evanescing, badly shot selfies that our diminishing set of users send each other on our app.

The reason why Snapchat is finding itself constantly imploding is because the international community of social media consumers turns out to be deeply disinterested in poor materials like IRL friends. Rather, the whole world of humans seems to be obsessed solely with corporately owned celebrities and face filters that make users look like sexy cartoon dogs. Our main rival Instagram is openly evil, and so its directors have long understood this quirk of human nature: Back in the teens, former IG Emperor Kevin Systrom divested brilliantly from authenticity and purchased the fake but rich materials also known as fashionista @alexachung, dangerous wellness person @gwynethpaltrow, and blonde songstress @taylorswift. Today, The Gram also owns such supernovas as movie star/lifestyle guru @milliebobbybrown and the adorably huge-eyed nonhuman social media mogul known as @pumpkintheracoon.

Snapchat, on the other hand, is a late adopter of influencers, and so has been able to scavenge only Justin Bieber, Hailey Baldwin-Bieber, and Brodie Jenner, people like that.

Will the NBC deal allow Snapchat to free itself from its obstructionist Arte Povera-like origins and finally Hulk out into a Facebook-like $500B tyranny? IOW, could NBC North Korean Nuclear Threat mini-features tempt Demi Lovato to dish on après-preggers beauty tips on Snap's Stories format? Might a two-minute network doc on Venezuela's failed state entice Rowan Blanchard to slip nips on a live feed? And will such stratagems redound to our Snapchat patriarchs the power to purchase yet more Gulfstreams and skew US elections?

Sadly, I don't think so: Our company still clings to the original "authenticity" story, which will create deadly brand confusion when synergized with the slick truthiness of NBC. Snapchat's problem is that in its attempts to be so uber-hyphenated—to "have it all"—its brand has become demented. But isn't that always the end game of multitasking? In my experience, constant pivoting between identities produces vertigo, which leads to vomiting, which leads to passing out in the hallway while clutching a breast pump in one hand and an iPhone with 162 new messages in the other.

And such is the future of Snapchat, I predict. I know this is the last thing you want to tell Allan Ides, but as far as I can tell, an NBC/Snap hybrid does not promise to turn into an escape velociraptor that will gnash Zuckerberg to death. Rather, NBC brand diffusion will yet further confuse Snapchat's "story" until the company resembles other doomed multiplatform misfits like MySpace or Napster or ConnectU or even unpublishable creative nonfiction essays written in the interstices of memos to you, Francesca Maroni, VP of Marketing.

You know, I used to do things well. I used to be able to concentrate. Way before I had my baby, and got this stupid job, I was a full-time conceptual artist. I wrote plays, declaimed on stage, painted, and even sculpted with kaolinite clay. I was young. I ran naked through Tokyo shrieking my shape-note hit *NED McCLINTOCK SHOULD BE IN JAIL* and I screened a doc at Slamdance. My Laura Aguilar intervention earned me a hashtag that trended for sixteen straight hours on Twitter, and I had a table read of my all-wymyn show called *Texit*. Time was, I would sit at my desk or my car's dashboard for ten, twelve hours and do nothing but write Latinx liberationist dialogue, drink water, and sometimes run out to a public bathroom to pee.

I was also a very, *very* poor material. I once made a $10,000 Franklin Furnace grant last over two years, at first by squatting at art residencies and then living for two months in my Prius. But then, after my girlfriend broke up with me and my father died in '16, things started to get a little sketchy. I was thirty-six years old. I contracted a bronchial cough that lasted for fourteen weeks. I had to talk myself out of a 5150 lockup after an Agnes Martin show at LACMA; later, I spent a year staring at Wikipedia after a gallerist beat me up. That caused my boyfriend Brandon to race away into the ether. And just before I began alienating my labor to Snapchat, I took on that lean, questionable appearance that either denotes a fully-lived capacity for independent thought, or the desperation that comes from surviving in that cold tundra known as the margins.

And then I found out I was pregnant.

I gave birth one month into the shelter-in-place order, and for some reason, I still had this idea that I could work for Snapchat, have a baby, and yet still be an artist, but by making the kind of art that does not destroy your life like conceptualism does. Writing, I thought. You could just kind of bang it out on the weekends. And creative nonfiction arts essays? Piece of cake.

But I now know that writing is for lunatics because it takes forever. Like, when I finally edit out all of the literary flourishes and digressions from this memo, it will probably be at least 6 p.m., which is when I have to get into my Prius, commute forty-five minutes back to Glendale, and take over parenting duties from my feminist male nanny. This will involve cuddling, dinner, bathing, screaming, pajamas, more screaming, and finally mutual sleep. But no literary composition, I predict. At least not tonight.

If you really want to be honest with Allan, Francesca, I recommend that you explain to him that the NBC/Snap osmosis will gel only if Snap abandons authenticity. All you have to do is look at history to see that authenticity is a dangerous bet. It has led to the gory demises of other hyphenates who tried to "be real," namely, those who tried to be more than the world would allow—Friendster, Xanga, Apple Jack, and the unfired clay cat-head that, flake by flake, atom by atom, is predestined to return to earth as so much dust . . . Why Marisa Merz herself escaped from this fate is unclear to me.

What I wonder is this: Did Marisa Merz make her art in spite of the octahedrons that converted her into a hyphenate, or did she become a GFA *because* she made art out of her hinged "real life?" Was she actually the octahedral layer the entire time, and created her career out of Nietzschean will-to-power? Or did she so embrace her tetrahedral misfit status that she accidentally plugged into that sparkling source of energy that exists in between identities?

Mother-artist.

Marketer-mother-artist.

Sleeper-eater-marketer-mother-creative-nonfiction-writer-woman-of-color-artist.

Here's a little-known fact: Whereas perfect kaolinite is characterized by its seamless integrity, *disadattata* kaolinite actually proves far less likely to crack under pressure. Perfect kaolinite may have no problem producing book after book after book, but its lack of plasticity renders it best used for items such as common bricks. Disordered kaolinite's rough conjuncture, however, can take stress without collapsing. As a consequence of its paradoxical strength, it is the type of clay preferred for making fine sculptures, such as Marisa Merz's crazy-looking and pink-lipped cat-head, *Untitled, Undated, 8*, which she materialized sometime in the 1980s.

Indeed, Marisa Merz's atom-bristling figurine is the apotheosis of what disordered kaolinite might achieve. It's true that if you look up the glum, pink-nosed, mouth-breathing *Untitled, Undated, 8* on Google, it doesn't make much of an impression at first. You have to really start thinking about it, and drawing it, and Instagramming it, and sculpting it out of tuna, and writing about it—but soon enough, you find that *Untitled, Undated, 8* makes you want to tear your clothes while sobbing even as you're laughing hard enough to wet yourself.

From where does this little goblin get its power? From where did Marisa Merz steal her Promethean atoms to make such a perfect piece of ugly dumbness? From work. From exhaustion. From apple and banana purées. From tuna. From loving. From heartbreak. From traffic. From survival. From grief. From having children. From falling apart. From poverty. From wanting. From refusing. From trying. From racism. From the virus. From not dying. From forcing. From being a woman. From putting yourself back together. From capitalism. From protesting. From yelling. From caring. From failing. From doing everything. From real life. From not stopping. From not stopping. From not stopping. From not stopping, Francesca. From being as busted and relentless as these very essays that I try to write, that I must write, that I can't write, that I will somehow not quit writing.

Yours truly,
Amanda Ruiz

POSTSCRIPT ON "I DIDN'T EVEN KNOW THESE EXISTED"

The Vincent Price Museum held an ambitious and well-received retrospective of Laura Aguilar's photography from September 16, 2017, to February 10, 2018. Titled *Show and Tell*, the exhibition was guest curated by Sybil Venegas, independent art historian and curator and a professor emerita of Chicana/o studies at East Los Angeles College. Professor Venegas hosted the event in collaboration with the UCLA Chicano Studies Research Center. *Show and Tell* featured work spanning Aguilar's entire career, and showcased her *Stillness*, *Grounded*, and *Nature Self-Portraits* series. The Vincent Price Museum is part of East LA College, Aguilar's alma mater. The college works to "serve as a unique educational resource for the diverse audiences of the college and the community through the exhibition, interpretation, collection, and preservation of works in all media of the visual arts."

Laura Aguilar died of complications of diabetes in a Long Beach, California, hospice on April 25, 2018.

San Antonio's Museo Alameda, the Latinx-focused museum that held one of the first shows dedicated to Aguilar's work in 2008, closed its doors in 2012 due to unpayable debts.

Museum nabobs successfully encouraged Jeffrey Deitch out of his directorship of Los Angeles's Museum of Contemporary Art (MOCA) in 2013. MOCA continued to endure financial and administrative difficulties, despite the 2014 hiring of former DIA Art Foundation director Philippe Vergne. On July 31, 2018, MOCA announced that it had named as its new director Klaus Biesenbach, former director of MoMA PS1 in New York and chief curator at large of the Museum of Modern Art. Biesenbach's appointment has been criticized as a missed opportunity to staff a top Los Angeles arts institution position with a woman and/or a person of color. As of June 2020, when the name "Laura Aguilar" is typed into the MOMA search engine, four entries come up, but none of them contain her name.

Still, as of July 2019, MOCA began to make Laura Aguilar's work available on its website.

Acknowledgments

The author thanks and remembers Patrick Samuel, Trevor Perri, Doug Carlson, Soham Patel, Gerald Maa, Andrew Tonkovich, Ladette Randolph, Medaya Ocher, Lisa Teasley, Tom Lutz, Boris Dralyuk, Ellie Duke, Stephanie Malak, Dr. Eila Skinner, Dr. Tina Koopersmith, Dr. Sia Daneshmand, Lisa Ampleman, Susan Straight, Alex Espinoza, Ginger Barber, Tulsa Kinney, Christopher Michno, Brendan Embser, Sarah Preisler, Allan Ides, Anne Gendler, Anne Tappan Strother, Evan Karp, C.J. Bartunek, Elizabeth Baldwin, Ryan Botev, Chris Jarvis, Fred MacMurray, Thelma Diaz Quinn, Maggie MacMurray, Maria Adastik, Walter Adastik, Kathleen Kim, Eric Miller, The MacDowell Colony, Loyola Law School, Lindsay Tunkl, Lisa Locascio, Viet Thanh Nguyen, Gianna Francesca Mosser, Jesse Gomez, Cathy Sudo, Colin Washington-Goward, Marina Castañeda, Liz Luk, Babs Brown, and my dearest Andrew Brown.

The author also wishes to thank the following editors and publishers, in whose pages some of the chapters were previously published, as separate stories.

"I Didn't Even Know These Existed" is based on two articles that I wrote for *Aperture* magazine and blog. See Yxta Maya Murray, "A Pioneer of Latinx Identity," August 2, 2018, https://aperture.org/blog/latinx-identity -laura-aguilar/ and Yxta Maya Murray, "Laura Aguilar Was a Proud Latina Lesbian, and She Flaunted It," November 12, 2019, https://aperture .org/blog/laura-aguilar-yxta-maya-murray/.

"I'm Not Sure I Should Have Pressed Send" was published originally as "Triangle" in *Joyland*, June 6, 2016.

"Is This Healing Me or Is This Propaganda" was originally published as "Overlong and Thus Unsuccessfully Submitted Yelp Review of the Agnes Martin Show at the Los Angeles County Museum of Art (Apr. 24–Sept. 11, 2016) by Anonymous" in *Ploughshares* (Summer 2019). It is based on an Agnes Martin review that I wrote for *Artillery* magazine. See Yxta Maya Murray, "Agnes Martin at LACMA: Why Mental Health and Sexuality Matter," *Artillery*, June 28, 2016.

"The Science of Invisibility" is based on a nonfiction piece, "Nothing to See Here," published in *Guernica*, March 20, 2017.

"Private Language" was published originally as "Is This What Feeling Feels Like (First Attempt Wide)" in the *Los Angeles Review of Books*, Dec. 31, 2017.

"The Disease of the Learned" was published originally as "I've Got It All" in the *Santa Monica Review* (Fall 2019).

"The Sucking One" was published originally as "Editing the Wiktionary for 'Female' " by the *Berkeley Journal of Gender, Law & Justice* (online) (2019).

"Björk's Kids Seem OK" was published originally as "Youtube Comment #2 to Björk—Sacrifice—Live @ Zénith de Paris, France, March, 8th (08-03-2013)" in the *Los Angeles Review of Books*, May 31, 2018.

"The Cry-It-Out Method" was published originally as "I Like America and America Likes Me" in the *Cincinnati Review* (Fall 2017).

"Own Your Emotion" was published originally as "Toba Khedoori's Untitled (Table and Chair) (1999)" in the *Georgia Review* (Fall 2018). It is based on a Toba Khedoori review that I wrote for *Artillery* magazine. See Yxta Maya Murray, "Toba Khedoor: Making It Your Own," *Artillery*, February 28, 2017.

"Make Something Out of It" was published originally as "I Will Be Like Claude Cahun" in the *Georgia Review* (Winter 2020).

"Arte Povera" was published originally in the *Santa Monica Review* (Fall 2018).

Image and Text Credits

33   Photograph by Yxta Maya Murray, 2017. Marisa Merz, *Untitled, Undated, 8* "Testine." Image courtesy of Fondazione Merz and the Hammer Museum.

86–97   Lindsay Tunkl, stills from the video *Is This What Feeling Feels Like—First Attempt*, 2013. Images courtesy of the artist. Copyright © Lindsay Tunkl.

107   Yxta Maya Murray, *Texit*, 2018. Silk thread and ribbon on undyed linen.

117   Yxta Maya Murray, *I've Got It All (variation)/we can form the idea of a golden mountain, and from thence conclude that such a mountain may actually exist*, 2019. Silk thread and sequins on undyed linen. Dimensions variable.

135   Yxta Maya Murray, *This Is Bad (1)*, 2019.

135   Yxta Maya Murray, *This Is Bad (2)*, 2019.

135   Yxta Maya Murray, *This Is Bad (3)*, 2019.

135   Yxta Maya Murray, *This Is Bad (4)*, 2019.

141   Yxta Maya Murray, *But I'm Too Panicked and Depressed to Work Right Now (1)*, 2019. Ink on undyed linen.

141   Yxta Maya Murray, *But I'm Too Panicked and Depressed to Work Right Now (2)*, 2019. Ink on undyed linen.

183   Claude Cahun, *Untitled* (1928). Image courtesy of the Jersey Trust. Copyright © 1928 by the Jersey Trust.

197   Yxta Maya Murray, *Marisa Merz (Untitled) (undated)*, 2019. Ink and graphite on paper.

Regarding Glenn Ligon describing his method of making his "Door" paintings, see Glenn Ligon, White # 19, MoMa.org, https://www.moma.org/audio_file/audio_file/1118/OE_106_WhiteNo19_edit.mp3.

Thelma Golden and Glenn Ligon's interview at Luhring Augustine may be found at "Glenn Ligon and Thelma Golden in Conversation," Luhring Augustine, March 12, 2016, https://vimeo.com/161058793.

Jean Genet's 1964 interview with Madeleine Gobeil may be found at Madeleine Gobeil, "Interview with Madeleine Gobeil," in Jean Genet, *The Declared Enemy: Texts and Interviews*, edited by Albert Dichy and Jeff Fort (Palo Alto, CA: Stanford University Press, 2004), 2–17.

In reality, LACMA hosted their Agnes Martin exhibition April 24–September 11, 2016. See *Agnes Martin*, LACMA.org, https://www.lacma.org/art/exhibition/agnes-martin.

Mickalene Thomas quotes are from "Mickalene Thomas by Sean Landers," *Bomb*, July 1, 2011, https://bombmagazine.org/articles/mickalene-thomas-1/.

Quotes from Linda Nochlin are from "Why Have There Been No Great Women Artists?," *ARTnews*, May 30, 2015 (retrospective), http://www.artnews.com/2015/05/30/why-have-there-been-no-great-women-artists/.

Aliza Shvarts's comments are from "Figuration and Failure, Pedagogy and Performance: Reflections Three Years Later," *Women & Performance: a journal of feminist theory* 21, no. 1 (2011): 160, https://www.alizashvarts.com.

The James Taratano quote is from "The Ethical Hoax," *Wall Street Journal*, April 18, 2008, https://www.wsj.com/articles/SB120853768406126721.

Sidri Eldon quotes are from "The Confessions of a Misanthropic Musician: The Sindri Eldon and the Ways Interview," *Reykjavik Grapevine*, October 17, 2012, https://grapevine.is/grapevine-airwaves-2012/2012/10/17/the-confessions-of-a-misanthropic-musician-the-sindri-eldon-and-the-ways-interview/.

Iris van Herpen's interview in *Dazed* magazine can be found in Susanne Madsen, "Q&A: Iris Van Herpen," *Dazed*, January 24, 2013, http://www.dazeddigital.com/fashion/article/15493/1/qa-iris-van-herpen.

Matthew Barney's comments can be found reported in Josh Saul, "Bjork's Ex Sues over Custody of Daughter," *Page Six*, April 1, 2015, https://pagesix.com/2015/04/01/bjorks-ex-files-custody-suit/.

Beuys's statements concerning his salvation by the Tatars may be found in Mark C. Taylor, *Refiguring the Spiritual: Beuys, Barney, Turrell, Goldsworthy* (New York: Columbia University Press, 2012), 21.